Drifter's Gate

Tales of Civitas Apex, Volume 1

Rachael S Lucas

Published by Rachael Lucas, 2024.

While every precaution has been taken in the preparation of this book, the publisher assumes no responsibility for errors or omissions, or for damages resulting from the use of the information contained herein.

DRIFTER'S GATE

First edition. April 23, 2024.

Copyright © 2024 Rachael S Lucas.

ISBN: 979-8224785032

Written by Rachael S Lucas.

Table of Contents

Chapter 1: The Drifter

After the Greenspark fire fell from the sky, it left the world in smoldering ruins. The coals burnt out and the world went cold. A barren wasteland of broken stone buildings, scorched shells and blackened skeletons was left behind. Technology and civilization had been destroyed. Of the survivors, everyone on the face of the earth was scorched, if not in body, than in mind. No one knew where the fire had come from, why it had fallen, or what they were living to gain.

Among the survivors was a man known only as Drifter, for the wide area he ranged over and his solitary habits. Rumors told that the Greenspark had destroyed his family when it fell, that he lived for vengeance upon whatever had caused their fall, that he was seeking death or simply that the scorch in his mind was driving him across the world purposelessly. Drifter himself told nothing and never camped among men.

One evening, as the reddish sun set behind the broken skyline of the horizon, Drifter sat beside a small fire on the crumbling ruins of great stone steps. They had once led up to a structure of white marble and vast slabs of dove-gray stone. It stood proud and tall on top of the low hill, a palace full of curious and expensive items. Now it lay broken, smashed as if a giant foot had crushed the palace beneath its heel.

In a nest of pebbles and step-corners, Drifter's fire burned, made of twigs and dry moss. He sat hunched over it, hood shading his face while his eyes gleamed oddly in the light of the coals. His dark grayish-blue cape was ragged on the edge from long use and travel, matching the worn dirt-colored uniform he wore underneath.

It had not been his originally. He was no soldier and never had been. But when Drifter needed a new set of clothes, he took whatever he could get and those who provided them never complained. Stiff, cold bodies do not have much chance of complaining.

The firelight gleamed off of a pair of metallic capsules tucked in Drifter's belt and the golden goblet he held carelessly between the fingers of one hand. After taking another sip of the caustic wine within, he reached down with his other hand and began rolling up the left leg of his pants. Underneath, a scar ran from just below the knee, almost to his ankle. Blackened and hard like melted plastic, it covered his whole shin. Carefully, he tipped most of the cool wine onto the scar. His eyes slid shut as the alcohol trickled in.

When his gaze cleared, he was looking into a pair of feral, gleaming eyes just outside of the fire's light. Deep, ragged breathing came to him through the dark air. Drifter took the last drops of wine and let them spill out onto the step beside him. The liquid flowed like dark blood through the dust, dripping off the hard stone.

"Breath of night, light's own bane, men they fight, truth disdain." Drifter's voice was low and rough like the broken gravel his fire sat in. And like the gravel, it held a spark of unexpected fire hidden within it.

The eyes approached after this invocation, a form gliding into the firelight. Something like a large, heavy mastiff with clawed, webbed feet and bulging eyes. Its breath sounded like low growling, thick and resonant. Keeping his eyes on its face, Drifter reached towards something lying beside the fire. It was a gristly chunk of roast meat, formerly skewered on a long knife. Gently, he held it out towards the creature. With a snuffle, the creature opened its fearsome jaws and took the meat, before disappearing into the darkness.

Drifter watched it go with no sign of emotion. Picking up the goblet from the ground, he chucked it over his shoulder into the heap of rubble it had come from. The empty bottle which had contained wine followed it, shattering on the hard marble edges.

Standing up, he moved towards a car parked on the lowest, widest step before the pavement. It was dark gray, angular, bearing no mark of make or number on its scuffed sides. Drifter's walk had a slight limp to it, due to the unhealed wound on his left leg. It was an old limp, with no sign of frustration or uncertainty to it. He could have moved just as fast with it as most men who went without.

The door of the car opened with a soft creaking sound while the interior stayed dark. Drifter disappeared inside.

AT ONE TIME, THE CITY was called Gylestown. With technology and history, it outgrew its name, spreading to cover two-thirds of the continent and be renamed Civitas Apex. The Crown City. Peak of Civilization.

Now the reddish sun rose on a vast plain of ruins and abandoned structures. Arches gaped blankly, filled with deep shadow. Pillars stood with blackened ends, walls bulged precariously and steps were crumbling. Puddles glimmered in the dust and icicles hung from the window ledges, all made of glass from doors and windows. The sun struck through them in shades of orange and crimson. Between these buildings, wrecked or standing, were the empty streets of the once bustling metropolis. The sun beat down on them, sending queer illusions of heat and water skimming over the pavement. Here and there, the burnt shells of vehicles stood beside the road. Sometimes they were too blackened and melted for looters to bother with. Others were torn apart in a spill of garbage and cotton threads.

One car moved wraith-like across the desolate scene, driven by the man, who was driven by the scorch. Drifter sat in the driver's seat with no expression on his face and no movement except what it took to pilot the vehicle. Shadows fell in stripes across him, sliding over the hood, across the dash and then off the car as if made of plastic tape. The light between was dimmed by the tinted window, keeping stray beams from blinding the driver.

The sun was almost half-way across the sky when Drifter noted a small movement on the road ahead of him. Slowing the car to a creep, he took the situation in with a flashing dart of his gaze. A man was laying half in the road, having just crawled from the shell of a house and collapsed. He was dressed in rags, a patchwork quilt drawn over his shoulders. One hand was outstretched in a pleading gesture towards the oncoming car. No other movements, no odd colors or shapes proclaimed the presence of other people nearby. The man had not been shot, stabbed or beaten, so far as Drifter could tell. He was so emaciated as to suggest that he was starving to death.

The car pulled to a stop a few yards away. Drifter stepped out, purloined military boots crunching on bits of gravel on top of the road. A few steps and he was standing beside the ragged figure. But though only a moment had passed since he saw the movement, the man was already dead. Drifter reached down to make sure, shaking his head once in affirmation.

When he started driving again, there was a patchwork quilt on the seat beside him.

The sun set that evening into a bank of haze. It was not a warm sun anymore, even when it shone. With the rays blocked, an icy wind sprang up across the ruined city. Drifter's headlights cut the night, dimmed to prevent them alerting the wrong sort of person.

He had just driven out of a narrow avenue between two leaning buildings when, for the second time that day, he noticed a movement in front of him. This time, it was a slight vibration. Someone shrinking back into the shadows, in the corner of a brick wall. The headlights illuminated the figure a second later. A woman, dressed in nothing but a sleeveless shirt and jeans so ripped they were little more than shorts. She had straight, dark hair falling around a narrow face. Her gaze was blank as she cuddled in the corner, hugging herself. Even from a distance, Drifter could see that she was shivering. His hand closed on the soft folds of the patchwork quilt beside him. It passed through his mind how comforting it would feel across his legs on a chilly night.

The woman was not looking at him as he stepped out of the car. She was staring straight ahead, skin white and prickling with the cold. Her lips were a purple shade, like the twilight sky. As he approached, Drifter noticed that the lips were moving. Soft, shivery words came out between them;

"It-it is not cold. It i-is not c-cold."

Even when Drifter stood beside her, she did not look up or stop this monotonous litany. She was so lost in a world of denial that she would freeze before admitting that the world was cold.

The faded blanket fell to drape across her lap. Drifter turned and walked away, not looking back to see the icy fingers coil into the fabric and pull it over the white shoulders.

He drove through most of the night, ever alert for signs of trouble on the road ahead. Too many people together in an area often meant problems for a lone stranger. Almost everyone was willing to grab what another man had if they thought that they could do it without repercussions. The smallest of injuries could mean death if untreated. With little vegetation and few surviving manufactured medicines, there was a dwindling amount of methods for treating a wound, other than water, bandages or mud. Even alcohol took plant sugars to make.

Food was almost as difficult to procure. Not many plants had come back after the Greenspark, not in Apex, even those known for being able to survive normal wildfires. And the small domestic animals, pets, that were often kept in a city, had either died off or gone feral. The survivors had become...odd. Mutated or adapted to the circumstances in abnormal ways. Such as the Chardogs, like the one Drifter had fed the night before. Clawed and fanged, unlike domestic dogs of any species, with giant, bulging eyes and a taste for things their owners would never have allowed. Roaming the city at night, seeking companionship with wraiths and eating human flesh, to mention only a few.

Rats, on the other hand, had hardly changed throughout the disaster. They increased on the bits and scraps left behind for them to prey upon. If a man dared, they could make a meal, but they were not affected by the plagues and contaminates they often carried. A person could not tell what the rat had been eating until he ate one himself.

But there was one place in this section of the ruined city that Drifter knew of where a small group of people had come together. Ones who were not normally dangerous and had even managed to plant a small field of eatables from seeds found in the wreckage. It was the next stop in his wanderings. He would reach it in the morning.

When the road blurred before his eyes, Drifter pulled to the side and shut off the car's engine. The doors were already locked securely. Reaching over, he opened the glove compartment and took out a pocket-sized book bound in stout paper, only a little frayed around the edges. Using just the dash lights to read, he opened it in the middle and cruised slowly through a few pages. All the time his lips moved as if memorizing something, and he used a finger to scan down the lines. When he was done for the night, he put the book away carefully, still mouthing words it had contained. Pulling his cloak around him, he lay full length along the bench seat and fell into a light doze, feet propped up in one window and head in the other.

The dawn found him driving again, taking a route through a tunnel-like underpass which echoed and glared eerily around him. The walls were marked with messages in various forms of paint, including the dark red-brown of blood. A torn blanket on the ground showed where a human form had spent the night at some point, but nothing remained to indicate what had happened to them. The rags were not worth stopping to pick up.

Leaving the tunnel behind, Drifter came out at a crossroads. Straight ahead of him was a wide alley between mostly ruined buildings. Stretching across the alley was the burnt hulk of a semi-truck trailer. It left a gap at one side just large enough for someone to walk through. A car could not fit without tearing itself up on the jagged steel frame.

Drifter pulled to a stop parallel the trailer and drew a slow breath. He disliked coming into contact with so many people at a time. It was like a mental assault which had to be held at bay until he was far away.

But they might have one of two things he needed. Feeling the cylinders at his belt, he got out of the car, keys slipping into a buttoned pocket of his uniform. There were no guards at the narrow space between broken wall and truck's trailer. He stepped through without a challenge to find himself looking into Apex Haven.

The long alley, a section of crossroads, and another alley like it beyond had all been converted into a sort of open market and village. Fabrics that had once been bright were stretched over the alley on each side, making awnings to cast shade on the pavement beneath. Under them, the ruined building fronts had been formed into homes, booths and workshops. Scavenged scraps of civilization were put to use, often in ways that had never been intended.

A row of blenders held various potions being brewed, showing in every morbid color through the glass containers. Half-burnt steel lockers were tipped up and used as storage containers for fruit and vegetables. The bed of a pickup truck sat in the middle of the crossroads, filled with earth and seeded with herbs which were growing in lush profusion. A clothesline held the skins of dead Chardogs, stretched to dry into usable animal hides. A portable cement mixer had been fit with a piece of metal on top of the barrel and a foot-powered pedal on the bottom, making it into a pottery wheel.

Everything was a little dirty, rundown and scrappy. Especially the denizens, who were at work all up and down the street. There were perhaps two dozen in sight, men and woman dressed in what they could put together from their past, all laboring to create a haven of safety and plenty against the cold outside world. It was hard work. Sometimes it seemed like they were failing by painful degrees. But somehow the community staggered on under its load of civilized pretensions.

Drifter looked at all the people and squinted. Too many, and this was perhaps half of the inhabitants. The other half would be out in the hidden field nearby, working it.

Quietly, he started walking down the village street, gazing at the wares displayed on each side. Food on racks, pure water in glass jars, herbal medicines in tins...all in tiny amounts, for a heavy price. He still had not found what he was looking for when a hand descended on his arm.

"Drifter."

The loner looked up suddenly. A young man, worn beyond his years by work and worry, stood beside him, dressed in clothes that were obviously too small. A reddish burn scar ran down the outside of one arm. He had a tired face, but his eyes actually held a pittance of genuine welcome. Drifter stared down at the other man's hand until it released him.

"Drifter, what brings you here?" The young man asked, stepping back a pace at his cold look.

Drifter knew that the people of Apex Haven would have allowed him to stay, if he had asked. Not that anyone there liked him personally; he never allowed that familiarity. But Apex Haven prided itself on allowing anyone to settle in their precincts, as long as they worked for their keep and caused no trouble. Drifter would have been welcomed quietly. He had no wish to settle there, and would have hurt anyone who tried to make him.

In answer to the young man's question, the loner said, "I need to find some crystal fuel."

He pulled out one of the cylinders, rattling it to show there were only a few bits left inside. A clear glass insert on the side allowed a small amount of blue light to trickle out.

Ryan, the young man, bit his lower lip in thought. After a moment he shook his head back and forth, "you're lucky to have what's in that capsule, Drifter. During the disaster—most of the fuel supplies exploded. Others were captured by gangs soon afterwards. We haven't had crystal fuel for a year, ever since we burnt the last running the minivan to look for seeds."

Drifter gave him a long, steady look, making Ryan step back again and hold up his hands in protest at the silent accusation.

"I'm telling you the truth. I wouldn't lie about it to you. You've never been a trouble here, Drifter, and always paid for what you took. We have no crystal fuel, for our own use or for sale."

"'Truth; Conformity to fact or reality; exact accordance with that which is, or has been; or shall be.'"

Drifter shrugged, tucking the cylinder away in his belt again. The one beside it had no cap, so it was open on top. Something made of thin bars of bronze-colored metal shaped in an oval was sticking up above the edge of the capsule.

"Is that a key of some sort?" Ryan pointed at it curiously. "It's too big to be the key for your car."

"Truth again," Drifter remarked, moving his arm so that a fold of his cape hid the cylinders from view. "Which reminds me. I have one other thing to ask for. Years ago, I knew a man who lived in this area. Name was Chelsea. Dick Chelsea."

He looked at the young man's face for recognition and saw none. With a sigh, he turned away. "Goodbye, Ryan."

Ryan jumped after him, remembering just in time not to touch him again. "Wait! I know someone who might remember your...the person you're looking for. Ol' George remembers a lot that is useful to us. He might know this Chelsea fellow."

Drifter turned back, making a sign for him to lead on. "But be quick. I don't enjoy lingering here."

As they walked past the truck's bed full of herbs, Ryan looked back at him curiously. "Surely it's better than the streets? The rest of Apex is an apocalyptic ruin for miles around!"

"The rest of Apex has a lot less inhabitants because of it."

As they went down the street, the inhabitants of Apex Haven stared at Drifter, some with curiosity or muttered greetings, many with suspicion. Drifter ignored them, all alike. Ryan cast a few glances back at him as they walked, compassionate but devoid of understanding.

Soon they reached a section of the alley where two semi-white pillars supported an overhanging roof of white marble, all mostly unharmed by the disaster. Underneath the overhang was a floor of cracked tiles. Some were missing, letting the hard-packed earth show beneath. Particles of soot danced across the floor in a light breeze. Dust adhered to the pillars on either side.

An old man sat in a wheelchair in the deepest patch of shade. One arm and the corresponding leg were missing. Scorch marks up his shoulder revealed the cause. They were black and hard, like the scar on Drifter's leg. A direct hit.

"This is Ol' George," Ryan introduced them, "and George, this is Drifter. He comes from outside."

The old man had tufts of white hair sticking out behind his ears and one on top of his otherwise bald head. His eyes were misty with all he had seen. Still, he had some work to do on his lap. A small string-winding machine, made of re-purposed parts. His one hand turned the crank even as he looked up and spoke.

"Drifter, 'ey? You lookin' to move in here, Drifter?"

"No." The loner crouched beside him. "I'm looking for someone. He thought you might know where to find Dick."

A thumb jerked at Ryan to indicate who the 'he' was.

"The man I'm looking for was called Dick Chelsea. He was an antiquarian, a collector of odd and ancient bits. Many of which he claimed had...strange powers. He used to live near this section of the city, before the disaster. Had a shop. You know of him?"

George was already bobbing his head slowly in thought. "Aye, Dick Chelsea. I recall that name. Tall, thin man with big spectacles, right?"

"That's it."

"Let me see...Dick...Dick...that's right." George stopped to slap his one hand on his knee, wincing and coughing afterwards before finally getting to the point. "Dick Chelsea moved out about a year before the Greenspark fell. Had an offer for a job teaching some fancy school on Terminal Point, in the Academy section of town. Don't know if he survived the Greenspark. I hardly did!"

Drifter sighed again and stood up, "that far...?"

Ol' George nodded. "Across most of the continent. Say, you want something from him?"

"I was hoping to have an artifact identified." Drifter felt at the brass object thrust in his belt. "I don't know of anyone else who would understand it—"

Ryan waved a hand in the air to get their attention. "What about that 'magic' lady? The sorceress. Remember her, George? Said she was going to check out 'reports' of a phantom in the Falel sector nearby."

"Oh yeah! Did magic tricks for the kids. If they were tricks and not real magic. Huh. Came through here about two weeks ago, she did, all mysterious and quiet-like. Lookin' for phantoms, too!"

Drifter's eyes sparked with interest. "'Magic lady'? Who is this?"

"She was a traveler from the outside, like you," Ryan explained, a smile appearing on his tired face, "but she was...well, different than anyone I've met before."

Ol' George snickered and a tight smile crossed Drifter's face briefly. The young man went on without noticing.

"She didn't talk much. Just asked if we had seen phantoms or wraiths in this area. Ol' George told her everything he knew on the subject—"

"Which is plenty!"

"Then she did a few conjuring tricks, or something, giving the kids a piece of candy each. Real candy! She seemed to know all about all sorts of things. Ancient relics, phantoms, the Greenspark..."

Drifter nodded impatiently, tiring of the narrative. "So you think she can identify old things? Strange old things?"

"I'm sure she can."

"Then I'll look for her first," Drifter decided. "And try for Dick if I can't find her, or she fails."

Turning on his heel with a nod of thanks to Ol' George, he began to walk away. Ryan fell into step beside him, saying nothing until they had reached the end of the alley, where the truck trailer was parked. Then he spoke with a grave face.

"What are you looking for, Drifter? There's nothing out there that you can't have in here, better. I know you aren't really like those human rats out there, scrounging and stealing from their neighbors. I've seen you be so kind—"

The loner cut him off with a sharp look. "What am I looking for, Ryan?"

Ryan nodded.

"Tell whoever asks; 'Eternity. Peace for all.' And let them chew on that."

He walked out between the wall and the melted trailer, leaving the young man behind him, looking puzzled and sad. Outside, the stark contrast between Apex Haven and the ruins of Civitas Apex was severe.

When the Greenspark had fallen, it not only burnt like no fire the city had ever seen before. It caused earthquakes where it fell in greater numbers, and sent odd interference like electromagnetic pulses through the air, destroying all electronic devices. All that were not specially shielded.

The ruby sun was climbing towards noon. Its rays crawled on the pavement and glimmered on broken slabs of stone. Shards of half-melted glass lay in the road, glittering. Drifter gazed up and down the crossroads, memory feeding him directions. The Falel section.

It had once held warehouses, factories, and living spaces for many of the accompanying workers. Drifter had been through it once or twice since the disaster. It was not a friendly sector of Apex. Except for Apex Haven, no sector was friendly, unless it was too empty to pose a threat.

Falel had a little more inhabitants than most sections. All of them tied up in, or terrorized by, the Falel gang.

It was also one of the few places that Drifter had personally seen a wraith. That, and on the broken Glass-Ebon Bridge, which used to span the Ebon river.

Phantoms were one of those things which had only appeared after the falling of the Greenspark. Many believed them to be ghosts, the spirits of people who had died violently in the disaster. Drifter thought otherwise. He knew what the vagrant spirits of people scorched to death by Greenspark fire would look like. It was imprinted on his imagination like a nightmare. And it was nothing like the phantoms.

As for this 'sorceress', Drifter thought that she was probably someone driven out of her mind by the scorch. It wasn't hard to let go of sanity under those circumstances. He had come near it himself more than once. But if she had any knowledge of artifacts still left in her mind, he wanted to use it. The object in his belt might be the key to more than anyone on Earth imagined.

Opening the door of his car, he slipped into the seat. He had enough fuel remaining to get him to the Falel section...with luck, enough to get out of it again afterwards. Perhaps along the way he could find a spot, unseen by others, where at least a bit of crystal fuel was left.

The dark gray car pulled away from its parking place, engine humming low as it disappeared down a crossroad.

Chapter 2: Falel

Gray clouds streaked the dawn like melted lead, the red sun spilling as blood across the sky. Spread out below, and all around Drifter, was the Falel section of Civitas Apex. While the rest of the city was stylized by heavy stone construction replete with arches, pillars and curlicues, Falel had been built on a more practical, industrial plan. Huge sheds with steel rails and aluminum sides, brick buildings with rusty iron stacks reaching towards the sky, and warehouses of composite materials. The office buildings were the only things stylized to fit the rest of the city, like an ancient temple set in the precincts of a mechanical cloister. Drifter crouched on top of one of these offices, arms resting on the low stone curb around the rooftop as he inspected all that was before him.

This sector had been hit less hard by the fall of Greenspark fire. Holes were melted in many roofs, a few buildings were knocked down in a heap of dusty rubbish and technology had come to a grinding halt. But many of the huge, industrial structures still stood.

Nearby, a water tower was upright, though one steel leg was mangled. Its sides bore the name of the sector in once-red words so faded that they were now a soft shade of periwinkle. The Falel company steelworks lay spread out in that direction, the huge corporation which had given the sector its name and owned many of the sub-companies throughout it.

Huge pipes, silos and storage yards bracketed the buildings, holding the furnaces, kilns and rollers of the steelworks. At one time it had refined metals for a large portion of Apex. Now it housed one of the cruelest gangs of all those which terrorized the fallen city.

Drifter scanned the area carefully, looking for any sign of movement. So far, he had not seen anything except for a few scavenging birds fluttering between steel frames in a yard below. The scene was broodingly peaceful. Grime, ancient and new, clung to the buildings, scraped off on one side of the steelworks to create huge letters reading, 'Steelfist Rules'.

Drifter knew from an earlier experience with the Falel gang, one which had nearly led to his own demise, that the name of the gang's leader was Steelfist. Drifter had escaped, just barely, by taking the life of a member of the gang. If they remembered him, they would have a vendetta against him. But so many victims passed beneath their hands, he doubted that they would recognize him again.

Still, better to be safe than captive. His searching gaze caught no movement below. The Falel gang seemed to be either out raiding in another area or sleeping off the effects of a raid in their rat hole. Probably the latter, as their one vehicle, a giant semi-truck with plenty of 'additives' was parked under the edge of a shed near the main building. Bent double to avoid notice, Drifter backed off the building's roof and descended an outside staircase on the far edge. In a dark alley nearby, his car waited in the shadows.

He had been unable to find any fuel for it on the way to the Falel sector. Now the gauge read close to the empty line.

After lifting the hood, Drifter unscrewed a cap beside the engine. Then he pulled a cylinder from his belt which held a faint bluish glow inside the sight-glass. Popping the lid, he tilted it over a tube which had been exposed under the engine' cap and tapped the cylinder gently on its rim. Five or six crystals slid out, disappearing into the tube with a faint rattle. Their pale blue glow disappeared into the darkness of the fuel storage container, swallowed by shadows. Drifter inspected the inside of the silver cylinder in his hand to find it empty, before tossing it away with a shake of his head. Those few crystals were the last of his fuel. Five or six grains of medium-small grind. Enough to go a dozen miles, maybe further if he went slowly. Not nearly enough to reach the Academy section of Apex. If he wanted to find Dick rather than the sorceress.

Swinging into the driver's seat, he piloted the car out of the alley, creeping down a nearby street. If the sorceress was looking for phantoms she would probably come, sooner or later, to the place Drifter had once seen such an apparition.

Guioletti's Cafe, once the favorite eating place of many mill workers in the area, now a haunted wreck of strange sadness and beauty. It was a place seemingly made for wraiths to haunt. It was the place that a magic lady would be drawn to like iron to a magnet.

Drifter set his mental compass for Guioletti's, careful to stay away from all streets opening onto the steelworks.

THE STREET WHICH GUIOLETTI'S stood on was narrow and winding. It was hemmed in on the west by a trashed apartment complex, while a collection of rubble, brick walls and the backs of buildings took up the east beside it. Girders and beams, which had fallen from the apartment building, lay over the avenue across the tops of lower buildings, making stripes of shadow on the cracked pavement below.

Drifter pulled to the side of the street, looking carefully up and down it before shutting off his car. In front of him, to the north, lay a gravel parking lot fenced with chain-link. Behind him the road curved away to where it met the main thoroughfare. All was empty and silent.

Guioletti's stood a little back from the curb, a tiled pathway leading up to it through the blasted sticks of what had once been a garden. There, it ended at what looked like a garden gate, made of wood and painted in peeling red. Curlicues of black metal acted as the hinges. There was only a hole where the latch should have been. On either side of this door stood a sooty white column, each supporting the fractured remains of a blue glass orb.

Drifter walked up to the gate and stopped outside of it to listen, before peering through the hole in the wooden planks. All appeared quiet inside. He pushed the door open with one hand. It creaked softly out of the way. Inside was a small courtyard paved in smooth gray stone. Cement walls ringed it on three sides, frescoed with images of trees, vines and flying birds. The forth side was made up of the cafe itself, which was entered through an open colonnade. Flimsy white chairs and tables were scattered about the courtyard, some still standing while others lay toppled. In the center of it all was a fountain sporting a statue which depicted a woman bearing a platter of grapes above her head. The marble statue had cracks all across it, stained reddish brown from age. Grapes of cold gray stone dripped from the upper basin, some laying broken off and lop-sided in the larger pool below. All of it was as dry as a bleached bone.

Drifter came in and shut the door behind him. He was just a pace beyond the door when he heard an odd noise. It was like far off singing, or a low humming, shimmering with sorrow. It sent a tingle all throughout him as it drifted nearer. Turning slowly, he saw something move in the colonnade on his right. A figure glided out between the columns, coming towards him.

The form was that of a pale woman dressed in a flowing, gauzy gown. Her hair swirled around her like snowflakes in a storm, her feet barely touching the ground. She did not appear to have any face. It was broad daylight and a phantom was haunting the cafe.

The song became stronger, wordless and sad, pulling at Drifter's mind. He felt the world blurring and fading as a strange sensation prickled him like the edge of a dream.

Memories.

As the phantom approached memories filled his vision.

'The man who would become Drifter stood on the porch of his house, one arm on the shoulders of his pretty wife. She seemed so young, innocent...a child compared to who he was now. And in her arms an infant, their only son.'

'They were looking up at the sky over the horizon line of Civitas Apex. Up in the blue, something was falling, streaking the air with neon green.'

"What is it? Some sort of meteorite?" his wife asked.

The man shook his head. "I don't know. My parents are watching the news inside. Why don't you take the boy and join them?"

He thought that they would be safer inside. Something fell with a sizzle a few blocks away, like a fist-sized rock, sparkling with fiery energy.'

Drifter saw the phantom float up before him, pale emptiness where a face should have been, tilting towards him curiously. It was singing, he thought, as the noise came from it, but how it made the sound was a mystery. He struggled against its pull, but was dragged down again into memories.

'Recalling his car, he stepped out and hurried to the drive where it was parked. The man had built this car himself, buying and fitting together the raw parts, painting it, installing every piece by hand. He had added one or two special ideas of his own to it as he went. Such as a force-shield generator.'

'The man thought that it would be quicker, and better, to turn on the shield generator rather than trying to get the car into the garage. Something fell to the lawn not far away, burning and fizzling in the grass. He paused for a moment to look at the clod of green, burning material before dashing to *his car. Throwing open the door, he flung himself half-way into it and reached for the shield generator switch. One leg stuck awkwardly out of the door, balancing him.'*

'He had just laid finger on the switch when something struck his leg. It was one of the curious meteors, which were starting to fall all around, thicker now. It seemed to melt into his shin like a fiery knife through butter. With a gasp of shock, the man pulled himself into the car, hitting the shield switch as he came. For a moment searing pain took him as he curled up on the seat...then everything went dark.'

Drifter saw the pale hand reaching towards his face. Even through the visions, he knew that it spelled danger. He fought to free himself, reaching for the kitchen knife tucked in his belt under his cloak—

'He awoke to a world of destruction, lived like a wraith in the blackened, charred ruins of his house. The pain in his leg ate at him as he teetered on the brink of sanity—'

Snatching the knife from his belt, Drifter struggled free of the visions and slammed it point-down through the phantom's hand. There was a pause in the singing as the wraith stared at him without a face, gasping emptily in shock. There was a snapping noise and it was gone.

The courtyard was empty except for himself and the smiling woman who was a statue. The knife in his hand did not bare a trace of blood, or any other substance.

Still, he wiped it on his pant's leg before returning it to the belt, tucked out of sight. That was the first time a phantom had approached him or made any sound which he could hear. He felt wary now, exposed, as if someone else was there sharing his feelings and watching him.

Turning, Drifter strode out of the courtyard to lean against a pillar outside. He had not remembered, not wanted to remember, for many days. Weeks, months even, had gone by without a thought of the past entering his head. Now he was forced to face what had happened; what it was like to live before the disaster. Having people and a place to call your own.

Closing his eyes, he shut the images out. Like a man hoarding gold, he locked them away again, somewhere they would not easily be seen. When they were gone, he let out a sigh and straightened, contemplating what to do next.

The sorceress was not likely to be in the cafe with that phantom. Or at least, be alive in it. Drifter considered going back to make sure, but he dismissed the idea with a rough shake of his head. The 'magic lady' would have to be forgotten. Whoever she was, wherever she had gone, he didn't want to get caught up with any more phantoms while trying to catch her. Instead, he would concentrate on finding more fuel for his car and going in search of Dick Chelsea. They had been friends once, in a light manner. Long ago, back a few years before the disaster had even arrived. Dick was the one to answer his questions if anyone could.

Fuel would be a challenge to find, but Drifter had an idea of where a nearby a store of it could reside. Anyone driving a vehicle, and there were very few, would have to possess a store of crystal fuel to run it on. The Falel gang had a semi-truck. They would have crystals in plenty.

Retracing his path, he went back to the top of the tall office building. He had no binoculars or other long-range vision apparatus, but his sight was keen. Laying along the roof, he propped himself up on the low curb in preparation to watching for a longer amount of time. His dusty-dark cloak contrasted with the pale beige stones, but there were no buildings nearby tall enough for someone to look down on him. Only the upper curve of his hood and forehead showed above the curb, with a pair of eyes watching from it.

All was quiet in the steelworks, except for an occasional clink, clank or shouting voice to show that it was occupied. Drifter lay perfectly still as the day passed above him. He had a small bottle of water sitting beside him, but no food. He had learned to go long stretches of time without eating, especially when physically inert.

There was a bit of scrounged hardtack in the glove compartment of the car below, for when he was done watching and he needed supper. Until then he just took small sips of the water and kept alert so that he would not fall asleep.

Late in the afternoon he noticed some movement on the rooftop of the giant structure in front of him. Focusing on it, he made out three figures walking out of a door towards the edge of the roof. Two were men, roughly dressed and carrying what looked like wooden cudgels with metal inserts. He could see the metal gleaming in the sun. The other was a slim person dressed in a long, flowing robe of either black or dark purple. He could not decide which shade it as at a distance. The robed person moved between the two men as if being watched or held prisoner.

They all three made it to the edge of the roof and paused. The figure in the robe reached up, pulling off the hood which hid its face. Underneath was a long, shining cascade of dark hair. Drifter squinted against the sun's glare. The third person was a woman. It crossed Drifter's mind with a sharp clarity that this woman was the sorceress.

The group on the roof had just turned and started back towards the door when Drifter was startled by a noise from directly below the building he lay on. He rolled to his knees, crouching for a moment in uncertainty. After a heartbeat he jumped to his feet and ran to the other side of the roof to look down. The sound was that of his car's engine. Looking down, he saw two men lifting the hood to look inside, while another sat in the driver's seat and at least one more crawled in from the other side to look at the objects piled on the wide shelf behind his seat.

Drifter clutched at his cloak in frustration. Feeling in his pockets, he found that he had left the car keys behind in the ignition. An easy steal for whoever came along. Gritting his teeth, he bent to continue watching. There were far too many enemies for him to risk an attack. Especially as he would have to descend the staircase in plain sight to reach them.

Laughing, one thief called to the other, "this is great! The boss will be pleased."

"Too bad we have to report it," another grumbled loudly.

The man in the driver's seat poked his head out, speaking with authority, "Alright you clowns. Shut the hood and let's take the car back. It's in good order, better than any we've found before."

"What about the owner?"

"What *about* him, you idjit?"

"Well, he has to be around here somewhere. The car still has a little fuel and runs fine. Why would someone leave it?"

There was a pause of silence as Drifter crept away from the edge, making for an emergency escape hatch in the center of the roof. Behind him he heard the words drift up, "Clance, Hugo, look around and see if anyone is in the area. The rest of us will take this back to the boss."

Drifter opened the hatch, careful to hold it so that it would squeak as little as possible. Inside, the building was dark, only the end of a metallic ladder showing near the hatch. Without a pause, Drifter swung onto it and started down, closing the door behind him. They had his car, and there was no way for him to get it back, at the moment. But with a little patience he could keep himself alive and perhaps regain what he had lost.

The shadows inside the structure became less dark when he was within them. The top story was gutted inside, garbage and insulation from the wall laying scattered on the floor in drifts. A shattered window, thick with grime, looked out on the steelworks, letting in only a little of the westering sunlight. Through the thick walls, Drifter heard the faint sound of two people ascending the staircase at the back of the building, arguing all the time. He couldn't make out the words, only the angry overtones. Looking about him, he found steps leading down another story and took them, testing cracked stones before trusting them with his full weight. At the bottom, he was in a hallway leading between office rooms. The doors were hanging open, all of them arched and set with round panes of glass in a fashion prevalent in Apex before the fall.

Down another flight of steps, past more office rooms and storage closets, he came to a place where the stairs were broken and fallen away. The walls were bulging here as well, shaken out of shape by the earthquakes. Looking around, Drifter spotted an entrance to the elevator shaft. But when he glanced into it, he saw that the elevator was at the bottom, smashed, the cable snapped. The emergency escape and repair ladder along the side of the shaft was also broken away. There was no easy way down to the next story.

Turning, he heard voices echoing from the level above.

"See the footprints in the dust? Someone went this way."

"Hush! Let's find them."

Drifter moved stealthily to a nearby office door. Slipping behind it, he waited, peering through the dusty glass pane with one eye. It was not long before soft footsteps could be heard coming down the steps. A moment later the two men came into view. The leader had a hand gun, small but powerful, held ready. The other carried a cleaver. Immediately, they became labeled in Drifter's thoughts. The one with the gun was Target One, the other was Target Two.

Target Two was lagging, falling behind to check office doors and peer out of the windows they passed. Target One led the way, intent on the footprints in the dust. He walked hunched over, gun pointing before him and head bowed towards the ground. Neither man was armored. They were wearing only ragged and worn clothing which looked second-hand, or perhaps third.

Drifter tensed himself, careful not to concentrate his thoughts too hard on either man until he was ready. But as soon as Target One was just past the door, Drifter's concentration focused on him like a laser beam. He slid out around the door.

He moved so quickly that Target One barely had time to look up before the gun was being kicked from his hand. It flew through the air to clatter off the wall, while Target One had just begun to tilt his head up, mouth opening in surprise. His head was stopped part way up by a blow to the back of it by the edge of Drifter's hand. A second blow took him on the side of the jaw, while a kick sent him sprawling. Target Two had more time to prepare himself. Swinging the cleaver upright, he advanced in a few hops towards their assailant. His face was set in a snarl and filthy words dripped from his lips.

Drifter was calm. Everything flowed from him and around him at just the right pace, not too fast, not too slow. He let Target Two advance until he was almost within striking range with the cleaver. Target Two tried a few swings, always just missing the dodging loner. Finally, Drifter slid to the side and forward, bringing his hands together in a double-handed grip on the other's wrist. With a wrench he twisted the knife from his opponent's grasp and unbalanced him. A kick to the ankle and Target Two was laying on the floor. It only took a few extra blows to pacify him.

It had all taken only a few minutes. Drifter stood looking down at his targets, panting lightly.

"Too bad for you, Clance and Hugo. Better luck next time."

Stooping, he picked up the pistol from the ground. It was a compact model in black, with a clip which slid into the grip. There were three bullets in the clip, none on the body of inert Target One. Ammunition was rarer than fuel, as there had been less of it before the Greenspark fire fell and just as much had been destroyed. Three shots was all that was in the gun. It was more than Drifter had owned since the disaster.

Tucking the weapon into his belt, he retraced his steps up the stairs, onto the roof space. Those two gang members were still alive, but they would be unconscious for some time. And unable to get themselves back to the steelworks, to report. Now was the time for Drifter to go after his car, before a larger group was raised to come looking for him. He would have to go carefully into the old industrial structures to find the car, make sure it was refilled with fuel, and perhaps pick up one more thing before leaving. And getting out of the area fast.

THROUGH THE LAYERS of iron piping as the sun set, into the shadows of the giant structure housing the steelworks, slipping through the halls to the room overlooking the main foundry. Drifter had pursued this route cautiously, giving time for a few sentries to move out of his way and an argument between gang members in a back hall to be settled with blows, before moving on. Now he was leaning against a wall in the shadows, looking over a dusty control console at the room where molten metal had once been poured from a giant crucible into molds on a conveyor belt below. The crucible and belt were gone, torn out with only bone-like frames and structures left behind. In their place, a heap of glittering treasure had been built, containing everything from silverware, through jeweled knives, down to silken gowns and rich rugs. All of it pillaged from ruined houses or extracted from terrorized refugees.

Sitting on a large armchair in front of this useless heap was the boss of the Falel gang. It had been more than a year since Drifter had last met him, and he had not appeared to age a fraction. He was still a young man, little more than a boy, sitting draped in the chair with a smirk on his face and a wineglass in his hand. He wore a shirt with the sleeves torn off, exposing arms corded with wiry muscle and decorated with a wrap of thin gray chain from wrist to elbow. His shirt itself was plain white, with khaki green pants below, sporting huge pockets stuffed with odd items. His face was difficult to describe, as it held a collage of expressions from cruelty, cunning and intelligence down to sheer boredom. His hair was long and black, sleeked back over his head and glistening with oil.

The men who had kidnapped Drifter's car stood before him, explaining what they had found and done. The car itself was parked over in a corner of the room, having been driven in through the large doors on the far side. Behind 'Steelfist' lurked a giant shadow, resting on the back of the chair. It was his body guard and chief thug, a fellow captured and spared because of his immense strength.

"You sent only two men to find whoever the car belonged to?" The boss sat up straighter, frowning at his minions. "Stupid. What if there were two people in the car?

Or more? What if whoever owns it is armed with a gun? Hugo and Clance can be picked off from a distance with that! Go find them and capture whoever owned the car! And if you do, try to bring the drivers here alive. There's something special about that car, I can tell. It wasn't bought stock off the market. Go!"

The men looked at each other and hastily beat a retreat out of the room.

Steelfist tilted his head to look over the back of the chair. "Melchior."

The giant moved out with a submissive bow. He was arrayed in faux skins, cut to look like a caveman's outfit, with golden bands at the wrists and ankle. The gang had given vent to their crude imagination in keeping the giant as a pet and dressing him for the part.

"Fetch me the woman. And no rough stuff, now! She's worth something to me."

Melchior bowed, moving out of the room. The boss pulled himself out of the chair and went to look at Drifter's car, running a hand thoughtfully down the hood. After a second, he moved to a chest against the wall, which had a blue glow leaking from under the lid. Thinking that it would be a good time to make his move, Drifter started heading for the door leading into the re-purposed foundry room. But he had only gone a few steps when Melchior returned, one huge hand around the wrists of the woman Drifter had seen on the rooftop earlier. With an inward sigh, Drifter returned to his post to watch.

The boss spun about and gestured for Melchior to let his captive go. The woman had her hood up again, so Drifter could not see much of her face, though he was closer than before. Her features appeared to be pale and refined, framed in inky hair, but he could tell little else. The deep purple robe flowed almost to the floor, showing a slim, tall figure.

"Witch!" Steelfist waved for her to step closer to him. "I want information."

When the woman spoke her voice was low and cold, hardly varying in tone. Drifter didn't hear the words. The boss looked at her with a frown for a moment, before slapping her across the face. The woman swayed to take the blow but offered no resistance.

"Melchior! Take her to the heap," the boss ordered. His giant pet had been looking on with what seemed to be a sorrowful expression, but he still did as he was asked. Using both hands, the giant grasped the woman around the waist and dragged her over to the pile of treasure, the boss following behind.

At the heap of treasure Steelfist seemed to be pointing out things and asking the woman questions, to which she answered in her cold voice, which was too quiet for Drifter to make out.

By now, Drifter had decided to make his move even with the giant Melchior and the boss in the room. From what he could see, no one else was present, so he crept to the door and opened it. Outside, a set of stairs led down into the open space, traversing the shadows opposite the chair and treasure. He followed them down and clung to the edges of the room, moving around it towards the car and chest. The blue glow from under the chest's lid attracted him. Stopping at it, he bent down and sniffed at the crack between. The unmistakable scent of crystal fuel leaked out, thin and acrid. Now that he was closer, he could see that other chests and barrels, better sealed, stood against the wall behind the front chest. They didn't let a blue glow out, but were probably filled with the same substance.

Straightening up, he pried at the lid. It was fastened with a hasp, which he found on closer inspection to be closed with a small, thin padlock.

"More! Tell me more!"

Drifter glanced over his shoulders at the sharp words, but Steelfist was still immersed in interrogating the sorceress about the heap of glittering goods. Slipping the kitchen knife from his belt, Drifter jammed it in the hasp of the lock and twisted. The latch was made of thin, poor material. When he put all of his strength to it, the hasp snapped and the lock fell away. It produced a thin clinking noise, making him look over his shoulder again. Still, the woman and boss were turned away, lit by a lantern on a stand near the chair, looking over the treasure. Melchior seemed to be lost in the shadows beside them.

Upon opening the lid, Drifter was looking into a trove of crystal fuel. The bits of blue crystal ranged in size from fine to medium-large grind, all heaped and piled together. Acting quickly, Drifter pulled a miniature leather sack from one of his pockets and began stuffing it. He had just filled the sack and tucked it under one arm in preparation to close the chest's lid when he heard a faint noise behind him. It could have been an in-drawn breath or a slight misstep. Whatever it was, the sound saved him from capture, perhaps death.

Whipping around, he saw Melchior swinging a massive fist at his head in a swift arc. Drifter tried to dodge it, but only managed on saving his head. The blow fell on his shoulder instead, sending him sprawling noisily to the floor. The sack of crystals dug into his side as he rolled out away from a kick from the giant's foot, trying to recover his breath. Melchior jumped at him when the kick did not connect, stooping towards him with hands like monstrous clamps. Drifter rolled again, hitting against the chest of fuel. With his free hand he reached into his belt and whipped out the gun he had taken from either Clance or Hugo.

Melchior swung towards him and Drifter fired twice in succession. The first shot took the giant in the shoulder, making him stagger back a pace. The second hit him square in the chest. Moaning, Melchior stumbled in a circle, growling in a bubbling voice, "I'll get the mouse..."

He crashed to the floor, blood staining his chin. Drifter jumped to his feet, noticing the boss running across the room towards him, shouting for his gang. Meanwhile, the woman had taken advantage of the situation to make a dash for the huge doors, robe flapping behind her.

Drifter only had a moment in which to act. With a grim smile, he considered that it was best to go out in a bright light than be captured by the angered gang. He spun around, discharging the last shot from his gun into the chest of crystal fuel. In the same breath he threw himself towards his car.

It started on the first crank and he gave it no time to wake up before demanding that it get him out of that place. The car complied, as always. He had only gone a few yards when there was a rumble and the first box of fuel exploded into a shower of burning sparks, like a enormous fire work. The sparks hit the nearby barrels and crates, starting to eat through the thin wood that bound them and creep through the tiny cracks between.

The woman had thrown open one of the wide double-doors in the far side of the room. Drifter aimed for it with the nose of his car, knocking the other door open, sliding into the huge hall leading outside. The woman had stopped against the wall, staring at his car in uncertainty. Hardly slowing, Drifter kicked open the passenger door.

"Get in!"

Without hesitation, the woman threw herself onto the chair. As soon as she landed they were flying down the hall, knocking over two hurrying gang members on the way. Behind them a series of explosions was starting to go off, fountains of flame and destruction shooting all throughout the room.

They shot into the gloom of twilight on the outside of the steelworks building, skidding into a parking lot ringed by chain link fence. At one point there was a gate, open just wide enough for a car to pass through. Drifter aimed for it, glancing once over his shoulder. Through the windows of the huge structure behind them he could see the reflected glow of hungry flames.

Once they made it through the gate Drifter slowed just a little, letting the bag of crystal fuel fall out from under his aching arm onto the chair beside him.

"Was that a planned rescue?" The woman on the passenger seat asked in her calm, frigid manner. She did not seem phased in the least by the circumstances.

"Not exactly." Drifter pointed his car down the nearest street, taking corners as often as possible without going in a loop.

The woman looked out of the back window with a slow nod. "I didn't think so."

Chapter 3: Relics and Phantoms

Drifter glanced into the rear-view mirror. "Even if it was, I'm afraid it's not over yet."

"That semi-truck?"

"Yes."

Behind them a large, scarlet shape could be seen now and then, weaving between the buildings. Its dim headlights proceeded it in the shadows. It was often lost to sight around corners, but the sound of a large engine could be heard gradually gaining on them.

"Some of them survived," the woman remarked.

Drifter shrugged. "Crystal fuel is not extremely volatile. It goes off in a burst of flame and gets hot, but is not the best material for blowing up buildings."

Glancing at his fuel gauge, he added, "which reminds me. We're still low."

"How will we escape the truck?"

"Some fast maneuvering. Hopefully not too much of it."

Flexing his aching shoulders once, Drifter took a better grip on the wheel and put his foot down on the pedal. The car jumped ahead, twisting down the narrowest alleys and taking the most convoluted paths. The truck slid out of sight behind them, engine noises fading away. The woman held onto the seat with one slim, white hand but otherwise appeared unconcerned. Her face was turned towards the window, away from Drifter. They burst through a heap of garbage at the end of an alley, spinning out onto one of the main roads.

Right in front of them the semi-truck was pulling around a building towards them, its lights picking them out in the dark. The woman let out a gasp and Drifter made a small gesture with his head as if about to say something in angry words. Instead, he whipped the car to the side and took off. The fuel gauge dipped ever lower.

With a roar and a belch of smoke the semi-truck came after them. It was weighed down with a heavy bumper in the front and various bits of armor all along the rear. But it had enough power to come after the car with an aggressive energy.

"Bad choice of roads," Drifter explained, "this time they won't catch us."

"And the fuel?"

"We'll burn what we have like Greenspark fire."

The car redoubled its speed. Choosing the straightest path, this time, Drifter soon pulled away from the truck and left it far behind. Eventually he took a turning which led into a broken, quake-streaked road where cracks gaped in the pavement between blocks of fallen stone from the buildings on each side. It was a barren, wasted street.

Drifter threaded his way carefully between the obstacles, coming out on a curving avenue leading up to the top of a low hill. There had once been a park on the hill, with trees and grass surrounded by a low hedge. In the center, a pavilion of white marble had once stood with a monument to a dead hero inside it. Now black sticks poked up in a circle around a weedy slope, with a pile of fallen pillars and broken roofing tiles at its peak. A pair of thin, twisted trunks stood together nearby like the legs of a charred skeleton left standing. The scene was outlined against the starry sky, drawn in shades of black.

Drifter eased up onto the hill and halted just over the crest, where they would be out of sight from the sector of the city they had just left behind. When the car was shut off, everything went silent. No roaring engines could be heard coming towards them. No headlights cut the gloom of the streets.

Picking up the leather sack of crystals, Drifter got out. He moved slowly over to open the hood. The woman stepped out to stand on the other side of the car, watching him. The light from the cab, coming through the window, illuminated the scene.

"Were you injured in the fight with Melchior?"

Drifter looked up at her with his bright gaze as if not comprehending.

"You are limping."

"Oh." He gave a grim twitch of his mouth like a stillborn smile. "I've always...well, I've had that for some time. It's nothing that can be cured."

"I see."

Carefully, Drifter poured the crystal fuel from the bag into his fuel tank. Grains of every size tumbled in, slowly filling the metal space until it was nearly full. After closing the cap and then the hood, he turned the key half around to check the gauge. Finally he let out a sigh and leaned against the car, observing his companion. She met his gaze unflinching.

He had lost all sense of beauty by now, considering it to be an innocent and youthful emotion of the past, buried with his memories of a world before the disaster. This woman would have been considered beautiful by some, he knew that. She was tall, slim and pale of complexion, with a face almost perfect in its symmetry. Except for the faint red mark where Steelfist had slapped her. Dark brows like the lines of an ink pen arched over her clear eyes, which seemed to hold a mystic intelligence.

Her attraction was mitigated by an expression which was cold and calculating. Every move was graceful, but planned and coordinated, with no pleasing artlessness to it.

After a moment, Drifter realized that Ryan had been speaking the literal truth. There was something different about this woman.

"You're not scorched," he said harshly, "it's mark is not in you."

"No," she returned, "I'm not. I knew of the Greenspark before it fell. My prophecies went mostly unheeded, but I and a few people who believed, were able to avoid its affects. We went deep underground and hid for a year, until the fallout was over and the world had gone cold. We survived without the scorch, but the disaster still affected us. Friends, family, our whole world was destroyed, blotted away in one burning incident."

Drifter turned away, crossing his arms and closing his eyes. After a moment he said, "so you survived and let the rest of us burn."

"I tried to warn the ruling—"

"It wasn't enough! If you knew the Greenspark fire was going to fall, then tell me, what is it and why did it come?"

The woman sighed softly, shaking her head under its purple hood, "I don't...perhaps we should start with an introduction. I don't even know who you are or why you rescued me from Steelfist. And you don't know me."

Drifter was silent, so she went on.

"My name is Loran. I don't know where the Greenspark came from or why it fell. It was only a week before it came that I received a prophecy of its coming. It was...just a vision. A few words. It warned me to go underground. I tried to tell the rulers of Apex but they would not listen. They forbid me from using any form of media to spread the word. They watched me. I wish my message had been allowed to reach more people."

Something she had said seemed to change Drifter's anger to acceptance. He turned back, his face impassive as usual.

"They call me Drifter. That about describes who and what I am. I entered the Steelfist gang's hideout looking for fuel, and to get my car back. But I had already heard of you and wanted your opinion on something I have. So I brought you out of it with me."

Loran inclined her head briefly.

He reached into his belt and pulled out the second cylinder, the one with the oval ring of bronze sitting sideways on its top. When he pulled on it, a shaft came out, followed by an end with a few teeth on it. It was a key. Large, plain and dulled by age, it looked like a key from a movie about a locked garden, rather than one used for cars and houses in the modern world.

Drifter set it gently on the hood of the car and slid it over to her. She picked it up, turning it over to look at the loop on the end of the shaft. Imprinted on one side was a symbol like a branching candle with a circle resting just above it.

"It's a relic." Loran narrowed her eyes. "This same symbol is on all of them."

"That's what I thought. I had a friend once...name of Dick Chelsea. He collected a few of those things. Do you know what this key goes to?"

The woman thought for a moment, then shook her head. "I'm afraid not. It isn't mentioned in the scripts I have read on the subject. But one would think that a relic key must go to something of importance."

Drifter nodded once. "That's it. I'll have to find Dick and ask him. I was hoping you would know...but that can't be helped. Perhaps you could tell me what these relics are and why they were made."

Loran perched herself on the side of the hood after giving back the key, resting her head thoughtfully on a hand.

"It is a riddle now, and was even before the Greenspark fell. The odd thing about all the relics is that, as far as we can tell, none of them existed before two hundred years ago. Yet, the relics themselves are definitely older. Thousands of years old, perhaps, though they are in such good condition."

"Buried and came to the surface by erosion and diggings?"

Loran shook her head. "That is the true mystery. The relics are always found in fairly obvious places. Laying in a park, on a shelf in an attic...all the records I have, show that they were never buried far under ground. Not only because they are found nearer the surface, but because some of them would have been harmed by long contact with damp earth. None of them are."

She gazed at the key in his hands for a minute before shaking her head again. "Once in a while, I almost feel that someone is playing games with us."

Drifter gave her another crooked almost-smile. "Whenever I tell that to an inhabitant of Haven they say it's blasphemy."

Loran let him have a long, cool look. "I don't mean by God. Someone else. Something more...mortal. And then there is the 'phantoms.'"

"Yes, I've had a few run-ins with those. I suppose you don't believe, either, that they are dead people?"

"No. If dead people walked as spirits on the earth in such a manner, we would have heard of it long ago."

"They say it's because of the violence of their demise."

The woman crossed her arms, pacing slowly up and down beside the car. "The Greenspark disaster my have been more wide-spread, but there has been isolated accidents and terrors just as violent in the past without that result. No, I don't believe that the phantoms are 'ghosts' or the spirits of dead people made tangible."

"Neither do I. What else they could be escapes me. Humans or beasts twisted by the scorch beyond recognition?" Drifter shrugged. "I just know that they are…powerful in strange ways. Dangerous. Or rather, dangerously attractive. It's odd to me that you would search for them. Relics I can understand. Not phantoms."

He gave her a searching glance, which she met with that look of deep intelligence and enigma he had noticed before.

"I have my reasons. Mostly, because I am trying to solve a mystery. The mystery of the Greenspark fire, and the things I believe are linked with it in some way. The relics and the phantoms."

Drifter bowed his head over the car's hood, his own hood shading his face in deep shadows. "Mystery: That which is unexplained or secret; A story involving a mysterious person; Secrecy."

"You sound like you're reciting from a dictionary."

"I am." Drifter gestured at the lit interior of the car. "I keep one in the glove compartment. It's one of the things which kept me sane when I almost lost it."

Twisting his head up to look at the stars, he added, "you must be tired by now. I have no great comforts to offer you, but feel free to sleep on the seat inside."

"I wouldn't want to steal your—"

Drifter made a motion to cut her off. "I've gone many nights without sleep before. I don't feel the need now. Besides, someone needs to keep watch in case the gang managed to follow us. You rest. I'll watch."

Loran hesitated before nodding in acceptance and thanking him. The only time her manner had not been cold and distant was when speaking of the relics and phantoms. Now she retreated into the car and wrapped herself in her robe, before shutting off the light.

Drifter stared at the window for a moment, a faintly gleaming surface which reflected the stars and night sky. Turning, he made his way over to the heap of marble that had once been a pavilion and climbed carefully to the top, where he perched on a chunk of level stone. The stars slowly moved across the sky.

Something padded closer in the darkness. One pair of huge, reddish eyes looked up at Drifter, followed by a second and third. He gave a dismissive wave of his hand towards them.

"Not tonight. I have nothing to spare and another guest besides. Beasts of the dark, disperse."

The Chardogs blinked, before turning and disappearing into the night.

IN THE MORNING, DRIFTER woke the woman by opening the door under her head. She gave a slight gasp and scramble, before regaining her composure. Sitting up, she made room for him on the driver's seat.

"Where are we going today?"

Drifter looked to her. "That's up to you. I'll take you anywhere you wish, in the area. Then I must be on my way."

"Where are *you* going?"

He did not answer until the car was running and he started to back it down the hill, turning around before continuing down the slope.

"Dick. I'm going to find him. Someone told me he may be in the Academy sector."

"Hmm..." Loran put her hands together on her lap. "Academy sector. They have a bigger library there—"

"Many of them."

"Many large libraries there. May I accompany you?"

Drifter once again did not answer for a few minutes. Eventually he shook his head. "No. I travel alone and could not provide for you. Provisions are hard enough to find for one."

Loran held up a hand in a commanding gesture. "I have supplies cached nearby. Food, water, coffee. Enough for both of us for some time, if we are careful."

"Coffee..." Drifter tasted that word like a foreign delicacy. But still, he shook his head. "No. Forgive me. I travel alone. Just tell me where you wish to be dropped off."

"The Academy sector—"

"Nearby, or else I leave you right here."

Loran sighed. "You're a hard man."

Drifter did not reply, just idled the car down and waited.

"The Workman's library. It's near here. Down that street and to the left." She gestured at an intersection ahead of them. It was fairly clear of debris, leading to a medium building of pale green stone. The roof had an ornamental dome on top of it, smashed and shattered so that only jagged teeth of glass was left in a ring where the dome used to stand. A blackened statue stood beside the steps, depicting a lion raising one paw over an open book. The face was broken off, leaving a blank hollow behind.

Around it was a space of gravel that had once been a parking lot, ringed by trees and shrubs that would never grow again. Even the seeds had been cooked by the heat of the Greenspark, giving no hope for the future. Where there had once been short spaces of lawn, there was only hard earth and the broken fragments of nearby structures, mostly less fortunate than the library. Glass from the building lay sparkling all across the area.

"There are rumors that the Academy sector was hit less hard than many others, in places." Loran looked at him once the car had stopped.

"Then perhaps Dick survived." Drifter motioned towards the door. "Your stop, I believe?"

With only a small nod in return, the woman opened the door and stepped out.

Her feet crunched on the gravel and she paused. "There is one more thing I should say before I go."

Drifter shot a glance at her.

"Thank you."

She did not wait for an answer and Drifter did not offer one. He eased the car away as she moved towards the building, robe swirling softly behind her. The woman had just disappeared into the sagging doors of the library when he rounded the corner and it disappeared from sight.

For just a moment Drifter felt as if he had made the wrong decision. He was going towards the Academy sector anyway, the woman's knowledge might be useful, and she had offered supplies the likes of which most modern inhabitants of Apex would kill their closest relative for. Not only that, but she had claimed to be a prophetess of sorts. Someone who could see the future might be useful to have around. Drifter had not disbelieved her, though it would have been easy for someone to lie after the fact and claim they had foretold it. But she was unmarked by scorch and that was a finger pointing out the truth of her words.

But the feeling of having left something important behind stayed with Drifter for only a moment. It was soon washed away by thoughts of how to reach the Academy sector in one piece, with his car.

The fuel he had stolen would not last all of the way there. At some point he would have to refuel, finding or stealing another supply of the same size along the way. He also had to find the usual food and water supplies while he traveled. The thought of food made him hungry, realizing that he had not eaten, even after the fight in Steelfist's hideout. Reaching over to the glove compartment, he yanked it open and took out the lump of stale hardtack. It was a grayish, amorphous blob in his hand, stiff with long baking and exposure to air. Someone had cooked it before the Greenspark fell, probably for a voyage across the sea or as an experiment. Now he gnawed crumbs off as he drove, thinking how good meat would taste instead.

The thought grew on him until, just a few miles from the library, he decided to stop and camp. He would get something more to eat, perhaps enough to take with him and last for some days. Then he would not have to worry about provisions during the first days of the journey.

Two buildings leaned precariously together over a sunken section of road. Drifter pulled up just outside of their shadows, reaching into the shelf behind his seat to push aside a few rags and tags before drawing out a slingshot. It was of the sort a person could hold in one hand, balancing it against the wrist while aiming and firing with the other hand. It had belonged to a boy before the disaster... someone Drifter had known. It had been left by accident in the car and the original owner had perished off the face of the earth. Not powerful enough to use as a weapon of defense, but it could flick a rock, bottle or bit of metal hard enough to stun small game. He only used it for hunting.

The buildings stood up starkly against the sky, one leaning on the other like a pair of drunks trying to get home together. Reinforcement rods and power lines dangled from the building's sides towards the deep shadows underneath, where all shapes became a dark blur. This pit was what Drifter made his way towards, picking up sharp corners of broken stone along the way. Perhaps half the size of his fist, they fit neatly into the sling and into the pockets of the military uniform, where he stored them.

Drifter slid into the shade, feeling it on his face like cool water. He had to watch his step here, so as not to trip over the rubble on the ground. Caved in underground systems created a hollow pit directly underneath the leaning towers. Cracks ran through it, rough and torn like shedding skin. A smell of damp pavement and burnt wires pervaded the space.

As soon as he was down inside the pit Drifter stood still, listening. Little squeaks and scuffles started up after a minute, running all through the cracks in the valley. This was the sort of place where Rabiters's and Vollans lived.

Those creatures had begun, once upon a time, as rabbits and voles. But the toxic influence of the Greenspark had twisted them into new creatures, which had received mutated names to suit them. Rabiters, as their name suggested, were known for sneaking up in the night and biting people as they slept. Especially on the toes, if the victims weren't wearing boots, or on the fingers. They bit hard, often severing the digit and running off with it to munch in peace. Vollan was a play on the words vole and villain. They were fat, burrowing creatures which stole whatever was not nailed down or watched, but were otherwise harmless. And better for eating than the hazardous rats.

It was not long before Drifter's eyes had adjusted enough for him to make out shapes and movements in the dark. Something scuttled between burrows dug into the cracks in the pavement. A split second later the shape resurfaced, carrying a bit of straw or a twig in its mouth. Drifter aimed carefully and let fly with one broken piece of rock. There was a thump, a squeak and the Vollan lay still. But the man did not go to pick it up right away. He waited until business resumed in the colony before shooting another one, then a third soon after.

Accepting this amount for the moment, he walked forward to scoop up the creatures one after the other and break their necks. Each was about the size of a normal rabbit, unnaturally plump in the back and narrow up front. Somehow they managed to survive on what seemed to Drifter to be little more than dirt and burnt twigs, even getting fat on them. Of all the rodents in the new world they were the only one he had come across really safe to eat, unless you studied the animal carefully first. Rats were often poisonous or diseased from their own horrible diets and the Rabiters seemed to have become indigestible while turning to carnivorous habits.

It did not take much to skin and dress a Vollan. After scouting around to make sure he was unobserved, Drifter started a small fire near the base of one tower. He burnt the inner woods of pre-charred sticks he found laying nearby, and some yellowish-orange moss from cracks in the buildings themselves. It just took a small jerk of the hand to harvest handfuls of these materials and they gave out a steady heat.

Laying the Vollans on half-melted metal gratings from a window, Drifter propped them over the fire on rocks. The ones he did not eat would keep better cooked than raw, especially as they were roasted right in the smoke of the fire.

As he sat watching them, another pair of Vollans crawled out of the pit on their own accord to be added to the improvised grill. Fortune was giving Drifter the benefit of a wink for the moment, making his life easy. He even found a hollow stone in the shade, full of rain water, which he put in his metal flash and set near the fire to steam away impurities of the organic kind. Any heavy chemicals collected from the buildings above he would just have to live with. So far, drinking that sort of water had not killed him.

When the Vollans were roasted, he ate one with the remaining bit of bread. Then he rolled the others carefully in rags and set them on the back seat of his car to cool. The water was also set aside to lose its heat, while he searched the bottom story of one leaning buildings. It creaked dismally in every gust of wind, all of its empty windows humming as the breeze blew through it. The bottom story was burnt almost bare from fire.

The only thing of interest he found in it was the head of a ceramic doll, broken and missing one eye. Holding it in one hand, he looked down at the curls that had once been painted yellow and the single eye with flecks of blue still remaining in it. This object had been held by a little girl once, probably loved in a childish fashion. Perhaps talked to, fed pretend delicacies, led an imaginary life. It had most likely even had a name once, just like the little girl who owned it. Now it was broken in two and there was no sign of the one who had held it before.

The eye seemed to stare up at Drifter with cold intelligence. With a tiny shake of his head, he dropped it to the floor. It shattered as it hit, the fragment with the eye flying away to land in a corner. Lost like so many other things of the past.

Feeling oddly reluctant to start on his journey, Drifter decided to camp outside the leaning buildings until the next morning. To justify himself, he hunted again and roasted one more Vollan. But they were wary now and did not show themselves often. Adding more sticks to the fire, Drifter let it burn on into the blue shades of evening as he sat beside it, listening to the night sounds.

Chapter 4: To Change a Mind

Drifter dozed off beside the fire, once the night got late. It was a foolish thing to do, sleeping out in the open beside a light source. Even if there had not been any other person for miles around, there were still Rabiters to deal with. Drifter knew better and would not usually have made such a mistake. But the reluctance he felt to leave had turned into a lassitude which he could not escape. Watching the twigs burn to coals he had simply closed his eyes once and not open them again until early in the gray morning.

It was a noise which made him open them again. A sound of gravel popping, the stealthy fall of feet on the ground. Drifter jerked awake and found himself staring at the end of an improvised spear pointed at his chest. It was tipped in broken glass and had a metal pole as a haft. Following the haft upwards, he met a bizarre face.

It was made up of the shade of a lamp drawn low over the head, a pair of swim goggles much greened and blurred by time, and finished by a hard mask of metal across the jaw. A pair of wires had been fastened hanging down on the sides of the lampshade, supporting the skulls of mice like earrings. Behind the greenish plastic of the goggles was what looked like a pair of cracked sunglasses, completely concealing the wearer's eyes and adding the the bug-like affect of the whole.

The spear menaced, poking close without puncturing. Drifter was about to throw himself to the side when there was another noise to either side of him and two more of the beings stepped out, each with their own, personal variations to the headgear. The rest of their clothes were a matching mess of rags, tennis shoes and recycled junk. Each of the newcomers also carried a spear with glass tips.

They hemmed Drifter in before he could move, threatening with the sharp shards of glass on all sides. The first one, in front of him, poked the spear forward until it touched the cloth of his military top.

Drifter slowly raised his hands up just above the end of the spear to show that he was unarmed.

The leader of his captors spoke in a husky, grating voice that could have been either male or female, worn to almost nothing. "Food. Where is your *food*?"

The others picked it up in the same tone. "Food...food!"

Without warning Drifter made his move. One hand came down and twisted the spear away from his chest, while he sprang up from the ground, pushing off with the other palm. Shoving the leader away with the haft of the weapon, he whirled and swiped the second spear away with a kick of his foot. But while he was doing this the third somehow tangled its weapon between his legs, so that when he turned to deal with it he stumbled to the side instead. The other two jumped on him, all three piling on to bring him down. Sitting on his chest and holding his arms down, they jabbed at his throat and shoulders with the spears so that he felt tiny prickles all over the exposed skin.

"Give us food or we eat *you*!"

Panting, Drifter realized there was only one thing to do. He pursed his lips up and let out a long, eerie whistle.

The attacking beings all paused, jerking their heads up and gazing around in fear. The gray twilight of dawn hung over the ruined city, damp cold seeping upwards through the ground. Drifter could feel it coming through his cloak, trying to sap his vital warmth.

"What did ya' do?" The leader of his captors demanded, pressing the blade of the glass spear against his throat so that he could hardly breath without cutting himself. "What did ya' do, huh?"

"Called; 'dinner time'," Drifter managed to rasp out.

There was a canine howl from behind a block of stone nearby. Thumping feet and loud panting was heard approaching from all sides. A group of large dog-like shapes burst out of the shadows, skidding to a stop around the captive and his odd captors. Huge eyes that gleamed red or yellow stared. Clawed, webbed feet scuffed the ground. The Chardogs began circling like wolves coming in for the kill.

"Hunters!" The leader of the attacking beings shrieked, leaping from Drifter's chest. The other two let go as well, following their leader's example. With grunts and cries of fear they backed up, staring in terror as the Chardogs closed in. Drifter sat up, rubbing his chest and throat. The leader had not been heavy, being starved into a stick-like figure, but having it there had been uncomfortable nonetheless. There was a fine line of blood on his throat where a jab had gone too far.

"Wait," Drifter commanded, and the dogs stood still, hackles raised.

Pointing at the leader, Drifter added, "that one. Let the others go."

"No, no, we let you—aghh!"

The leader was pounced on by all of the Chardogs at once. Rags and bits of junk flew through the air as he was lost to sight in the mass. The other beings fled for their lives.

Drifter pressed his hands to the side of his hood and looked away, muttering darkly, "that will keep them from bothering me again."

Soon the dogs fell to snarling and snapping among themselves, still arguing in their own way as they dragged the kill off to their dens. Drifter stood up without watching them, straightening his cloak and shirt. Moving over to the car, he lay a hand on the door. But as soon as he touched it a strange sense of hesitation came over him again.

"I have to get to the Academy sector and find Dick." Closing his eyes, he leaned his head against the edge of the roof. Still, he did not feel like leaving for his intended destination. Instead, he felt a draw to...

"That woman." He straightened up, eyes flashing. "She is a witch after all. I should have known, since she can prophecy."

With a sudden decision, he jerked the door open and got in. A moment later he was driving towards the Workman's library.

It did not take long for him to reach it. The broken glass in the gravel glittered just as it had the day before. The doors hung open and an air that was silently forlorn sat over the building. His car crunched to a halt before he shut off the engine. Pocketing the keys, he walked up to the steps leading to the doors. The porch was shadowed, early-morning light streaming sideways past it in the dust of his coming.

She would know he was coming. Or at least, that someone in a car had pulled up outside. And there were not many of those left in the world.

Feeling as if he were about to go into battle, Drifter walked up the hard stone steps and went through the rickety door. Directly inside was a wide hall, showcasing scorched pictures in tarnished frames. The carpet on the floor had been burnt for a certain length, before the fire fizzled out and left the rest to be chewed by mice. Not far past this cutoff point was a wooden desk, one leg crooked. The bones of a human hand lay on the floor a few feet from it, blackened and gnawed but still in place.

Beyond the desk the library opened out into tall metal shelves which had once held books. Some of them still did, the spines stiff and bleached with age. Other books had fallen into heaps of dust or been burnt by falling debris from the open dome above. A circle of light beamed down in an opening between shelves, where couches and chairs had once stood.

Drifter walked into this, before flinching into the shadows. Following them around the edge of the room, he came to where a set of brass plated steps had been leaned against the book case. Below it a three-legged stool stood, having survived the disaster. It was backed up against the shelf behind it. Loran sat on the stool, robe flowing around her as she held a book open in her lap. One finger rested against her chin as she raised her eyes slowly to look at him. There was no surprise on her pale face, no emotion at all.

"Did you change your mind?"

"No." Drifter gave her a flat look. "You changed it."

Loran returned a long, curious stare. "How did I do that?"

"You tell me. You're the sorceress."

She stood up, pushing back her hood and placing the book carefully on the shelf before saying anything in reply. When she spoke it was in a brisk, dismissive tone. "Come now, if you've had a change of heart don't blame it on 'magic' or anything I could hold over you. You're subconscious is guiding you to make a new decision, tha—"

Drifter moved so quickly that even a person prepared for it would have had a hard time stopping him. Loran was unprepared, face partially turned away to look at the shelf of books. He grasped her by one arm and jerked her closer, looking into her dark eyes with his light ones.

"You see these marks on my throat? The only thing that was going to change what's left of my heart was a glass-tipped spear pointed at it this morning. Other spears made those marks. It wasn't because I am naturally stupid or was absent-minded, either. I don't have time for playing games. Your spell almost got me killed."

For once the woman seemed a little surprised. She pulled out of his grip when he slackened it a fraction, and looked him up and down with something other than coolness on her face.

"How would a spell to change your mind almost get you killed?"

Drifter made a gesture of disdain. "I guess you wouldn't understand. Sheltered living is all you have known. But a person needs all of their mind to stay alive, out there. Lose even a fraction of it and you've lost yourself."

He shrugged, glancing behind him towards where the door stood. "Just take the spell off and I'll leave."

Loran narrowed her eyes, arms crossed on her chest. "But I still wish to get to the Academy sector. I have offered you every sort of payment I have. Is it so hard to accept a companion for a few days?"

It had been many days since Drifter had experienced an argument of this solid type. He seemed taken aback by it, though he only showed it by a tilt of his head and a sideways stare.

After a minute he said more softly, "why do you wish to get there so badly?"

Loran held herself in cold silence for a moment, before suddenly bowing her head. "Forgive me. I did not mean to harm you. It is no true spell I put on you. I don't have the power for that, or else you would never have left until you agreed. Just a compulsion... you don't understand my power, do you?"

Drifter shook his head once. "I don't need to. The world has gone insane; that you should speak prophecies and cast spells is no stranger than many things I have seen. Even things that I have become, myself... But I do want to know why you want to go to the Academy sector."

"I told you before." The woman gestured at the books with a graceful sweep of her arm. "I am trying to solve a mystery. The mystery of the phantoms, relics and Greenspark fire. There is knowledge that I need in the libraries."

There was a long moment of silence before Drifter returned, "there is only going to be one way to solve the mystery, that I can think of. I suppose you could say that I am on the same quest as you. Very well, you may come with me."

He held up a hand. "But. You will do as I do, go where I go and judge nothing."

Bowing her head again, Loran nodded agreement.

"And you will take your own path as soon as we reach the Academy sector."

"Yes. Thank you."

Drifter shrugged uncomfortably. "Just take the spell off and pack your things."

Loran looked up with a gleam in her dark eyes. "The compulsion ended as soon as you came here. I will show you where my cache of supplies is and you may take whatever you want as your own, before we pack the rest for traveling provisions."

Loran led the way back through the library, to the entrance hall. There she raised a tile in the floor, one which looked much like all the others. But, underneath it a hollow had been made in the foundation, larger than the tile would have seemed to indicate. It was big enough to contain multiple packs of food and bottles of water, all wrapped up in separate bundles of white cloth tied in black yarn. Drifter refused to inspect the goods or take anything for himself. Instead, he picked a few of the packs up and carried them out, stowing them in the back of the car, before returning for more. Together they hauled all of the bundles out, which seemed to Drifter to be a wealth of supplies. Even the fabric they were wrapped in was worth much, being clean, unworn and strong.

The back shelf in the car was fairly packed with them when they were done, all sitting on top of Drifter's own rag-tag goods.

"I hope no one sees through the windows too clearly." Drifter waved at the pale cloth inside. "A large enough gang would mob the car and tear us apart to get at those."

Once everything was stowed, they were ready to go. Feeling the pressure of his self imposed mission lessen a little now that they were on their way, Drifter slid into the left-hand seat. Loran settled herself beside him, purple robe flowing almost to the floor of the car. She gazed out at the Workman's library as they backed away from it. Drifter pointed them down the main road.

"Ready?"

Loran gave him a cool look. "You're in charge, now."

The dark gray car rolled away with the quiet rumble of engine noises.

AS THE DAY PASSED IN driving, hardly a word exchanged between the driver and passenger. Loran rode with an unfazed calm, rarely moving even her hand or foot to a new position. Often, her head was turned so that she could look out of the side window, dark eyes searching the landscape as they passed it. Or perhaps looking inwards to some hidden realm of mystic thought; Drifter could not tell.

For his part, he did what was necessary to keep the car going and watch for trouble. He was not a restless man, but the demands of driving did not allow him to sit perfectly still. And always, his light-colored eyes swept the landscape of broken and burnt ruins around them.

Midday they stopped briefly, having hit a dead-end road. It was a cul-de-sac between marbled palaces, the way ahead blocked by the face of one structure that had fallen across the street. Gilded blocks of stone were piled across the pavement, intermixed with snapped-off pillars and the rags of what had been inside. The clean-picked bones of a human arm protruded from underneath one of the heavier blocks. An inhabitant crushed under the weight of his own grandeur.

To either side the less blighted buildings looked at their brother with empty eyes, devoid of pity. The tears of glass which dripped from open windows were only for their own pain.

Drifter stopped for a few minutes when they hit the dead end, allowing Loran to eat something while he scouted among the broken structures. In one of them he found a cupboard against the wall, with patterns of grape leaves carved into it. The latch was locked, but it only took a sharp twist of his knife for the wood to give way. Inside was a bottle of deep red wine, sitting beside a collection of delicate goblets. Three of them were fractured, having fallen over sideways against the wall from vibrations. The other six stood gleaming proudly, untouched by human hands for years.

Drifter took a pair of glasses down and wiped the dust from them, carrying them and the bottle back to the car. Loran was eating bread and cheese in neat nibbles. Even when she ate it was not with an excess of movement. Each time she bit, a piece of food moved a fraction closer towards her, arm poised a few inches in between.

Setting a glass on the driver's seat, Drifter stood in the open doorway and filled it.

"Have a drink. We surpass the kings of old, because we can throw away the glasses when once used. They'll never be used again, though the world spin for a million years."

Loran gave him an odd look. "Does one become better by wasting more?"

"Following fashions is supposed to make you better," Drifter returned ironically, "waste is the fashion of the world at the moment."

He gestured at the buildings around them, waiting for the woman to pick up her glass before sitting down where the cup had stood. He didn't pour himself any wine, corking the bottle with a blow and tucking it between bundles in the back for later. He put his glass safely there as well, before starting the car again.

When Loran had finished her drink she moved as if to set the cup on the bundles, but he took it and tossed it out of the window. It shattered into glittering bits on the pavement. When it had gone by he gave her a hard look.

"I told you. You must do as I do while on this trip. It's the only way I'll take you."

They drove on again until darkness was settling over the world. The car had moved away from the Falel sector of industry and into a section of upscale residence. Blasted parks, crushed palaces and statues missing arms or faces surrounded them on all sides. When the night was getting late, Drifter parked between an avenue of columns, the standings ones topped with spikes of alabaster in the shapes of reaching flames. Round, blue pebbles had once been set into the sides of the pillars, but now the stones all lay about on the ground.

When he turned off the headlights and flicked the interior light on, Loran's face became reflected in the glass of her window. It hovered there like a pale ghost surrounded by purple shadows, before she turned towards him.

"Are you going to eat something now?"

It had strangely rankled her that he would not take lunch earlier in the day. Neither would he eat later, in the orange sunset when she had her supper. He looked at her sideways for a moment before nodding once.

"Give me something."

"What do you want?"

"Food, woman. They're your bundles. Give me what you will."

Loran did not argue. While she picked out his dinner from the traveling rations he took the wine glass and filled it from the bottle. What was left in the bottle he set beside him on the floor by his feet. Once he was given his dinner he gestured at the glove compartment.

"Open it and take out the book inside."

After raising one fine eyebrow at him, Loran complied. She looked at the stout little book and read the faded title.

"World Dictionary."

"I need you to test me. Find a random word and ask the meaning."

"An odd amusement for someone who lives alone. Being wordy."

"Just because the world has gone to ruin doesn't mean we should neglect a good education, does it? Find a word."

Still appearing bemused, Loran opened the book with her fine fingers and looked down the page.

"Helical."

Drifter shrugged. "Of or pertaining to, or in the form of, a helix. In the shape of a coil. Pick something more difficult."

She scanned down the page, flipped ahead a space, then spoke again. "Stultify."

"Meanings," Drifter leaned back on the chair, taking a sip of wine. "One; To make foolish; to make a fool of; as, to stultify one by imposition. To regard as a fool. Two, law; To allege or prove to be of unsound mind, so that the performance of some act may be avoided."

Loran's eyes slid over to him to make sure that he was not reading over her shoulder. But his eyes were half-closed, the edge of his blue-gray hood blocking his gaze in her direction. The wine glass sparkled in his hand, held delicately between roughened fingers. His expression was one of concentrated abstraction.

"Well?" He asked.

"Almost perfect, word for word. You only missed that it says 'To regard as a fool, *or as foolish*.' How many words have you memorized?"

"Most the dictionary. I'm going through it a second time now, to embed the meanings better. Any past S and I might not get them as thoroughly. Try me."

Loran flipped even further ahead and continued to quiz him. A few of the words he did not return the meanings of, just as they were written down. One he did not recall the meaning of at all. This seemed to frustrate him and he had her stop the game.

Loran did not think it was surprising that he had missed a single word out of a dozen from the whole dictionary. In fact, she was more astonished that he could remember all of the others. She did not show it in expression or tone of voice, but her gaze held a reconsidering gleam.

"You started memorizing those directly after the disaster?"

Drifter opened the window to send his glass spinning into darkness. "When a bomb goes off, every tiny crack in the window in front of you is impressed on your mind forever."

He paused before turning towards her, adding, "that's when I learned words the quickest. Ever since, I've just been keeping it up. But, enough of this. You should get some rest."

Reaching down, he picked up the bottle of wine and took it outside, disappearing into the dark. Loran settled herself across the chair, turning off the interior light.

Wondering when Drifter would sleep, while she was always there, she wrapped her robe tightly around herself to ward of the cold of night time.

Out in the dark, Drifter found a place to sit and bathe his old wound with the wine. It had not healed past scarring over in the last years, no matter what he put on it. The wine kept it from getting worse.

IN THE MORNING THEY had not driven far when there was a blasting noise from the front of the car, followed by a series of rubbery thumps as the wheel turned. Drifter slowed it to a halt, jumping out to look towards the tire.

"Flat." Kicking at the dust on the street, he turned up several rusty nails and a few shards of glass. "Not surprising."

Loran got out and moved around to his side with a concerned expression on her face. "Will we be able to continue in the car?"

With a shrug, he leaned back into the vehicle and began digging through his ragged supplies under the white bundles. Taking out one packet, he unrolled it to reveal a sort of patch kit, including various pieces of rubber, a tube of some sort of glue, sandpaper and a few hook, and needle, shaped instruments.

"I'll patch it. It will take a few minutes. Do as you like."

Moving a few steps away, Loran muttered to herself, "for a man who knows a dictionary of words, you use a small amount of them in speech."

She set herself the task of standing guard, while Drifter found his bottle-jack and a brick to use with it, jacking up the front of the car until the wheel could spin freely. He worked efficiently, his hands always sure and swift. Loran was gazing between pillars next to a ruined building when she saw a small movement. Concentrating on it, she soon spotted a small figure coming into view, followed by a second, larger one and then a third of mediocre size.

"Drifter," she warned.

He looked up and they watched in silence as three children trooped out between the pillars, each carrying a bowl in their hands. All of them had burn scars on their arms and legs, clearly visible, as their ragged cloths did not cover more than was strictly necessary. One of them wore a cape of flapping, dirty-white fabric. It appeared to have once been a curtain from a fine bedroom chamber.

As they neared, the kids began to chant, their voices echoing eerily through the broken city.

"Some like it hot, some like it cold, some have it in a pot, nine days old!"

There was a small pause, before they continued with another rendition, slightly altered,

"Some don't get it hot, some don't get it cold, some don't get it in a pot, nine days old!"

They proceeded to chant and walk in step until they were not far from the car and the two grown spectators beside it. Then, the children all arranged themselves in a semi-circle and sat down on the ground with a thumping suddenness. Bowing their heads over the bowls, they held them out without looking at the spectators at all.

"Beggars," Drifter explained, leaning back over his work. "Harmless monks of a minute size."

"Are we going to give them something? They look starved."

"If you wish. They're your supplies."

"So you've said." Loran moved to the car and opened the door. Taking out a bundle, she untied it and removed sticks of dried meat, a loaf of bread and a bar of chocolate. Adding three bottles of water to the mix, she went over to the waiting children. They did not move as she apportioned the meal out equally between them. But when she was done they all arose at once, bowing to her deeply over the bowls.

"Thank you."

"Bless you, kind lady."

"Many thanks."

Turning about, they carried the bowls away, holding them above their heads in triumph, singing a new variation of their song.

"We have it hot, we have it cold, we'll have it in the pot, nine days old!"

"No one takes care of them." Loran remarked, clutching her robe in one hand as she watched them go. "Yet, I would guess that the youngest is little more than eight and the eldest fourteen."

"No one hurts them, either." Drifter gave her a thoughtful look. "Strange, I've met a few bands like that. Children so resigned to their fate that they make an ascetic life for themselves, living on prayer and other people's mercy.

Every other survivor will be the target of gangs, aggression and thievery. Even the worst leave the beggar children alone, through superstitious fear."

"The Lord watches the helpless." Loran decided.

Drifter gave one of his small, grim smiles. "So, that's why I've always had ill fortune. Because I can change a tire and hunt for myself."

Loran showed him a heatless, exasperated look but said nothing.

Once the tire was patched and replaced, the jack put away, they continued on their course westward.

Chapter 5: The Adobe Houses

Watching the fuel gauge, Drifter tried to calculate how many miles they had come. He had put about three pounds of fuel into the car when it was almost empty. It got an average of a two hundred miles to the pound. The fuel gauge was a little more than two-thirds empty. Perhaps five hundred miles.

"How far to go?" Loran asked him as if reading his mind. He wouldn't be surprised if she had. When the people of Haven had spoken of her, he thought she must be scorch-mad. Meeting her, he knew that was not the truth; she wasn't even touched by it. Instead, she had some talent for empathy and understanding of the future. Dangerous gifts for those around her.

"Another five hundred miles, at least," Drifter answered her question, "it's out on Terminal Point. That cinderized sign we passed said 'Grish sector'. Never heard of it before, but I can judge how far we've gone by the fuel the car's burnt."

"I believe," Loran touched a finger to her lips, "that it said 'Grisk', not 'Grish'. The letters were too blackened to read easily. In that case, I have heard of the Grisk sector before. It lies in between the lake of Gloutan to the south and the mountains of Grisk, which gives it their name, to the north."

"Nice," Drifter grunted as he navigated around the front of a building laying shattered across the road. "What sort of sector was it?"

"Partially small businesses and contractor's yards. Nearer the lake, it is mostly vacation homes and the like. I believe it was a much-envied sector."

"That means that whoever lives here now will be even more off their rocker than most. And it will probably be packed with phantoms."

"You don't like people, do you?"

Drifter simply cut her a look like charred twigs caught in ice.

The buildings here were a little less ambitious in scale and style than those in the sectors they had recently left. Some had even been built of wood, which had charred away, or thin metal that had melted. Foundations stood bare beside gravel parking lots, water pipes sticking crazily into the air from the stranded plumbing. Rows of buildings constructed of the typical stone had their roofs smashed in, fronts faced by broken colonnades. Old signs hung half destroyed from rusty iron posts, advertising items and stores that were long gone. The wind picked up as the travelers drove down one of the many avenues, dust and bits of garbage blowing before them.

In one yard, Drifter's gaze was attracted by a vehicle with its hood open, cab burnt out. Someone had come more recently and yanked the doors off, leaving one laying on the ground while the other was carted away. For a moment, the memory of how he came to survive in his car flashed through his mind. He shook it away, distracting himself by asking Loran, "you've been studying it. Why do you think the Greenspark fell?"

She leaned her small chin on one hand by the window. "I'm not yet sure. At first I wondered if it could be some sort of meteor fallout. Perhaps one struck the moon and sheared off an avalanche of stone blocks? But then I thought about the odd nature of the Greenspark fire, how it caused electromagnetic type disturbances and earthquakes. I'm trying to find out now: was it man-made? A satellite or weapon gone wrong? But there are the wraiths, too..."

"Yes, what about them?" Drifter encouraged laconically.

With a sigh, Loran shook her head and looked at him. "The same questions and answers apply. What about you, what do you think?"

The driver's eyes seemed to light up for a moment at the question, but not with pleasure. "I think that the Greenspark is the beginning of the end of the world. The 'abomination of desolation.' We've just lived through the apocalypse and are waiting for the very end in the post-apocalyptic world. As for the phantoms...? Angels perhaps. I don't know."

"Not very likely." Loran raised an eyebrow at him. "How many phantoms have you seen?"

"It's hard to say how many. They could all be a single being, shifting shapes, or many creatures coalescing into a single shape. I've seen them a few times."

"What was it like?"

Drifter's expression became bleak. It reflected the world outside of the window, which was shifting past them as they drove. Stores, homes, yards of wrecked equipment. All emptied of the life that once sang within them. All scorched. All silent.

"I only ask for my research, not to pry."

For a time it seemed he still would not answer the question. Then he chose the memory least likely to awaken others from the far past.

"It was out on the Glass-Ebon bridge. Ever been there?" Loran shook her head.

"They built it out of glass. Like icicles and cobwebs all strung together with silver cables. It spans the Ebon river, known for its dark color and strange fish...but the bridge shattered, of course. Despite all the precautions built into it, half of the bridge fell into the river. The other half still stands, connected to land. Like a skeleton without a head. A monster reaching across the darkness. I drove out on it one night to...watch the water flowing underneath."

Drifter paused, moving his head so that it was hidden by his hood. "At the jagged end. I had been standing there for some time when I caught a movement behind me. Turning, I saw a white shape glide out into the road on the bridge perhaps fifty yards away."

"No one ever sees where the wraiths come from or where they go," Loran murmured.

"That's true. Unless you call watching them disappear 'seeing where they go.'" Drifter took a hand from the wheel to gesture once with it, sharply. "Anyway, the wraith slid out into the middle of the road. I couldn't tell what it was shaped like. A human, basically. Man or woman could not be discerned. Tendrils floated around it, waves of white rippled from its limbs. It started to dance. Without a noise it whirled and twirled in the middle of the bridge. I watched...before suddenly it vanished. That's it."

The woman sat quietly on her side of the seat, one hand resting on the window. She seemed to be thinking over what he had said. Every once in a while, she would nod her head slowly as if his words agreed with something she had known before. Drifter did not offer any further explanation or press her for her own thoughts.

This silence had gone on for some time before Drifter noticed something odd beside the road up ahead of them. They were driving down a long, straight avenue between ruined buildings that had once housed small businesses. Rusted signs and lights with the glass melted out overhung the street. When he first saw the odd shape he thought that it was a signpost someone had hung old cloths and a backpack on. But when they had come a little closer he realized that it was a man, an extremely thin man, standing on the curb with one arm sticking out.

Drifter began to slow, taking in the whole scene to check for danger. The man seemed to be alone, and the only building behind him was turned into low rubble, too broken for people to be hiding in. It could still be a trap, though the figure did not seem too concerned about anything around him. He was dressed in an orange shirt, not too worn, with sunset and palm tree stylized on the front of it. His shorts were denim, cut off too neatly to have once been jeans. On his back was a dull green backpack, stuffed with junk, including what looked like a thermos tied to the top of it. His right arm was sticking out as if made of wood, the thumb pointing upwards.

Loran and Drifter exchanged a glance. Pulling up in front of the man, the driver rolled down Loran's window with a push of a button. His gaze took in the jutting, cliff-like jaw of the fellow and his squinty eyes. He did not appear to be looking at them, or at anything else, but his thumb stayed stubbornly upright.

"You trying to hitch a ride?" Drifter queried.

The figure finally moved, hand straightening and raising to brush his long, bleached hair back out of his face. "Yeah."

His voice was surprisingly deep, with an edge of surf and wave to it.

"Where to?"

"'Bout ten miles down the road."

"Well, what's one more?" Drifter said with a note of irritation. "Move over, Loran."

The woman did not look pleased, but scooted over until she was in the middle of the bench seat, robe brushing the shifter. The hitch-hiker took off his pack with a serpentine, gradual undulation and insinuated it in the back of the car on top of the other packages. Then he slid himself onto the seat, bony knees sticking up like more knobs for the dash panel. His huge feet were stuck in sandals with curling velcro straps. The toes sticking out of the front looked almost the same as the straps, nails blackened and curling upwards.

"Thanks," the hitch-hiker said once he had slammed the door. "I heard you coming and thought I would try for it. Don't get much traffic here these days. I'm Colgrin. Clarence Colgrin. You folks?"

In his usual terse style Drifter introduced both of them. Loran kept giving small, distasteful movements of her hooded head towards the newcomer and shifting away from him. But this soon put her right up against Drifter, who gave a snort and scooted right up against the door himself.

"Hold still."

Without any preamble Clarence remarked, "I don't eat people, you know."

"Glad to hear it." Drifter shrugged, steering them around a washing machine sitting half-melted in the road.

As if he hadn't replied, the hitch-hiker went on, "it wouldn't be, like... cool."

Then, after a minute he added, "not to mention it's bad for the diet. Makes your hair fall out. And you never really know what a person's been eating or doing with themselves, do you?"

"No. Not really."

They drove on in silence until the hitch-hiker seemed to feel they needed more conversation, though he still would not look at the others or acknowledge they were there.

"I eat algae."

"Algae?" Loran was finally drawn out of her frosty silence.

"And pigeons. Algae and pigeons are healthy as well as easy to catch. Algae doesn't even run away, you know?"

Both of the other occupants of the car showed that they did, indeed, agree that algae couldn't run away when you tried to catch it.

"The pigeons haven't changed much. Just a little more rubbery, *I* think. And their red crests are kinda grotesque. A lot of things have changed lately, haven't they?"

This was another undeniable statement. Clarence Colgrin did not appear to notice their lack of response. After a polite pause in case they wished to make a remark, he continued in a dull monotone.

"I don't care for how some things have changed. Just isn't cool. Like the... uh... like the... uh..."

Every word he said began to go up in tone, until he was almost screaming on last ones. "Uh... like the Chardogs that eat people in the middle of the night and tried to bite me! Agh, *tried to bite me*!"

The last sentence was screamed, hysterically. His long, knobby limbs began to thrash and flail around the cab. A long, drawn-out shriek issued from his cavernous mouth as he convulsed terribly.

Drifter slammed on the breaks, reaching for the door, about to jump out and drag the hitch-hiker from the other side. But before he could make his move, Loran had reached out and lay her hands on their hysterical companion's head.

"Calm. Calm my friend, quiet. Everything is peaceful here."

At the sound of her firm, cool voice his thrashing slowed. He gulped and the shriek came to an end. Loran took her hands away, and a moment later Clarence was sitting as calmly as he had been before.

"Sorry." Even his voice was back to the monotone. "Sometimes life gets to me. Been a lot of changes around here lately."

Hoping to distract him from another outburst along the same lines, Drifter waved a hand out of the window. "Look, we must have gone almost ten miles by now. Will this spot do for you?"

Clarence turned his head to look out at the scene around them. It wasn't much different than where he had been standing before. There was a long, dusty-red firetruck parked nearby, ladder extended towards a collapsed building and hoses melted all about it. Emergency vehicles had been dispatched when the Greenspark had first started falling, sent to wherever the first meteors touched down and conflagrations ignited. But the amount of emergencies was soon overwhelming. There were not enough response vehicles to go around. What had been sent out was being destroyed faster than the fires could be put out. Fuel tanks were hit and exploded, airplanes struck down out of the sky and the emergency personnel died in agony.

"Yeah, this will do," Clarence said, nodding at the side of the road. But he did not make a move to get out. Instead, his voice went on as he stared out of the window.

"You know, I met this strange guy once. He was really weird, far out. Had glowing eyes. And he said...uh...he said that...uh..."

Once again the hitch-hiker's voice rose without warning to a screaming note, "he said that he *came from another universe!*"

The tuneless shriek began to issue from his mouth again. This time his limbs were perfectly still, ridged and tight as he gripped the chair in his fingers. Loran tried to calm him, as she had before, but this time her words and touch had no effect. He continued to sit staring into the distance, fingers like talons and squinted eyes blank. The scream of mental pain did not cease.

Drifter jerked open the door, moving around to the passenger side in a few strides. Opening the door, he grasped Clarence's arm and leg, pulling him bodily from the car. His hands ripped loose from the seat. He continued to make his endless, inhuman cry. Drifter dragged him over and left him sitting on the cement sidewalk, pulling his backpack from the car to slam down next to him. Clarence did not seem to notice.

Sliding back into the car, Drifter drove away.

Loran looked over her shoulder through the back window, watching as the miserable figure dwindled away. Like the thin, far-off cry of a hunting bird his voice faded with him.

Once they were had gone some distance, Drifter turned his head to Loran. "How did you do it the first time?"

"Calm him?"

Drifter nodded once.

"The human mind is always hungry for assurance, sympathy. I gave it to him and it calmed his immediate fear of loneliness and pain. But he is still deeply shocked from the disaster. Certain memories will bring it out. The fear becomes so strong I can do nothing."

"I see." The driver turned back to pay attention to the cluttered road. "We're all just enigmas for you to work out."

"But I—"

"What about the last things he said?" Drifter interrupted. "Do you believe what he said about someone from another universe?"

Loran's gaze was long and slanted before she answered, "I'm not sure. It sounds far-fetched to me. Perhaps it was just someone he met who had been so altered by the disaster it was hard to recognize them as human."

"Perhaps." Drifter grunted. He waited some time before murmuring, "or it could have been one of the riders of the apocalypse, eyes flashing with vengeance. Sent from another realm."

With a small flutter of her hand, Loran brushed his remark aside. "You're too caught up in the idea that this is the end of the world. Just because things are bad now doesn't mean we can't rebuild."

"Oh?" A grim quirk twisted the edge of Drifter's mouth. "We'll see about that."

MILES LATER THE ARCHITECTURE had shifted once again, this time to a type they had not met with previously on their trip. It seemed to be an experimental sector, though they could not find a sign still standing to tell its name. There was a sort of division line between it and the last sector, an open space of charred ground with nothing on it but the blackened sticks of fences that had been destroyed and trees that had died. Beyond this strip of 'open range' a line of beige walls rose in tiers one upon the other. Arched doors and round windows opened empty eyes out onto the charred ground. Streaks of black ran up the sides of the adobe walls, along with the jagged lines of cracks. Few of the buildings looked to be fully destroyed. Being made of cured clay they were impervious to heat. But any decorations on their outside had been charred off and the earthquakes had made many of the walls break, even fall down.

The road ran into a canyon between the adobe houses, crossed high up by an arch tinted dull red. If it had once held the name of the sector there was nothing left now. Drifter aimed for it but slowed as they neared the entrance. To each side of the road posts had recently been rammed into the ground. Something hung from each post like a ragged sack with holes torn in it. But it was not sacks. It was corpses, their clothes in rags and faces torn by the ravages of scavenging birds. It was impossible to tell what they had looked like before, but they had become a easily readable sign since they were hung there. The sign read 'Warning' in crimson flesh.

"This place is bad." Drifter came to a stop, eyes cutting from one side to another.

"Why don't we go around?" Loran made a small movement with her hand, the first she had made in some time.

"Not enough fuel."

The sun was hanging on the western side of the sky behind them, throwing long shadows in front. It made the walls of the houses an each side of the road seem darker, looming into the street streaked in black and peach.

Drifter looked at the fuel gauge again and shook his head. "Not enough fuel to go around, because this is the best place I've seen so far for finding crystal fuel. The buildings aren't completely destroyed, so it won't have sparked off as easily."

"Despite those things?" Loran tilted her head towards the warnings without looking at them directly.

"Yes." He started driving again, car sliding into the shadows of the adobe houses. "Those probably mean that there is a gang controlling part of this place. But no gang is omnipresent, or can have found all of the hidden supplies. I'll take my chances with them rather than with running out of fuel and having to go the rest of the way on foot."

"*Our* chances." Loran reminded him dourly. "I'm trying to get to the Academy sector as well."

With a grunt and a shrug, Drifter pushed her words away. His foot pressed on the accelerator and they glided forwards.

Some of the buildings in the section had evidently been more than houses. Taller office buildings, garages with scorched metal doors and medical offices with worn signs depicting bones, teeth or eyes were set into the homogeneous flow. Most of the adobe houses did not have individual lawns or spaces around them, only drives and small patches of shriveled grass in front. They made a sheer canyon wall on each side of the car, many with balconies, ledges or flower boxes protruding beneath the openings of windows and doors.

Charred lines showed where rugs and banners used to hang from these protrusions. Large cracks gaped in the walls here and there, displaying teeth made of steel where support rods ran through the adobe.

Drifter flicked a gaze at the top of one building, then returned his stare to the road. After a minute he pointed the gray vehicle down a different street, running between buildings tinted faintly green. The shadows were deeper here and his car almost seemed to creep into them like a living thing.

"Someone was posted up there." Drifter jerked his head back the way they had come from. "Watching the entrance road. I saw him move off to report to base."

"So they already know we're coming," Loran commented in a soft voice.

"But they won't know where we are for long, unless they have scouts all across the sector." Turning down another street, Drifter kept to the shadows and drove slower, so that the engine noise would not travel as far. He took one path between buildings after another, until they came to a dead-end lined in garages and stacks of private dwellings.

"This will do." Piloting the car over to one side, Drifter slipped into a garage of which the door had fallen down and been blown aside. Inside there were a few cardboard boxes, marvelously whole, a shelf containing rusty tools and a workbench empty of everything except for a cracked coffee mug. It was shadowy inside, the darkness deep and menacingly quiet in the corners. Once the car was shut off, the inside of the garage felt like a swept tomb.

Stepping out onto the cement floor, Drifter gestured to his companion. "You can come with me. If the car's going to get stolen it's better that you're not in it."

"I could watch over it," Loran offered, looking up through the car's open door.

He shook his head in a negative. "Too dangerous. They might come in numbers. The best we can do is hope it keeps hidden here."

With a shrug, the woman stood out of her side and closed the door without a soft sound, before settling the purple skirt around her and making sure the hood of her robe would stay up. She seemed put out by Drifter's abrupt commands.

"Why didn't we put it in a garage with a door?"

"Those things are so unkempt they would shriek like a banshee. And if we need to make a quick getaway it's best not to be fenced in."

"I see."

Drifter waved her after him and stalked towards the inner door, which led from the garage into the house it belonged to. The door opened with a muffled sound, letting them into a dim hallway. There was a carpet on the floor, woven in shades of orange, plum and coral. It was thick with dust, which came up in little poofs as they trod on it. There was no ornamentation on the walls, and the light fixtures in the roof were hidden under tinted shields. At the end, the hall opened out into what had once been the living room. It was in shambles now, the tables broken up around the room, deep cracks inches wide across the floor and burns running down the walls in dark stains from the open windows. Beside one window a wide, low picture hung on the wall, depicting a horse galloping across the open plains. It reared its head, wearing various watercolor hues that a horse would never be seen in alive.

After this space Drifter led the way through a warren of more rooms and halls, all ruined to various extents. Some of the chambers were so unharmed that it felt like they would walk in and find a family still living there. Others were cut through by cracks and scorches, marred by broken furniture strewn across them.

Eventually, they exited through an open, arched doorway into a courtyard placed in the center of one adobe block.

It had once been tiled in bright shades of green, blue and yellow, with potted plants growing in the corners to give vibrancy and life to the scene. Now the tiles were broken and gone, the plants hairy sticks of black in their containers. Reddish spears of sun slanted over the roof tops, striking into the shadowy court. A few scraps of dirty fabric blew skittishly across it.

They stood in a shaded porch overhung with the upper story's balcony, supported by beams of sculpted adobe which had once held creeping vines. Drifter paused here, surveying the courtyard. When his companion made a move as if to go forward he put out an arm to stop her.

"Wait." His eyes narrowed as he gazed around. "I heard something move..."

Loran stood still, cocking her head to one side. After a moment she nodded in agreement, touching his arm to draw his attention to a doorway on the left-hand side of the court.

"Someone is in there."

Drifter's eyes narrowed at her. "Instincts. Someone or some thing?"

"A human."

Moving away from her, Drifter nodded at the porch. "Stay here. I'll check it out."

He strode to the cracked tiles and, keeping to the deeper shade, began to make his way around the yard. Loran stepped back to lean against the wall, a worried frown on her face. Drifter looked back once to make sure she stayed put. With her purple robe about her, it was hard to make out the woman's shape against the dim walls.

The noise Drifter had heard was a faint clinking, rattling noise, akin to gravel being sifted through someone's hands. It had fallen silent as he started to move, before beginning again with an odd consistency. He followed the sound as a wolf stalks a scent, carefully moving across the court to the door.

Inside was a room brightly lit by a pair of olive oil lanterns set on the seats of chairs. Between them a large bowl sat on the floor. An old man, with white hair trailing to his shoulders crouched over the bowl, picking up the contents and letting them roll off of his fingers. It was crystal fuel, pale blue and glittering.

The old man's fingers were stained with this activity. The thin, bony hands had an odd green-blue tint that only came with long handling of the fuel. He did not seem to see anything around him except for the pale hoard. His clothes were good and he did not look starving, but all he saw was the fuel. As he sifted it the old man muttered in a high, panting tone, "my jewels! My treasure! Oh, my lovely treasure..."

Drifter's gaze became sharper. Crystal fuel was just what he was looking for. One weak, old man should not be able to stop him from getting it.

Striding into the room, he came up beside the bent figure and looked down into the bowl along with him. The old man hardly seemed to notice until Drifter spoke,

"you have a few pounds of fuel there."

With a little gasp, the old man looked up at him, eyes becoming round and luminescent like milky marbles. "My treasure!"

"I'll trade you for it. Bread, meat, coffee...?"

"No, no..." The old man hunched over the bowl, putting out his stained talons in an attempt to cover it. "Mine, mine!"

Drifter crouched in front of him, meeting his gaze. "Look, old one, I need some fuel. I have goods to trade. The fuel's doing nothing for you in that bowl. I will give you things to make your life happier, for a time, if you give me that fuel."

But the white head continued to shake in a negative and the hands to tremble over the bowl in defense. Standing up, Drifter decided to use harsher methods. He was about to employ them when he heard a high-pitched whistle from outside. Turning away from the old man with a start, he peered out of the door. The shadows were becoming deeper away from the lantern light, darkness eating the sky. A form moved swiftly through the dark and stepped in at the door, followed by three others.

"Look what we have here, brothers. Some sort of scorched scum bullying our father!"

The first man was tall and square-faced, an ugly burn scar running down one cheek. Other than that, he showed no signs of the Greenspark disaster. His clothes were strong and clean, a jacket, vest and jeans which all fit him. A wide-brimmed hat sat on his head, and there was a pistol in his hand. The three men who followed him were all much alike, except for the weapons they carried. One had a semi-automatic rifle and a belt of bullets, another a pair of machetes at his belt and the last a long staff with a metal ferule on the end. They did not look like brothers one should mess with.

"I wasn't tormenting him." Drifter's voice was gravelly in the small room. "I was trying to make a trade."

"Hah, what have you got to trade, scorched rat?" The eldest brother stepped forward. He was in his early thirties, perhaps, while the youngest brother could have been anywhere between eighteen and his mid twenties.

"Your cloak? That empty fuel cylinder in your belt? Come on, what would you trade?"

Drifter wisely held his tongue. The brothers crowded up on one side of him, while their father continued to crouch over his bowl like a hungry rat on a carcass.

"Won't talk, eh?" The eldest's voice became darker, rougher. "We'll just have to kill you. You might even be part of the Adobe gang. Don't look it, but it's better that you're safely dead than we're sorry."

Drifter tensed himself, eyes flicking between the other men.

"Not here!" The old man shrieked, "don't want his blood in here!"

"Outside." The leader jerked his head at a lantern. "Josh, bring a light. It will only take a moment."

His hand reached out and gripped Drifter's shoulder. The youngest boy, with the stick, grabbed up one of the lanterns. They began to lead the loner towards the door.

At that moment he made his move.

Josh had fallen a little behind with the lamp. Jerking free of the eldest, Drifter kicked at the lantern. His toe contacted and flung the fiery glass to the side, where it exploded on the floor. In a split second Drifter was whirling to knock the pistol from his main captor's hand. It flew across the room as he felled the man with a series of blows to stomach and face.

But by now the brothers were reacting. Josh swung his staff at the loner in a whistling arc, almost taking off his head. Drifter ducked it just in time, jumping towards him to grasp at the wooden haft. The brother with the rifle whipped it up, pulling a lever before pointing the gun at him. He did not yet dare fire because of the proximity of Josh, but he was ready if Drifter moved away at all. The third brother drew a machete, pushing his way into the fight with it upraised.

"Stop!"

Everything froze as if a spell had been laid on it. Even Drifter paused as the icy, commanding voice reverberated through his bones. All heads turned towards the door.

A tall, slim woman with a pale face and inky dark hair stood framed against the darkness beyond. The hood of her purple robe was pushed back, while the folds of the garment fell gracefully to the floor. Her hands were out in front of her, cupped under a glowing orb of crackling blue light.

Loran moved slowly into the room between the skirmishers. Halting, she let the light go. It fell with a splash to the floor, exploding outwards in tiny droplets of blue before disappearing in mid air. Looking around, the woman said, "I think there is no reason for us to fight and kill each other. If you do not wish to accept Drifter's offer of trade, we'll leave."

The old man was still holding his bowl in his talon fingers. "No! No trade!"

Loran beckoned to Drifter with a flick of her finger. "Then we will go."

Very calmly, without a twitch of his face, Drifter joined her and they walked out of the door into the gloom of the twilight. As soon as they were out in the dark he grasped her wrist and started running, pulling the woman after him through the doorway on the side of the courtyard, down a hall and into a pitch-dark room. From there he led them at a quick walk back through the warren, to where the car sat in the darkened garage. He took no wrong turns.

Drifter stopped in the garage, turning to her with a quick motion. "So, it isn't just a mental sensitivity. What was that blue light?"

Loran extracted her wrist and brushed down her robe, panting. "There was no reason to run so fast. They were letting us go."

"For the moment. Now answer my question."

The woman hesitated, face a blur in the dark. When she spoke it was with firmness, "I do not question you about your secrets too closely. Do not question me."

There was a space of silence.

"Fine."

Drifter surprised her with his answer, moving over to open the door of his car and start it. They both slid into opposite seats and the driver looked over at the woman. "I've been fighting too much lately. It's time to play a new card."

She forbore from asking as the car slid out into the darkness of the gathering night.

Chapter 6: A Gathering at Night

The bullet-gray car rolled through the dark, headlights on and reflecting from the adobe house walls. Drifter did not take the twisting back alleys now, choosing the widest, openest streets to follow. A few times they had to back-track because of chasms in the street, or buildings crumbling across it. The driver almost seemed to know where he was going, though he had never been to this part of Apex before. Loran was forced by her own words to hold her tongue.

She did comment after a moment, "whatever gang rules this place will certainly come to know our movements now."

"Certainly," Drifter intoned, before adding in an abstracted tone, "without doubt or question; unquestionably."

His dictionary quotations were a habit.

"Those men were not part of the gang, were they?" Loran asked after a moment, as this was not a direct questioning of him or his motives.

"No. The Adobe gang is their enemy, I gather."

After this terse reply a sliding, cold silence fell on the car. The heater worked with a light hushing sound to keep the chill of the air away, but it could not hold out the iciness of their thoughts.

It was not long before they pulled into a central plaza. A strange, oxidized, bronze statue stood in the center of it, surrounded by tiles of dull brick in a large, open square. Haughty buildings with their roofs cracked and faces falling at their feet stood around the square, shutting out most of the sky with their balconies and walls. Arched windows and open doorways looked out, hardly visible against the blackness of the buildings in silhouette. It felt as if a face or terrible eyes might peer out of the apertures at any moment.

Above, the sky was half-starry and half covered in gathering clouds. An abnormal oppression was starting to build in the air.

Drifter parked the car on the edge of the square, turning off the lights so that everything inverted into shadows. The walls of the buildings gleamed with a faint starlight, the statue was a dark shape like a grim reaper bending over his scythe. The tiles on the ground caught the most of the little light, throwing it back in a hazy glow.

As if drawn after him by an invisible force, Loran stepped out of the vehicle when he did. Without a word, Drifter pulled a few items from the back of the car and tucked them under one arm, walking towards the statue in the center of the plaza. He came to a halt in front of the sculpture, apparently studying it in the darkness. Loran glanced around with a shiver, feeling as if she were being inspected as well. Her eyes met a pair of gleaming red orbs only a few yards away and she gave a jump.

"Drifter." Her voice was tight and low. "There is a Chardog."

His hooded head turned towards the red orbs as a low growl rumbled out of the shady shape supporting them.

"I know."

Moving towards it, he held out a hand and continued to speak in an even tone.

"They sense fear and hate, you know. They're still dogs, under their twisted forms. Most people see one and are afraid. The dog feels it and it triggers his attack response."

Standing right beside the Chardog now, Drifter reached out and rubbed it under its huge, hanging jaw. The growling had stopped. Now, as the man stroked it gently, a low whimper came from the beast. Like a domestic dog, it tilted back its head and rubbed it against the man's side, flipping at his elbow with its snout for more attention.

Drifter removed a dead Vollan from where he had tucked it under the opposite arm. The Chardog took it from him with a snap and a grumble of satisfaction.

Drifter edged away and walked up to the statue again.

"That old man's fuel would not have been enough to get us to the Academy sector anyway. I need more than that to complete my mission. Perhaps even more than what would take me to Dick Chelsea. I don't have the time or inclination any longer to hunt for it like a rat."

Feeling that what was coming was somehow unnerving, almost evil, Loran protested weakly, "you did not search long. We could..."

Her words trickled away to nothing as Drifter flicked her a glance over his shoulder. The Chardog was still crunching and cracking at the Vollan carcass in a slobbery joy that could be heard but not seen. Other than that, the only noise was a a cold wind flowing through the night, sharp and hissing against the walls. It twined around Loran's feet and crept up her robe. She shivered. Drifter's enigmatic actions made her harden herself against whatever was to come.

Taking out three more dead Vollans, Drifter arranged them beside the base of the statue in front of him. Once they were to his liking, he stepped back and spread his hands wide, intoning words with the fire running through them stronger than the gravel.

"Beasts of the dark, winged and wild. On four legs and on two. Come from the regions of utter night, I have need and pray for you."

Turning from the statue he looked like some sort of grim reaper himself, or a prophet of doom. His hood made his face an utter darkness except for a faint gleam of eyes, while the cape down his back blurred his shape to blend with the bronze figure behind him.

"Beasts of the dark, winged and wild. Gaping jaw and beak. Come from the region of shadow's spark, I need your bright eyes to seek."

When his words had echoed out across the plaza and gone silent, he let his arms drop and moved a step towards Loran, seeming to shrink back into the wandering, scorch-driven Drifter he was.

With a shrug he said, "nothing to it."

As he finished speaking the darkness filled with the flap of soft wings, the prowl of padded feet and an even softer swish, as of smaller, fuzzier feet stalking. Shapes began to gather in from the gloom. Some landed on the statue, others crept in along the ground. With a swoop, something landed on Drifter's shoulder. Loran looked closer to see a thin, black bird with a raven's blunt beak and twinkling eyes. But the feathers along its belly, legs and the centers of its wings were missing, so that pale flesh showed there almost in the shape of human arms and legs. All down its back were crinkled, white stripes, like those of certain woodpeckers.

"Charwings," Loran said slowly, glancing around at the luminous red eyes and hulking shapes gathering on the ground. "And Chardogs."

"That's not all." Drifter clicked his fingers and a smaller, more lithe shape detached itself from the darkness. It was pale, bone white, a blurred mass in the dark. It walked without a sound and its eyes were blue-green circles that glowed like the eyes of the Chardogs.

Loran did not even have a name for the feline that came to sit at Drifter's feet. It would have been simply a cat except for that its face was longer, more pointed like a rodent's. Its ears had grown long and thin, standing up in peaked lines, while its paws were wide and fuzzy-soft. There was no sign of toes in that glimmering fluff, only talons which slid in and out with horrible glints.

"There are so few of these," Drifter told her, bending to touch it once on the back of its head, "that I have had to name them myself. Moonhunters."

The feline tilted its head as if understanding the name, before taking fright at Loran's involuntary movement and whisking away into the deeper shadows.

The heavy breathing of Chardogs was all around them now, and a pack stalked up to sit on their wide haunches a few yards away. The Charwings on the statue rustled around impatiently. Drifter stepped over beneath them and picked up one roasted Vollan. Holding it up on the flat of his hand to the Charwing on his shoulder, he whispered something near its beaked head. It took the fat body and flapped away. The Moonhunter also came back for its share, while the last one was tossed to the largest of the Chardogs.

"Crystal fuel, my friends," Drifter told them, "bring it here."

And as the creatures streamed away into the night with soft cawing noises, bubbling breath and the pad of many feet, a different sort of congregation drew nearer from where they had been watching around the edges of the plaza. Men. Carrying shuttered lanterns which they opened up, along with weapons of every description and type, they gathered around Loran and Drifter in a wide semi-circle. They were barbarically dressed, their arms and legs painted in patterns of bright red and blue. Many of them seemed to have a darker-skinned blood in them and those wore bones in their curly hair or bangles in their ears. They did not seem to notice the cold, though few had on the clothes for anything other than a day at the beach.

If there was a leader among them, they did not show it. They gathered and stared with glittering, hostile eyes. But not one stepped up closer than his fellow or made a move to communicate. Loran drew herself straight and looked back coldly, hands folding together in her sleeves. Drifter stood at ease, putting more weight on his uninjured leg. His bright eyes moved over the crowd without a spark of emotion.

Like a field of grain they all swayed forward and bowed low. No sound was made except for a low moan or hum, either of fear or awe.

The whole gang straightened itself and retreated into the gloom until they had become only flickering, jouncing sparks of light. These faded away between the buildings until Drifter and Loran stood alone in the plaza with the statue positioned over them.

"I believe we've just met the Adobe gang," Drifter commented in a rough tone.

The woman turned her pale face towards him, still stiff and regal as a queen. "They seem to have feared you."

With a tired sigh, Drifter slid down to sit at the base of the statue, back propped against it. His eyes shut and he leaned his head on one hand. "They are only afraid of the creatures. And that because the creatures have been affected by the scorch in different ways, more deeply, than most humans."

The silence became inflexible. Clouds slowly rolled up to cover more of the sky. Their edges billowed out like angel's wings, brushing the stars away. The darkness grew deeper until neither of the people in the plaza could see the other.

Drifter broke the stillness without apparent remorse, "bring me something to eat, woman. We haven't had dinner yet."

Without a sound Loran groped to the car and went inside. The door slammed. She did not come back out.

The sky thickened, the wind became moist. A drop of rain hit the tiles of the court, sending up a puff of dust. After the disaster particles from the burning and destruction had filled the atmosphere the sun had turned red. Both from a mixture of that and perhaps some harm that had reached out and touched it during the fall of Greenspark. Imbalances had come over the planet, shaking it to its core. The seasons had been altered in their patterns. There was no longer a wet season and a dry one, cold and warm, winter, summer, fall or spring. It rained rarely, but at odd times, without long warning. It was always colder, dimmer and dryer out in the open. Under the deep shade of buildings, ponds stayed for weeks. Moisture festered without leaving.

Another drop of water fell from the sky, splattering on Drifter's hood with a light sound. It was followed by the fluttering of wings, which came out of the dark to settle all around him. The Charwings had returned first. Their leader hopped to the man's shoulder and let a few precious grains of crystal fuel fall from its beak to glow in his cupped hand.

"Thank you, my friend."

Each of the Charwings jumped forward to lay a few grains at his feet. Soon there was a tiny heap of the glowing stuff in front of him. The rain held back, seeming to wait for the other beasts to return.

Soon they came, carrying odd little containers or the raw crystals in their mouths. Leather sacks the size of a golf-ball, cylinders which gleamed with blue streaks and boxes of every color were set before him. The creatures almost seemed to bow as he thanked them, touching a head or flank with his fingers.

As the beasts of the night faded away the rain began to come down. Drifter pulled off his cloak and threw it over the precious pile in front of him, wrapping them up from the damp. Large, hard drops hit his head and soaked through his hair. In only a moment he was wet through.

He did not dare call on the beasts of the night too often for aid. They might grow weary of serving him or even not respond to his call once he got further away from his home range. He reserved summoning them for the times of greatest need.

The fuel they had given him, he took over to the car and, opening the door awkwardly, stowed in the back among the bundles of provisions. Loran did not look at him as he stowed himself in the front seat and wiped the wetness from his face and head, before dragging his cape from the back and wrapping it around himself.

Rain thundered on the roof, running down the windshield in long strings and streaks. It pattered to the ground around the vehicle, turning dust to sticky mud. Red lightening flickered in the sky, the thunder growling dully many seconds later.

"I think," Drifter remarked, leaning back against the seat, "I'll sleep in here tonight. As long as that doesn't frighten you?"

His eyes cut through the dark. Loran's shape could be seen, dimly, to be sitting very upright on her side of the seat.

"No." Her voice held nothing, not even contempt. It was a hard, slick surface like glass. "I know you would not hurt me."

"Good. Because the underside of the car would be much less comfortable for either of us."

Without more ado he stretched his legs out under the steering wheel, pulled his damp clothes tighter around him and appeared to fall directly asleep. Loran sat stiffly for a few minutes, before muttering under her breath, "humph!"

But after this last protest she wrapped up in her robe and leaned against the cold window with her hood, weariness overtaking her.

IN THE MORNING THE rain had stopped, leaving the sky a ragged mass of clouds slowly being torn apart by upper winds. The air was raw and cool, bringing out the scents of pavement, dust and moldering buildings. Drifter awoke in the gray of predawn, one hand resting on the wheel and the other arm flung over his eyes. Quietly, he rummaged out bits of bread and dried meat from the back.

Loran was still asleep, forehead resting against the opposite window. He could see the outline of her back through the purple fabric of her robe, rising and falling steadily in slumber. Without waking her, he ate his breakfast, flicking the crumbs from his lap into a heap on the palm of one hand before dumping them down his throat. When he moved his left leg he felt that the scar had stiffened in the night. The rain soaking in through his pants had made it soften the evening before. Rolling up the pants leg, he gazed at the wound dispassionately. There was no wine in the car. It would have to fend for itself this morning.

He had just started to unravel the garment again when there was a slight movement and he realized that Loran had awoken without a sound. Her eyes were also on the old wound.

"I have some medicine—"

"Thanks," he cut her off, jerking the pant leg back into place. "I've tried various medicines before. Nothing helps."

"Mine might be more effective than any you've tried."

"I don't think so." Drifter opened the door and stepped out. A handful at a time, he brought the bags, boxes and grains of crystal fuel out of the car around to the front, where he poured them into the tank under the hood. The creatures had brought him pounds of the stuff, one bit at a time. Now he had enough to fill the tank and still keep two full cylinders to stick in his belt beside the key in the empty one.

"We can make it to the Academy sector now," he said as he came back to sit in the driver's place.

Loran had been eating her own breakfast. The crumbs from her robe she shook out of the door. "Good."

They started driving again, snaking around the statue and out of the plaza into more of the canyons between adobe buildings. There was no sign of the Adobe gang in the cool morning air. It seemed as if they had been washed away by the rain like so much dust.

The walls were a little cleaner, the colors brighter shades of orange, red and yellow. Pools of grimy water formed in every depression in the road, turning into rainbows as the car splashed through them. The reddish sun gradually beat a hole in the clouds and poured its depressed rays across the city.

After a time they left the adobe sector behind, leaving under another arched sign which had lost all of its lettering. There were no gruesome corpses here to warn the unwary away, only a Charwing sitting on top of the arch watching them. When the car had gone by, the bird rose on striped wings and soared away, letting out a victorious cawing sound.

Soon they were in another sector of smashed, ruined buildings made of heavy stone slabs and white pillars. Garbage blew across the streets. Slabs and shards of rock often blocked their way. It became slow and arduous to pick a path through the buildings, so often did they have to backtrack or take round-about streets to go further east. Once their way was blocked by burnt-out fire engines and other emergency vehicles, all piled up by human hands some time after the fire. But no one was in sight and the wall of vehicles did not seem to shield anything in particular from the rest of the city.

Days past by as they traveled through blasted sections of Apex. Without the need for fuel or food they stopped rarely, only to stretch their legs or scout a way ahead. They met few people in this last leg of the trip. Once they ran into another group of the children monks, begging for food on the ruined steps of the foundation of some large building. Other times they saw a glimpse of someone disappearing around a corner or flitting between wreckage. Otherwise, all was still and dead.

They spoke rarely. Twice more Drifter had Loran quiz him on the dictionary, stopping when he could not answer one question or answered it incorrectly. Loran would occasionally comment on the surroundings or ask a question. Except for this, they made few conversations in the many hours of driving together.

If the highways had been open and the streets kept usable it would have taken them much less time to do the distance between the Falel sector and Terminal Point. As it was, progress was often slow and obstructed. They did not reach their destination for many days.

The first signs of the Academy sector were odd, high towers and pointed roofs like those of a cathedral rearing up on the horizon. The jagged bits of smashed glass domes also glinted in the noon light, rising like icicles towards the sky. A stone plinth beside the road, a few miles on, bore the figure of a man in a robe and flat hat, pointing towards the sector with the words stamped beneath him 'Academy Sector.'

By now they were out on Terminal Point, though the coast was too far away and too hidden by buildings to see. The only indication of the change was a soft taint to the air, a distant saltiness and moisture. As they both knew from the maps they had seen when they were younger, the Academy section filled almost all of Terminal point. Except for Anchorage, on the furthest tip and a strip of seaside homes, fishing docks and other coastal installments which ringed it. Off the coast lay the Sea of Storms, a deep, cold and leaden ocean which ponderous freighters used to move across on their journeys to far lands.

The jagged, towering walls of the cathedral-like buildings loomed closer. The road became paved in closely-set gray bricks, worn smooth on top. They were laid in a herringbone pattern, running lengthwise down the street. In the shadow of the first huge building, with its roof smashed in and circular window broken, Drifter pulled to a stop.

The car idled down and both passengers looked out of their separate windows at the looming structure with its classic arches and jagged walls.

"Well, we made it. This is where we part ways." Drifter nodded at the building.

Loran slowly turned her head to look at him. There was little expression in her eyes except for a calm acceptance. "Thank you."

Drifter glanced away, shrugged and turned back, "I was fortunate you were there the night I tried to take crystal fuel from the old man. All scores are even."

Opening the door, the woman stepped outside. She did not reply to his words, though she gave a slight inclination of her head.

"Don't forget your supplies." Drifter gestured at the bundles and packages behind them. "We'll have to unload the stuff so you can cache it somewhere nearby."

"Half of it is yours," Loran reminded him. But Drifter shook his head, stepping out of his own door and leaning in to start pulling out bundles.

"I don't need that much provisions. I can always find something to eat."

The woman gave him a small smile with her head cocked on one side. "And I can't?"

"You're not experienced." With another shrug, Drifter continued to pull out what was left of the packages, piling them beside the car. At her insistence, he kept one small package of bread, dried meat and fruit for himself. He also had the lengths of fabric left from the empty bundles.

Once it was all out he gave a nod to Loran and got back in the car. She raised a hand in farewell as he drove away.

The tall, slim figure disappeared gradually from his mirrors, fading away into the buildings of the Academy sector. Drifter felt a small twinge of guilt, leaving her undefended against the broken world. But he shook it away in disgust. Loran had traveled Apex by herself for at least a year before he picked her up. She was not helpless. And even if she had been it was none of his business. He had a mission of his own to carry out.

Chapter 7: Alone Again

The huge places of learning, libraries, schools and colleges, swallowed the gray car like a fly. Its engine echoed quietly down the side-streets, reverberations soon muffled by marble and brick. There was no way to tell where the car should go next, which buildings to search or what Drifter should be looking for. He needed to find Dick Chelsea. Years ago that man had been living in the Academy sector. There was no guarantee that he still was or that he had even survived the fall of Greenspark fire.

After driving aimlessly for some time Drifter pulled over to the side and stopped. Beyond the sidewalk a patch of open ground spread, black trunks of destroyed conifers jabbing at the sky. The chain-link fence that had once ringed it was fallen to the ground, laying in torn, rusty heaps. In the center of the space a large building rose up, columns and arches of white marble supporting an angled roof of gray tiles. Three of the pillars had fallen, laying broken in the dirt. What looked like a blackened human skeleton was decomposing into the ground, trapped under a fallen pillar.

On the opposite side of the street was a monument of rough gray and tan stone, formed into a huge edifice of learning. Archaic symbols were carved into the stone above a dim opening, a colonnaded entrance like a gaping mouth. Drifter looked from one building to the other, then pocketed his keys and chose the larger building of gray and tan. It had windows, some of them surprisingly intact, which could be used to look out on a large portion of the surrounding city. He might see movement from there, someone he could question or follow secretly.

As he strode towards the building Drifter realized that he was alone again. No one followed in his footsteps, questioned his next move or watched him from coldly calm eyes. It was a feeling of release, a freedom from worry and care. Everything was as it should be. He moved alone, a solitary figure bent on his own projects.

The shade under the portico engulfed him. He walked under it to where the glass doors were still intact, dust filming their smooth surface. Recently, someone had scratched words on the wall beside the doors. Drifter leaned over to look at them, eyes narrowed.

'step inside and learn your lessons,
life and death together making fun.'

There was nothing else to the poem except for a vague scrawl on the wall which could have been a signature or words that were never written, stopped by some violence. It did not give Drifter a clue as to where Dick might live, though it did confirm that someone was still alive in this sector. If the poem was supposed to be a warning, Drifter did not know what it meant. Life and death walked hand in hand across all of Apex, death as the elder brother.

He pushed carefully on one side of the double-door, swinging it open soundlessly. Inside, a hall carpeted in moth eaten plush led past office and bathroom doors to the main chamber of the academy. A huge, soaring room with a pillar of dark blue material holding up the domed ceiling in the center. All around the upper edges of the chamber ran a wide balcony, bound by twining banisters of steel. Windows looked out upon the city at regular intervals around this balcony, most of them still intact. From them spilled light tinted silver and gold by dust. It pooled over the lip of the walkway and cascaded into the huge chamber, striking blue glints from the central pillar.

All this was quiet and harmonious. It exhaled an air of deep thinking and peace left over from its days as a college. But there was an incongruity in the scene which Drifter eyed warily.

Hanging from the balcony was a number of long ropes, bound to the supports underneath it. Dangling from each rope was a lynched body. Charwings hopped from one corpse to the next, picking and pecking. It did not look like a warning, unlike the pair of bodies outside of the adobe houses. These hanging forms had been executed for some crime or destroyed in a fit of revenge. The birds fluttering between them were horribly alive, the bodies grimly dead.

Drifter now understood the writing by the door. It had been done more recently than he thought, sometime within the last week, by the state the remains were in. But their faces were too destroyed for him to make out if any were the man he was searching for. He did not know if he would even recognize Dick should he meet him alive.

A stench of decay drifted through the large chamber, along with the golden dust motes in the window's light. Drifter hunched his shoulders against the smell and passed through the room, ascending a wide staircase at the other side. This did not lead to the balcony, but up to another hall with many doors leading off of it. The dormitories and living quarters of the academy.

Still, it was not the highest vantage point of the building. Drifter found another set of steps, narrower this time, leading him up to a series of school rooms, libraries and dining chambers. Eventually, he found the last set of steps leading upwards, even narrower than before. These took him to a tall pinnacle above the domed roof, set on its peak. In it was a sort of observatory, a circular room with windows all around its walls and a dome of shattered glass on top. Bits littered the floor like stars, reflecting the sunlight above. The floor was scorched but, being thick stone, still stable enough to walk on.

Moving over to a window, Drifter leaned on the thick stone lintel to look out. Directly below him was the dome of the lower chamber. Beneath it, the scene dropped away suddenly, plunging down a few jagged towers and subsidiary roofs to the herringbone pavement of the street. The white palace across the way could be seen clearly, tiled roof glinting with a dull light. Beyond it, and all around him, the structures of the Academy sector reached out. Massive, hulking buildings with domes and gables, towers of a brownish-gold stone with tops wider than their trunks, bubbled of shattered and sparkling glass. It spread all around him, with shadowy, bricked avenues in between. And, here and there, the burnt hulks of conifer trees with tops singed to a single spire.

He saw nothing moving, but Drifter was patient. Hoisting himself onto the wide edge of the window, he sat with his back against the inner wall and legs resting along the sill. With a turn of his head he could keep watch on his car below and everything that stirred in this part of the city.

Charwings hopped in and out of the lower story of the building. A few other birds, pigeons perhaps, winged their way between structures. Other than that, everything appeared to be silent. Drifter became as still as the scene, as motionless as the stone. Sitting in the window, he would have looked like a mere dark smudge from below. No one would have thought the shape alive, as it did not even twitch as the sun moved across the sky and began its descent into the gray mists of the far west behind him. For a few minutes the sun outlined the man in fiery red like a halo. Then it sunk beyond the edge of the opposite window and he became an even darker outline as the sky faded to blue. Gray tones gradually ate into the sky, bleaching color from the air until all was darkness, with a sprinkling of blurred stars above.

Finally Drifter shifted, legs swinging down to meet the floor. He had seen nothing to indicate human life as he watched, no movements, lights or smoke from cooking fires. But he knew people must be out there, as the lynching below proved it.

Retracing his steps down the stairs and through the halls in the dark, Drifter found his way to the main hall. The stench of decay still hung in the room, frosted by the cold air. No light came in through the windows except for the faintest starlight. The bodies were looming shapes of black in the gray darkness. Drifter moved through the hall quickly, coming out between the pillars of the academy's entrance and onto the sidewalk. Above him, the sky was clear and cold, stars burning silver in the deepest blue. His car was a faint gray sheen across the road, outlined against the ghostly white of the opposite building.

From the shadows by the pillar, he surveyed the road up and down to make sure that nothing was stirring. It was on the second sweep of his head that he saw something detach itself from the whiteness of the opposite structure. A shape just as pale as the stone it came from. Mist seemed to swirl around it, long strips of gauze floating on the chill air.

The wraith moved across the open space at a tangent to Drifter, heading towards a group of buildings on the far right. He could see no clear legs on the thing, but it glided in long strides over the desolate ground. As it came nearer, he heard an eerie, bell-like noise proceeding from it at intervals. A mellow, deep gonging would sound, before fading away into the still night air. Once each note had evaporated it would be followed by a second exactly like the first. Drifter crouched back against the pillar behind him at the sound. It was so inhuman, precisely placed, yet softly reverberating, that he felt a fearful chill as it repeated itself.

The phantom wafted by, gradually disappearing into a cluster of buildings which looked like storage sheds or outbuildings of some sort. It did not re-emerge. After waiting for some time Drifter went cautiously across the street to his car. He felt oddly shaken at the sight of the wraith. It brushed uncomfortably close to his memories of the last time he had met one, which in turn evoked remembrances further back...

With an effort he shook the spooked feeling off and turned the key to start his car. Almost without meaning to, he checked the passenger seat, before realizing that there was no reason for him to look towards it. No one would be there, whether he looked or not. He did not have to wait for Loran to get in, or argue the meaning of the apparition with her. A momentary twinge of disappointment traveled through him.

"Fool," he muttered to himself, wrenching the car around onto the road. "Forget it. Forget her and everything else. They won't matter once your mission is done."

Driving into the darkness, he ran without his headlights on so as to attract less attention. His eyes searched for any light that another person might have lit, any smudge of smoke against the sky. Seeing only stars and shadows, he drove through the whole sector from one end to the other. Late at night, past the deep-blue middle, he came out on the wharf of the seaboard. At the very tip of Terminal point, a long beak reaching into the sea.

The cement of the wharf was cracked and mildewed, the fence around it broken and dragged aside. Drifter drove out onto the edge of the docks and stopped, staring out over the deep sea.

The water was a black so alive it was like the hide of a sleeping beast, undulating at every breath. Tints of blue and gray ran through it, streamers of phosphorescent green glinting on the horizon. The swells were oily and shifting, so that not a star was reflected in it. The sky might as well have been covered in the thickest clouds. The noise of the breakers slamming against the pier filled the night with a melancholy solemness, healing and bitter as a tall glass of wine.

Drifter stood out of his car and moved to a stop beside the hood, leaning on it slightly. The cold sea air misted against his face, bringing the sharp scent of brine. Far to his right, along the wharf a huge ship lay crumpled against the cement, sides peeling and rusting as the bow was gradually jammed into the hard land. The name on its side was almost gone, the company logo worn away. It was no longer a machine, one of the tools of men to move and accumulate wealth. What had once been a ship was a ghost, the bones of a memory.

Turning about, Drifter looked back at the silhouette of the Academy sector. It stretched all along the landwards horizon, clasped by thin arms of sea on either side. Dead structures raised their heads to the sky, blotting out stars with their immensity. Gray tiles gleamed, walls blackened by the absence of light stood solidly. The jagged ends of broken rafters bristled out of one nearby warehouse, making inky lines straight as a ruler. Far away, a tall tower rose above the rest, head a bubble in the sky.

At first there was no sign of inhabitants, no light or movement in the city. But as Drifter watched, something happened which made his gaze sharpen with excitement. A tiny yellow light, a golden glow blunted by distance, appeared in one window of the tall tower. It was small and far away, a fairy drifting in the night air, but it meant life.

The tower was somewhere near the center of the sector. Drifter tried to fix its location in his mind, using the roofs of other buildings and towers near it to create landmarks. Once the outline of the city, with its one glowing spark, was imprinted on his mind he got back in his car and turned it towards the nearest street. The Academy sector was not wholly dead.

TANGLED IN THE MANY avenues between looming buildings, Drifter eventually lost his course. Whether the light had gone out, or was impossible to view from a closer perspective below the tower, he could not tell. Usually, he was adept at making his way through Apex with perfect precision. But the Academy sector was built on different plans, and once you came near their base all of the towers looked the same in the dark.

Frustrated, Drifter slapped a hand on the seat next to him and gazed all about in the shadowy alleys. The tower above him could be the one he had spotted from the pier, but it did not appear to be the tallest in the sector, from his perspective at its base. He had already tried two towers, both of which had appeared to be in the right place. But each had been empty, one even half-destroyed by the disaster. More than that, neither looked like they had been entered or disturbed in many days. Cobwebs hung over their steps inside, the dust was unmarked before Drifter stepped there, and sections of staircase were missing in the broken one. Sections too large to be bypassed, even by a great effort.

It felt as if the right tower were eluding him on purpose, a ghost losing itself in the mass of ghostly buildings to avoid his contact. Closing his eyes, Drifter recalled the scene on the pier and tried to bring up an image of the roof shapes around the lit tower. But all of the shapes in the sector started to blend together, slanted roofs, domed roofs and peaks all repeated in hundreds of buildings.

With a snort, he turned off the car and got out. He would try this third tower and if that failed, keep lookout in it for the light to reappear or, that failing as well, wait for morning in an attempt to spot the tallest tower in the area.

The area the third tower stood in was nondescript. More ancient buildings and the burnt twigs of scorched hedges stood around it. The road ran by on its right side. In front of Drifter, on the far side of the tower, lay a tall dividing wall of gray stone. There was nothing to show that a human dwelt in the tower. Even as he walked up to the tower's melted aluminum door, Drifter could not make out footprints in the loose dirt in front of the it. His hope was low as he walked through the arched doorway, metallic nuggets crunching under his feet. Inside was a large, circular room that had once been carpeted and set with comfortable couches like a waiting room. Now ash lay thick on the floor and small wooden beams stood like skeletons with the fabric burnt off.

Drifter was not sure what the towers had been used for before the disaster. They almost appeared to be wizard's retreats or the homes of sorceresses. But, as magic was not one of the studies in the Academy sector, he theorized they must have belonged to high-ranking professors who lived in them as status symbols.

A staircase of polished stone led up in a spiral towards the upper stories. Along its edge was a previously gilded banister, gold peeling off like flaking skin. The steps were more solid underfoot than the last tower stairs Drifter had tried. Walking up them, his senses were stretched on the alert for any sound from above. Nothing stirred, no light glimmered down the steps or feet echoed on upper floors. Drifter ran a hand along the banister as he ascended, gold flakes crackling off under his finger tips. He passed doors leading into other rooms and open landings strewn with dusty furniture. Finally, he reached the top, where an open square of paleness indicated the entrance to the upper chamber. Drifter came up through it like a man emerging from deep water, head and shoulders breaking above the darkness below.

A gray predawn light was just starting to cut the horizon, pooling in through the windows set all around the chamber. Some of the glass was cracked, one or two pieces missing from their corners. The earthquakes had not taken as great a toll on this part of the city, leaving many of the towers and buildings upright. Perhaps it was their older form of construction which gave them unexpected stability. Or maybe it was just one of the peculiarities of the Greenspark fall.

The room had a swaybacked bedstead, a few dusty chairs and what looked like a child's play pool set on the floor. Other than that the room was oddly bare, as if someone had stolen the very carpet and knickknacks. Drifter moved across the empty floorboards to stand by one of the cracked windows, peering out at the night. This tower was unoccupied, as he had expected. Even the dust of the floor was undisturbed. But somewhere out there was a lantern, flashlight or hearth that had been lit for a brief space of time. Enough for him to see it and fix it in his mind.

Going from one window to the next Drifter looked over the city. There were two or three towers in the vicinity, each appearing taller than the one he stood in. A huge, ancient library blocked his view in one direction, peaked eaves looming towards him. Drifter skipped those windows and came around to the ones facing east, in front of the tower, towards the divider wall. From this vantage he could see over the wall, into a open space on the other side. It was paved smoothly in dark gray cement, ringed with the wall on three sides. Standing on the cement in the center was a large, domed shape which glimmered in the early morning light. It was a dome, a huge bubble resting directly on the ground. Drifter's eyes focused on it with surprised intensity.

The dome was glimmering with the shades of unbroken glass. Not only that, it sparkled with a blue sheen, as if a net of silken cobweb lay across the whole thing, tinted a brilliant azure. Underneath the dome, hues of vivid green flickered and shifted. A shade of green Drifter had not seen in many days. But it was the blue which most held his attention. There was only one thing he knew of which had that color. One thing which could keep a huge dome of glass from being shattered or melted by the Greenspark fire. A force shield.

Force shields were not a widely known or used technology in the days before the disaster. If they had been, more of the world could have been saved. As it was the technology was mostly in development, an experimental idea being put to the test. Drifter had known a man, been close friends with a fellow, who worked in the development of force shields. This was why he had been able to put one in his car in the first place. It had been a sort of joke between them, a laughing gift his friend had helped him install.

"Because, who knows?" The words of his friend suddenly came down to him through the years, forcing their way out of the box of his memories. *"Maybe one day you'll be chased by mobsters or in the middle of a wild fire and need a force shield."*

Before the disaster he had only used it once, when out driving with his wife. They had been driving through a nature reserve of some sort, a national park. He had taken a rough back road through the trees and come upon a waterfall at the base of a rocky cliff. With a silly desire to scare her and have some fun, he had driven through the waterfall, putting up the force shield so that the water cascaded around the car without touching it, falling in beautiful, sun-lit streamers...

Drifter broke away from the memory with a gasp to find himself still standing in the abandoned tower, looking out across the cold, ruined city at the force-shielded dome. He was shaking and had to grip the window ledge to stop himself. The cold air seemed to cut through his cloak with unusual intensity. Staring at the glimmering circle of color, he forced the last vestiges of memory away, tamping it down beyond the dark scars of his mind.

He was in the ruined remains of Civitas Apex. In the Academy sector, to be precise. He had to find Dick Chelsea. Whoever had turned on the shield around the dome might still be living there. If so, they might have a clue as to where Dick could be found. Or if he had perished in the fall of Greenspark.

For a moment, Drifter turned this idea over in his mind. If Dick had died, what then? Where else could he go to discover more about the key in his belt, find out if his theories about it were correct?

The libraries, perhaps. Loran was still out there, searching the great libraries for knowledge. She might have found something by now that would help him. Or he could look through the books alone, hunting for any mention of a relic key and the gate it went to...

But for now the sun was starting to tint the sky lemon-lime and he wanted to find out more about the dome below.

THERE WAS A LOW, RUMBLING sound like an engine running coming up from below the cement pad. Drifter walked out onto it in the first streaks of dawn, having passed around the end of the division wall. Below him, the noise rumbled, far away. In front of him the force shield glimmered with silent blue flame. The glass dome underneath of it came down to an entrance on his side, a door set into a frame in the glass. Beyond it, vague green shapes stood reflecting the morning light in a million shades.

Attracted by the burst of color in the gray landscape, Drifter moved quietly up to the edge of the shield. His shoulders felt tight with inward tension as he turned to view the whole courtyard suspiciously. A moment later he pivoted back to peer at the glass in an attempt to see inside. But between its thickness and the sparkle of the force shield he could make out nothing except flighty colors and insubstantial forms inside. If anyone was watching his movements, they blended into the scenery too much to be made out.

Reaching out a hand, he ran it gently down the smooth surface of the force shield. There were no markings on the ground or handles outside to indicate a way through. It might have been remotely activated or enabled from inside.

As he touched it there was a faint flicker through the whole thing, a shift of color from blue to yellow around his fingers. The shield shifted in a way he had not expected a shield could, forming itself around the door, opening up in a rectangle just as big as the entrance. In front of him the force shield was cleared to the glass door. Everywhere else on the dome it still flickered sky blue.

Drifter blinked his eyes slowly, like a lizard, before stepping forward and trying the handle of the door. It turned easily, the door swinging open on smooth hinges to let him inside.

The first breath of air that touched him made him realize how stale the outside world was. Inside, it was not just breathable, not simply a gas to take in and exhale. It was alive, moist, warm and full of delicate scents. Breathing it in was like drinking a refreshing draft of water.

Once he had stepped inside and shut the door he stood taking in the sights, dazzled by color and living form.

A large deciduous tree grew in the center of the space, gnarled roots digging into a huge pit of rich, dark loam. Its branches reached for the sky beyond the dome, spreading forth leaves as big as a hand and greener than anything Drifter had seen in years. Like the air, it was not a stale, dead green. It was the verdant color of something that was alive.

All around the tree and in every available space between paths stood buckets, tubs and raised beds of growing things. Bushes, grass tufts, delicate annuals and flowers in every shade of red, orange and yellow. Their foliage varied as much as their forms, leaves of dark green, lighter shades or veined in red. Leaves the shape of spears, hearts, spiders and tongues. Some grew in thick profusion, making it difficult to see through them. Others sprouted in traceries so fine they were like vivid lace.

Drifter had never seen the hidden fields of Apex Haven. If he had, the greenery of this sheltered spot might not have come as such a shock. As it was, he felt like he had stepped into a different world, one he could remember imperfectly but had never understood so well as he did at the moment. For a few minutes he stood gazing all around, then up at the oak leaves, in a state of awe. Gradually, he awoke again and walked over to the edge of the path by the tree, laying a hand on the rough trunk.

"If the world could be like this again," he muttered huskily, "there would be no need for it to end."

With an effort, he shook free of his absorbed state of mind. The soil around the plants was moist, their stems carefully trimmed of any dying leaves. Someone had taken the time to build this place and was still maintaining it. They could not be far off, either in the dome itself or living somewhere in the city...

At that moment Drifter heard a noise in the dome. A clink or clunk like thin metal struck against something solid. He tensed, hand straying towards the knife at the back of his belt. Whoever owned this place might not be happy that he was trespassing. In fact, they would have every right to want him gone and seek to kill him if he resisted. Drifter would have understood it perfectly. This place was too precious to share with anyone who wandered in.

At the same time, he had entered looking for a person to question about Dick's whereabouts. He eased his hand away from the blade and began creeping stealthily towards the location of the noise, trying to see around the shrubs and flowers in his way. He was part of the way across the dome when he heard another noise, this time the shuffle of footsteps followed by a soft sound of running water. The owner must be watering their garden at the very moment.

Perceiving that the noise was just around a thick shrub, Drifter steeled himself and held out his hands in a gesture of peace before stepping around the bush. He found himself in an open space boxed in by flowering bushes, with a slight figure in front of him holding a watering can tipped towards one shrub. It was a boy, thin and pale, with hair the color of oat sheaths and round glasses perched on his nose. He looked somewhat less than sixteen, though his skinny frame and fine face would have been deceiving if he were older. He was watering the plants with an absorbed expression and did not appear to notice Drifter at all. The lone man stood for a moment with his hands out uselessly, then crossed his arms on his chest with a curious expression. His light eyes showed some impatience. How long would it take for the oblivious youth to notice him?

The drifter stood in his dark blue cape and hood, arms crossed over his tan uniform, while the boy watered and hummed lightly to himself. Finally, the boy's can ran out of water and he began to turn, presumably back towards the faucet set on a post nearby. But he had only came around a little when his gaze fell on the figure watching him and the eyes behind his glasses widened hugely.

"I mean no harm," Drifter assured him hastily, holding out one hand again to show that it was empty. The watering can slipped from the boy's fingers to the ground and for a moment Drifter thought that he might fall onto his knees or even collapse in a faint.

But the youth seemed to rally himself and picked the can back up, ducking his head awkwardly.

"Hello sir," he said, in a voice surprisingly young for one who lived in the later days of Apex, "I don't mean any harm either. You're...you're welcome to enjoy the garden."

"Thank you." Drifter nodded towards the bushes. "It is a sight for tired eyes. I haven't seen greenery like this since...well, for many days. Did you make all this yourself?"

"Oh no." The boy colored like a maiden. "I just help take care of it. The Shielded Garden was planted before the disaster, by some of the academy students. It was an experiment to see if plants could grow under the distortions of a force shield. As you can see, it worked."

There was a touch of pride in his voice as he waved a hand around at the growing things under the dome.

"And you helped plant them?"

"No, I wasn't even in the Academy sector then. Not long after they planted it, I came to attend upper grade school. A few years after that...well, you know what happened." The boy shrugged, smiling shyly. "I just help take care of it. Water the plants in the morning, make sure the water turbine underneath is still running on the underwater stream, trim leaves—"

Drifter interrupted him with a small gesture. "You said 'help take care'. Does someone else keep this place?"

The boy nodded, moving over to place the watering pot on the cement drain under the faucet. "My guardian. He saved me when the Greenspark fell, by having us hide in here. No one else...no one else made it into the shield. Some died right outside."

His face became long and solemn for a moment, memories of the horrible deaths playing behind his eyes. "Afterwards, most everybody ran away from the sector, afraid. There are a lot of phantoms here. Other people died of sickness...so there aren't much here except for me and my guardian. You must come from a different sector?"

With a nod, Drifter explained, "far to the west. They call me Drifter."

"I'm Bard. Bard Wently." The boy stuck out a thin hand, expecting it to be shaken. Drifter just touched his finger tips briefly and nodded once. "Not many people kept their last names after the disaster. It didn't seem worthwhile when there were so few people to become confused and so few families to keep it with. I came here looking for a man...his last name used to be Chelsea."

"Dick?" Bard gave another of his shy, eager smiles. "Dick Chelsea?"

Suddenly Drifter was gripping his hand tight, though he had only brushed it a moment before. "Do you know him? Where he lives?"

Bard extracted his hand with a wince. "Of course. He's my guardian. We live together in a tower near here. The tallest one."

Seeing the intense expression on Drifter's face, he added quickly, "I'll take you to him. He would like some company. I'm afraid he's...he's been ill lately."

Recalling the boy's previous words about sickness, Drifter took a step back. "Plague?"

Many people in Apex had succumbed to various plagues and diseases after the fall of Greenspark, with the lowered conditions of living and water quality.

But the boy was shaking his head in reassurance. "Oh no, it's not catching. Dick's had illnesses like this before. It's something...I think he has a weak heart. Or something else wrong, inside, that it would take a doctor to fix."

Looking away, he hid the tears in his eyes. His hands stripped the green leaves violently from a bush without noticing it.

"Well." Drifter took refuge in brusque manners. "We'd better get a move on before he goes. I have something important to talk to him about."

Bard nodded silently and led the way out of the shielded dome. When the door opened, the shield moved aside, slipping back into place once they had gone through. Drifter looked back once to see the shimmering bubble behind them, catching a glimpse of the wondrous world it hid inside. Outside, the sun was striking off the cold cement, glowing on the sides of cracked and abandoned buildings.

The boy led him around the far side of the division wall and through a sunken, damp street between high buildings. After just a few turnings they came out in a barren stretch of open earth, with a tower sprouting from its center. Drifter looked at the tower, then around at the buildings. Their roofs matched the image in his mind of the lit tower he had seen in the night.

There was no easy way to approach the tower by road. The sunken street they had traversed was narrow and dark, while walls and buildings cut off most direct access from any other direction. It was not surprising he had missed it in his car.

Taking him up to the door, Bard looked back over his shoulder cautiously. "You'll be gentle with him, won't you? You won't hurt Dick? He's awful weak."

Though it would have been easy for anyone to lie to the sensitive boy, Drifter nodded gravely. "We used to be friends, long ago. I don't know if he'd remember me, or recognize me now. All I want is a piece of knowledge he might have."

The door at the base of the tower opened with a creaking noise and Bard took him into the first room. It had been converted into a sort of processing room for produce from the garden, junk from the city and the water that was stored in barrels nearby. Benches, cutting boards and bins stood all around it, only leaving space for the stairs.

It was immediately obvious that someone lived in this tower. Going up the steps, the floors all had signs of recent activity in them. Odd inventions being built, food being stored or just muddy footprints on the floor.

When they reached the opening onto the final level Bard paused, whispering over his shoulder, "I like to let him know I'm coming."

Then he called up the steps, "Dick? I'm coming up now, with a friend to visit!" "Come up, young Bard." The voice which replied was cracked and weak, but Drifter still recognized some of the scholarly tones of his friend from so many years ago.

Chapter 8: Dick Chelsea

The room was filled with a golden glow from the morning sun coming in the windows. It turned everything shades of yellow and gold inside, striking off of shelves full of odd objects and ones full of books. It played on a desk covered in homemade ink and papers and across the well-swept stone floor. On one side of the room lay a huge four-poster bed with the sunlight gleaming in the creases of a silken coverlet spread on it. The blanket molded to a thin, long shape laying under the covers. A head rested on the white pillow at the top of the bed, face shrunken and black hair thinning.

Bard came to stand beside the bed on the far side. "I've brought someone to see you, sir."

Drifter came up on the near side and Dick's head turned towards him, arms pulling out from under the coverlet as he sat up a fraction on the clean pillow. His eyes were bright and alive though his frame was so wasted.

"Young Bard said 'a friend,'" he said, voice not as cracked now that he could speak in a quieter tone. "Do I know you from before or are you a new friend?"

Drifter looked down at him, taking in the bony, fallen face which he recalled as long and academic from before the disaster.

"Do you remember," he said slowly, "a young man who used to visit you in your antique shop on Falcon street? He always asked you about the relics and fingered the one like a dragon made of jade. One day he bought an old ring which came from a sunken wreck, with a red gem. He told you...it was for his bride."

Dick's eyes narrowed as he studied the visage above him, then widened suddenly as his face seemed to collapse even further and cheeks suck inwards.

"Leith Summers."

The loner turned away, face hardening into set lines. "They call me Drifter now. That is all I have become. It is who I am."

"Drifter," Dick whispered the word, turning his eyes towards one of the far shelves of objects. One of his thin hands pointed. "I still have that dragon. See there?"

Moving over to the shelf, Drifter swept his gaze over the items lined up on it. Book ends, a gilded box, statuettes of animals and even a pair of tongs. All with the branching symbol of a relic stamped deep into them. In front of him was a gleaming white shape of faintly opaque stone, a coiling dragon rearing its head. He reached out and touched it, feeling the familiar dips where his finger had sat many times, years ago. He picked it up and cradled it in one hand for a moment, before laying it gently back on its shelf.

"I've been looking for you, Dick," he said quietly, "I've come all the way from a place near the old Falcon street to find you."

"Why?"

"I have something I want you to identify."

Walking back to the bed, Drifter took out the long key from his belt and lay it on the coverlet. "This. It's a relic. And one I think you mentioned to me before."

Dick sat up further with Bard's help, eyes alight with interest as he reached out to pick up the heavy bit of metal. His delicate fingers held the key and turned it for those eyes to inspect from every side, the morning light gleaming off of it. Except for the symbol on its side and the apparent simplicity of the object it was not one to attract much attention.

"Di, Tidum and Kveth," Dick murmured under his breath like some sort of magic spell. Finally he lay the key back down on the blanket, though he kept the tips of his fingers on it as if to prevent its leaving his side.

"Do you have a guess as to what this relic is?" There was excitement in his voice now, though it was held back by his weakness.

Drifter nodded. "I have a guess, or else I wouldn't have cared so much to find you. But I want confirmation. And further information."

His eyes sliding closed, Dick leaned his head against the wall. "Relics are a mysterious thing. They only started appearing in the world two hundred and six years ago, in a corner of Apex that was under development at the time. The very first one found, the Mask of Di, was laying on a shelf in an old building marked for destruction. Studies showed it to be about three thousand years old. No one had ever seen it before."

Drifter made an impatient gesture. "I know the basic history. I want to know more about this key."

Opening one eye, Dick gave him a disapproving look before going on, "researchers have also found papers about a few of the relics, though no one remembered studying the papers or hearing of the writers before the relics themselves began to appear. One of these papers...the writings of an unknown 'Kveth'...claimed that there was a gate in a part of the land now in the Native sector of Apex, a gate which could only be opened by a certain key."

His fingers tapped on the key triumphantly. "A key hidden in a place mysteriously called 'Tidum'. A key which no one ever found. The gate was discovered, but no one could open it. After a time of intense excitement interest waned. No one could find Tidum or the key."

"I found it." Drifter bowed his head. "In a box of mixed junk in an underground garage. I was looking for fan belts for my car."

Dick smiled slightly. "Odd, like all the findings. But the real interest lies, of course, in the name of the gate and the legends which surround it."

Bard was listening with rapt expression as his guardian spoke the name.

"They call it the Gate of Eternity."

Drifter's head jerked up and his piercing eyes showed extreme excitement, though his face was set and hard as stone. "This is the right key, isn't it? It will open the gate?"

With a nod, Dick pushed the key towards him. "It should, if the paper was correct. But you know what all this means, don't you?"

Solemnly, Drifter took the key and slipped it into the cylinder at his belt. His eyes flicked to Bard. "Can we continue this conversation alone?"

Bard gave him a startled look, not comprehending right away. Dick gestured to him softly, with an affectionate expression. "Go for now, my boy. I'll call you back later. Check on the new sand clock and see if it's keeping time, would you?"

Though he seemed reluctant, Bard bowed his head in acceptance and trotted away. Drifter waited until he had been gone a few moments before moving closer to Dick, perching beside him on the edge of the bed. But it was the antiquarian who spoke first:

"I'm dying, Drifter. Not many more days will pass before my eyes close for the last time."

The loner lifted his shoulders philosophically. "The whole world is on its way out."

"It's a cruel, cruel world, now..." Dick Chelsea's eyes were still closed and his voice had dwindled to little more than a whisper. "The only thing I've lived for is that boy. But there is no future for him in Apex. No friends, no space to carve out as his own. Nothing...you know that, don't you?"

The words had a hint of sharpness to them, a touch of strange, dark hope.

Drifter took the sick man's hand and squeezed it lightly. "That is why I brought the key to you. I wanted to know if it was the right one. And if you are sure—"

"I am sure." Dick's eyes came open, surprisingly intense in his emaciated face. "It is the Key to the Gate of Eternity. And you know, Drifter, you know where we stand now."

There was a hard spark of fire in Drifter's voice as he answered, "at the end of the world."

Dick did not answer, but they both knew what the other was thinking. They sat for some time as if in silent communion. The sun had shifted so that the light no longer struck directly through the windows, but played on the roof, giving the room a soft ambient glow. The row of relics on the shelf almost appeared to be illumined with their own light, objects of every shape and material, each carrying the many-branched mark.

"Are you going to find the gate and open it?" Dick asked eventually.

Drifter nodded. "It's the only thing left for me to do."

"Then I have one favor to ask of you." Dick's hand moved restlessly on the pale silken coverlet. "I can't last much longer and I would not have Bard be alone. Take the boy with you."

Drifter leaned back against the far bed post with a sigh. He still disliked the thought of being with another person in his travels. But he did owe something to Dick for answering his questions and *not* questioning his answers. The boy seemed naive and weak because of the comparatively sheltered life his guardian had given him. Drifter dreaded having to hold his hand and walk him through the brutalities of the ruined city. On the other hand, it would only be until he found the gate. And Bard might as well learn what he could, while he could.

"Fine."

He stood up, flicking a glance at the man on the bed. "Will you be able to take care of yourself until your time comes?"

Dick's smile was surprisingly sweet. "I don't need much now. Send Bard up to talk to me one last time and then you may both go."

With a bow of his head the loner walked out of the room. His boots clattered softly on the stairs as he made his way down until he saw, inspecting a machine in one room off to the side, the boy Bard.

"Dick wants you. I'll be outside when you're done."

Giving him no time to ask questions, Drifter continued down until he reached the lowest story and could exit the door. The sunlight was a warm gold-red on the roofs of the old academic structures around him. He waited at his ease until he heard the sound of footsteps inside the tower. Turning to the door, he saw Bard come out, a sack over one shoulder, a scroll of paper in his hand and tears fogging his round glasses.

"My guardian says I am to go with you." His words were on the brink of unsteadiness. "And that you'll need this."

He held out the scroll, not meeting Drifter's gaze. Drifter took it with a brisk nod and glanced at the contents. It was a copy of ancient writing, part of the manuscript of the writer Kveth. It laid out vaguely where the Gate of Eternity could be found. At the bottom were notes added by Dick Chelsea explaining where some of the still existent landmarks were now, in the Native sector of Apex.

"My car is this way." Drifter jerked his head in the right direction. "We'll be taking it."

"Yeah." Bard still looked away, stealthily wiping at the tears which trickled down his nose.

Without further conversation they walked back through the twisting streets and sunken avenue to the courtyard where the shimmering dome stood. Bard came up and touched the smooth force shield once before following Drifter around the end of the division wall, past the stubby tower to where the gray car was parked in the shadows.

BARD HAD NOT TRAVELED by car since the disaster. He was uneasy at first, stowing his bag in the back and perching awkwardly on the seat. When the car started to move he gripped the door handle and his pale face seemed to become another degree white.

Once they were in an open avenue without slabs of stone or too many corners in the way, Drifter poured on the power. The car leaped ahead and Bard gave a little gasp of surprise. Looking sideways at him a second later, Drifter saw a smile growing on his face.

"Not so bad, eh?" Drifter prompted with a touch of pleasure in his grim voice.

Bard nodded his head enthusiastically. "I like it."

The driver kept the car moving at a good pace until their way became too torturous, down narrow lanes with burnt branches laying in them. Then he was forced to slow and pick his way more carefully. Their course was back out through the Academy sector, towards the land off of Terminal point. They threaded between large buildings, avoided the wreckage of a smaller one that had been toppled by quakes and came out on a main street. Drifter instantly recognized it and scanned the buildings they passed as they neared the end of the academic section. As one loomed up, tall and jagged with a smashed roof and gaping round window, the car slowed further.

"What is it?" Bard followed his gaze towards the structure.

Drifter shook his head. "Nothing...I wonder what that building was before the Greenspark."

"Let me see," the boy said, tapping a finger on his nose, "I think it was the Library of Mechanical Thought. Or maybe the school for the same thing. I'm not sure."

"Doesn't matter." Drifter turned away and increased their speed, giving up on the faint hope of seeing a purple robe moving through the windows.

Now that he had a solid destination and it was not far off, Drifter did not stop the car except for a brief halt at mid day for food. They had plenty of fuel to burn and Bard had brought a small amount of provisions with him in the sack, so there was no need to go scavenging. They made miles fast until places where the road was so ruined that they were forced to pick their way at a maddening crawl through the broken city.

It was late in the afternoon when the car began to have problems. First, it was just an odd note in the engine's running that caught Drifter's notice. But soon there was a cough and a splutter, then the engine went dead. The vehicle coasted to a stop and Drifter made a sound of frustration.

"What's wrong?" Bard flashed him a frightened look.

"I haven't found out yet." Drifter opened the door to get out.

Outside, he popped the hood and began to fiddle with the engine underneath. Bard got out and joined him, peering shyly at the mass of parts, half of which he did not know the names for. As Dick Chelsea's pupil he had studied ancient history, relics, physics and other old-fashioned knowledge. He had also learned to take care of and run the water turbine in the dank, dark underground beneath the dome of living plants. But he had never studied modern crystal-fuel machinery and had not often seen vehicles serviced before the disaster.

After plugging and unplugging various wires, checking connections and inspecting the air filter Drifter shook his head, "I think the fuel feed's plugged. Get in and turn the key half-way to the left, will you?"

Bard scrambled to obey. He felt nervous turning the key, but when the gauge lights jumped on and Drifter did not shout at him he guessed that he had done everything correctly. After a moment the driver told him to shut it off again.

"Can you fix it?" Bard asked breathlessly, hopping out and pushing his glasses further up his nose.

"We'll see what happens." Drifter fixed a tube back into its place and shrugged. "It's clean, now."

They returned to their seats in the cab and started rolling again. The sector of town they were in was typical to many parts of Apex. Structures of white marble lay scattered in ruins or stood valiantly despite everything the Greenspark had thrown at them. Their wounded brethren leaned on them or stood staring in surprise at the hunks of broken stone broken from their sides, laying on the ground. Unburned garbage blew gently across the road or lay in disintegrating heaps down alley ways. Piles of charcoal and partially melted metal showed where other pieces of people's lives had been scorched away.

Bard had rarely been to the edge of the Academy sector and had not left it since the fall of Greenspark. He looked at the widespread ruins in wonder, frowning nearsightedly at places the earthquakes had hit particularly hard. After passing many empty streets and buildings made of too much destruction to be inhabited, he ventured, "but what happened to all of the people? The ones who ran from the Academy sector and the others who lived out here...where did they go?"

"Mostly to their graves." Drifter gave him a hard look. "You saw them die. It happened all over."

Bard bit his lower lip at the harshness of the answer, before pressing on, "I didn't mean those. I meant the ones who survived it all. Like you."

Drifter snorted, "the ones like me are few and far apart. More than that, they are hard to find."

The boy turned in his seat to stare at the driver for a long space of time. His gaze was wide and naive, but not afraid. He seemed to be inspecting Drifter and trying to find the answer to him, as if he were a riddle.

"Were you a soldier, before?"

"No. I stole the clothes from a dead soldier's body."

"Even the cape?"

Drifter shot the boy an exasperated look. "No, not the cape. I got it elsewhere."

"Then what were you before the fall?"

"A human being."

"But, I mean—"

The driver cut him off by pulling to an abrupt stop and turning towards him.

"I forgot to tell you the rules about traveling with me. You go where I go, do as I do and make no judgments. Forget my past. And yours as well, for that matter. We're traveling to the Native sector to find the Gate of Eternity. That's all you need to know."

With this statement, roughly as it was given, Bard was finally cowed into silence. A minute later Drifter noticed that tears were rolling off the tip of his nose again. It made him wonder if all children vibrated so easily between extremes of emotion. One moment asking questions curiously, the next weeping in bitter silence.

But Bard *would* be sensitive because of being recently parted from his guardian and thrust into the outside world. Drifter let out another sigh, soundless this time, bracing himself for what could be days of having to travel with a youngster's swinging emotions. Drifter decided that he would simply say as little as possible. Wounds would either heal themselves or, he thought with a wry shift of his injured leg, become part of life.

They drove the rest of the day through a hard-hit section of the city, where buildings and burnt-out vehicles often lay across the street, forcing them to find new routes around them. Progress was slow and the only variety to the scene was even more pathetic mini-scenes of human misery. Such as the tableaux of an ambulance parked in the middle of the road, back doors hanging open on rusted hinges. The tires were burnt off and the sides scorched, especially on the wall facing the curb, where decorative trees used to grow. Behind the ambulance a gurney sat burnt and rusting on the cement, its cushions and blankets long gone in a chance gust of wind, blowing the ash away. All that remained in it was a few bones, too blackened for any scavenger to pick over. Of the medics, no sign could be seen, though they would have been gathered around the gurney at the time of the attempted rescue. Or, more terrible to think of, caught trying to flee with their patient left helpless behind.

As evening drew on, the car's engine kept givings signs of distress, hitting odd notes in its functioning or almost stalling when power was applied. Drifter looked grim (more than usual) and began considering pulling over. Before he could decide, there was a cough and the engine suddenly died for the second time that day.

He looked slowly across to Bard. "I'm afraid we might have got some bad fuel. It was all scavenged stuff...some of it could be impure."

Once again he swung out and went around to look under the hood. After a moment he gestured to Bard, who hopped out to join him.

"While I check it out, you look for fuel for a fire. We'll just camp here for the night. Charred sticks and browned moss both work fairly well."

Bard nodded. Leaving the loner picking apart the car's internals, he scouted around for the best place to find fuel. On their left-hand side, towards the west, stood tall apartment buildings with pillars and rubble laying all around them. They cast long shadows on the car, darkening Drifter and his work space. Their lowest stories all seemed to have walls and supports missing, giving them the precarious look of being poised to fall over. With a shiver, the boy turned to gaze in the other direction. Towards the east, where the shades of evening were coming on, was a sagging chain-link fence with gaps where hedges used to stand between sections of wire. Past it, was what had once been a small park, hedged in on all sides by more living spaces. Now a great pile of ruined stone and cement lay across the center of the park, hiding most of the stubs of trees which had stood there. But near the center of the broken pile Bard could just make out the bare, charred branches of a great oak, buried in rubble but still reaching valiantly above it.

With a nod of his narrow, pale face, he set off between the sections of wire, crossing a bare lot of brown earth and bone-like gravel before reaching the base of the heap. Finding a way up the cold slabs, jutting rebar and dusty cement was somewhat of a challenge, just what he was looking for to take his mind off of the rest of life. He probably could have found other fuel in an easier to reach location, but the physical hurdle of climbing the rubble lured him on, as well as the picturesque stance of the surviving tree.

Drifter would not find fault with him, he thought as he scrambled up onto the first layers of stone. He was hunting firewood as he had been told.

"But," he grunted to himself as he reached one thin arm up to haul his body to the next slab, "I'm also getting some fun."

Frustrated with his quiet companion, angry and saddened by the dismissal of his guardian, Bard took his pain out on the climb. When he reached the edge of the pile he was out of breath. Without looking around, he rolled onto a slab and lay still for a moment. Getting up, he turned around to look towards the tree. It stood on the edge of a low depression, reaching its thick bole and wind-torn branches up through the coarse material. Its base was hidden, buried feet deep in the broken stuff. Filling the center of the depression was an object that Bard did not at first understand. It was wide, black and glittered with a moist sheen like snake skin. The thing was spread out in a low hump, with one curling limb stuck to the side. Thinner, membranous sections lay crumpled beside it like deflated rafts. Strangest of all, the hump was slowly billowing in and out, as if breathing.

It was breathing.

All in a moment Bard realized that what he was looking at was not an inanimate object at all. It was a creature. A large creature all covered in scales with a short, thick head tucked under one bat-like wing. Three of its legs were hidden under it, tucked like a cat's. The forth stuck out with the toes twitching in its sleep. Claws as curved as a sickle slid in and out from each of these four splayed extremities.

Bard gasped, freezing. Either this small noise or some deep instinct made the creature shift in its sleep, gradually uncoiling its head. A huge yellow beak was unsheathed from under its wing. The bird-like head turned with a majestic slowness to take Bard in with one black, glittering eye. It was a beautifully shaped eye, curved and bright like a cat's. So dark that no pupil could be seen, only the depths of midnight.

With a grunt the creature heaved itself to its feet. A body like a lion's, but three or four times as large in every dimension drew itself up on poised limbs. The claws rasped out of their sheaths, grating on stone. Large, bat-like wings unfurled, veined in somber purple. The scales glittered black all along its body and a leonine tail lashed as the murderous beak angled the other way so that its opposite eye could take him in.

The boy felt locked in place, glasses slowly fogging with fear. The thing stood so close that its head curved above him, cocked as it tried to decide if it should kill him in a moment or let the pale, shrimpy being go.

With a scream, Bard broke free of its gaze and scurried for the edge of the rubble. In a moment he was tumbling from one slab to the other, bruising his arms and cutting his hands as he scrambled to the ground.

Drifter looked up from his work, hooded head turning in his direction. The dark shape of the huge creature reared up on the broken mountain, hopping to the edge to look down at the fleeing shape of the boy. Some hunter's instinct was aroused in the creature by the sight of a smaller being running from it. In deadly silence, it spread its wings and jumped into the air. The wind rushing past them was the only noise it made. The creature blotted out a section of blue sky.

Dropping everything in his hands, Drifter began to run. Bard was coming towards him, panting and stumbling as he dashed with frightened speed in the direction of the car. Drifter met him part-way and jerked him aside as the flying monster stooped.

Made wary by the entrance of a new creature into the scene, it missed its aim and landed on the ground a few yards away, claws digging up tufts of earth as it landed. Making small, inarticulate clicking and creaking noises, the creature folded its wings and reared back the curved yellow beak to fix the newcomer with its shadowed gaze. For a minute, dark eyes met light ones in a seizing up of fighting spirits. Bard leaned gasping on Drifter's right arm, sobbing with fright and the shock of his run. The wind of the griffin's landing blew strands of his hair awry across his face.

Drifter continued to meet the beast's gaze and held out his free hand in a gesture of peace. "Beast of the night, relinquish the day. Back to your sleep and forget the prey."

A long, drawn-out croaking sound, like a chicken would make when curious about an unknown object, gurgled from the griffin's throat. One set of talons dragged through the ground, leaving furrows half a foot deep. It made no other move to advance and Drifter began to back away, murmuring to the boy, "walk slowly to the car. Don't run whatever you do."

Bard drew in a struggling breath and tried not to look back, walking as if in a bad dream towards the parked vehicle with its hood open. Drifter followed him, backing up, keeping his one hand held out in a sign of peace. The beast stood regarding him with one eye for a moment, before twisting its head over on one side in a motion full of curiosity and chained fury. Gradually, it began to edge towards them, but not in a direct line. Instead, it crab-walked sideways, claws retracted so that it made hardly a noise moving on the bare earth. Like a cat stalking a mouse it came after them as they went through the gap in the fence and arrived at the car. Bard went first, skipping around to the other side of the vehicle to look back with a frightened expression. Drifter came second, leaning against the car with his face still towards the creature. It had reached the fence by now and stood on the other side, head lowered as it peered through the gap at them. First one glittering eye showed, then the next.

"Beast of the night, bane of light—" Drifter began another invocation, hoping to send it on its way so that it would not stalk them. But instead of calming the scaled griffin, his voice seemed to have the opposite effect. It had been standing quite still, shoulders hunched and head down, tail jiggling behind in a threatening manner. When he started speaking its head jerked up, tail went still and shoulders rippled in a muscled movement. With wings half-furled it leaped high into the air over the chain-link fence. Curved talons glinted in the late afternoon light.

"Run," Drifter ordered, turning to vault over the hood of the car and slide off the opposite side. "Under the buildings!"

He grasped Bard's shoulder and dragged the boy after him, moving with surprising speed. Behind them there was a sharp impact as the creature hit the cement, claws clicking and weight slamming into the ground. In another leap it was beside the car, wings brushing heavily off of the raised hood, making it crash down into a closed position. Drifter dragged Bard into a narrow space where the stone-work had given way, shoving the boy into the dark crack ahead of him. He heard the griffin pouncing, shoved himself under the stones just as the creature landed outside.

Claws scrabbled off of the wall as the two travelers huddled back into the dark, finding themselves in a small hole walled off by old ducts and crumbling wooden planking. Above them the building shook as the griffin battered against it. Dust sifted down and a few slabs of stone fell from the top of the little opening, slamming down onto the ground in front of it. A yellow beak was inserted in the remaining gap, clacking off of the hard material.

When it retreated, the claws started scraping again, making vibrations move all throughout the precariously suspending structure.

One paw reached in, claws extended to catch at the hiding human mice. Drifter saw his chance and jerked forward, whipping the knife from its place in his belt. Using it like a spike, he drove it down into the soft, fine scales at the base of the creature's leg where it branched into a foot. The griffin finally made a loud noise, a screech like nails dragged over sheet metal. Drifter barely got the knife back as the foot was pulled away.

After the screech, a heavy silence ensued outside. Both of the travelers' breathing was loud in the little space and Bard was still sobbing quietly in fear. The musty, tingling dust lay heavy on their shoulders and in their hair. Outside, there was a soft scuffling and scraping, followed by a hoarse mixture of croaks and soft cawing noises. After a minute, footsteps thumped with a sheathed sound away from the hole, gradually getting quieter until they could not be heard. Bard had fallen silent, too afraid to make a sound, and too intent on listening.

Chapter 9: On Foot

After a long space of time, sitting in the dark with their ears strained, they still had not heard the beast returning. Eventually, Bard's wish to learn overcame his terror enough for him to whisper;

"What was that thing?"

Drifter shook the dust from his hood. "I don't know. I thought I knew the creatures of the dark by now...but it would not listen to me."

Moving over to the hole, he peered out cautiously. Nothing could be seen except for the parked car and the evening sky spreading reddish-purple over the ruined city. There was no sign of the marauding griffin or any other living thing on the move. Kitchen knife still held in his hand, though it was hardly a lethal weapon against something so large and armored, Drifter made his way out over the fallen slabs of stone into the open.

"It's clear. Come out now."

Bard crawled out, wiping dust and the mud of tears from his face. His glasses had survived the ordeal intact, though he carried them in one hand. Standing up, he blinked around shortsightedly before fixing them in place. The only signs that the monstrous beast had been there was the scrape marks on the stone and the fallen slabs in front of the crack. That, and a few dings on the hood of Drifter's car.

"I don't know what sort of animal could have become a beast like that," Drifter muttered, moving over to make sure the hood could still open and shut easily. "Mutations abound in this wrecked world but no completely new species can appear...unless it isn't a regular beast at all but a sort of demon..."

He paused, face tilted up to the sky as he considered this idea. Bard had gathered his wits together again and felt a little ashamed of his obvious terror. Shuffling his feet on the ground, he put on a sullen frown.

"Drifter, I was terrified."

"Mm?" The man turned back to him, eyes focusing on the present.

"I said, I was afraid!"

Drifter shrugged. "So was I. When I looked up from my work and saw that giant thing hopping off of the rubble I thought we were both dead."

Bard stamped a foot on the hard cement. "But I was so afraid I didn't know what to do! You acted fast and saved me because of it!"

"True." The loner nodded once, moving around towards the driver's door. His limp was a little more pronounced than usual. "Self-preservation takes some practice. You'll learn."

He opened the door and leaned on it, giving the boy one of his withered half-smiles. "If the world doesn't end, first."

THE GREAT, DARKENED halls of the Academic Archives echoed to a soft footstep. Reddish light came down through one unbroken window, beaming onto a desk piled with books and papers. A woman in a long, purple robe with the hood pushed back came to stand in the light, the better to see the words on the page of a book she held in one hand. The paper was old and yellowed, faint brown marks showing where it had been creased or accidentally dampened in years gone by. But the ink was still dark and crisp, the illustrations gravely legible. Loran's eyebrows rose as she read down the page.

She had been digging through the great archives continually since Drifter had dropped her off. Except for brief pauses to rest and cache her food supplies, she had been reading books and papers. Now she looked from the words to the old ink illustrations, following each line and curve of two pictures on the opposite side. One showed a door set into what looked like black stone. There was nothing else depicted around the door or stone, no sign of what the entrance led to. It was a plain, dark-colored door with a large key hole in the front and no other mark on it. The other drawing was of a key. A large key stamped with a branching symbol.

"The Gate of Eternity," Loran read over the words again, this time aloud, "no one has been able to open the gate with any means, technological or otherwise. It is said that only the key made for the lock can budge it. The legends also say that the door will only be opened at the end of our world, bringing on the end of the apocalypse. This is what earned it the name it now bears. When the gate opens, eternity begins and the world ends."

The woman let the book sag to hang limply at he end of her arm. Her gaze traveled slowly to the window, her dark eyes squinting against the light.

"Rubbish."

After a moment, she slid the book onto the desk with many others, folding her hands into her sleeves. A chill not related to the coldness of the huge, dark building had come over her.

"But he believes it."

She stood for some time pondering this enigma, before turning back to the desk and carefully tucking a few of the papers into her robe. With decisive footsteps she began to trace her way out through the vast labyrinth of shelves and halls which made up the little-ruined structure. Whatever was behind that gate, it would most likely be dangerous if it was so carefully locked away. But it might also be important to her quest, hold some clue as to why the Greenspark had fallen and what the meaning of the relics really was.

BARD FROWNED AT HIS traveling companion for a few minutes, not understanding his reference to the end of the world. Deciding that it was just a pessimistic view of life, he asked timidly, "so, what now? I mean, did you find out what was wrong with the car?"

Drifter nodded, sliding into the driver's seat. With a gesture, he asked the boy to go around and sit in the other side. Once Bard was in place, Drifter explained, "impurities in the fuel, like I thought. But worse than I imagined. Some of the crystals must have been bad. The processor, feed tube and cogitation chamber are grimed. Junk's got down into the distribution needles and plugged them."

"Well...can you fix it?"

"It would take hours," Drifter shrugged. "Maybe even days. Without cleaning solution of any sort it would be a slow process of taking things apart and polishing them by hand. It's not worth it."

Bard's forehead contracted in worry. He was feeling utterly worn from the shock of the griffin's pursuit and his mind was fuzzy. "So what do we do?"

"Forget making a fire. Sleep here tonight." Drifter patted the seat affectionately. "Pack our more important possessions and continue in the morning. On foot. It will be dangerous, hard work and I would give almost anything for the car to be running again. Anything but the key. As it is, we aren't too far from the Native sector. Ten or twelve miles. It shouldn't take long to walk, if we're lucky."

"If we're lucky..." Bard repeated the words, taking off the glasses to rub at his eyes. He couldn't imagine being more unlucky than they had been so far. The car broken down, a griffin attacking them and his guardian left behind dying. The only thing that could be worse is if there had been nothing to eat for supper.

As if knowing his thoughts, Drifter slung the bag from the back into his lap. "Eat something."

Bard picked out a few dried fruits and other traveling rations, eating them slowly as he felt weariness pressing down on him. He fell asleep afterwards, just pushing the bag aside and curling up with his head on it. The boy had put his glasses back on, but now they hung askew on his face.

Drifter watched him as the light failed, remarking the openness of his pale face. He had not been burnt, physically, by the fall of Greenspark. Only the vision of the people struck down and dying outside of the dome darkened his brow with a touch of the scorch. He understood the harshness of life much more than most teenagers his age would have in the world before. Yet far less than Drifter did now.

The next morning Bard awoke to the dim rays of the morning sun playing on his face. He sat up stiffly, righting the spectacles on his nose. Everything came into focus and he saw that he was alone. No one sat on the seat beside him or was in view outside. A fear crossed his mind that he had been abandoned. Maybe Drifter thought him too useless to bring with him. Curling his hands into fists, Bard wondered how long he could survive on his own with what was in the car.

But his foolish fears were banished a moment later when Drifter came stalking with his peculiar gait around the corner of an imploded building and approached the car. Slung over one shoulder was a thin, charred stick with some sort of small, dead animals strung on it. Under one arm was a bundle of blackened sticks and dry moss.

Bard got out of the car with a feeling of relief and waited for him.

"Hot food for breakfast." Drifter dropped his burdens on the cracked sidewalk, untangling a slingshot from one arm. "I even found a fancy lighter to start the fire."

He reaching in a pocket and withdrew a large, silver lighter with green four-leafed clovers inset on the side. It made a sandy noise when he shook it, proving that it still had fuel.

"Are those Vollans?" Bard asked of the meat.

With a nod, Drifter dropped to one knee and began arranging the fire. Soon they had a nice flame, low and hot, burning sheltered by broken slabs of stone. The little creatures roasted over it, skin crisping while letting out thin, tasty aromas. Bard brought a slice of bread to toast for each of them, eating it with the slivers of meat picked from tiny Vollan bones.

"We had pigeon a lot back at the tower," he remarked, "Dick stewed them in a crock until they were all brown and tender, just swimming in gravy."

"Sounds good." Drifter flicked a bone into the nearby ruins. "Someone else recently told me that pigeons were worth eating. I didn't see many of them in my sector. Then again, that fellow also said he ate algae."

Bard grinned. "Well, seaweed's good. You ever eat seaweed? We had that and fish, too, when we could make it to the seaside for a day."

Drifter closed his eyes as if searching his memory. "I think I've eaten seaweed, in the time before the disaster. They wrapped it on little crackers, pale orange crackers that crackled when you bit them..."

"Norisenbei."

"What?" Drifter's eyes came open sharply.

"Norisenbei. Rice crackers with seaweed," Bard explained, "Or Norimaki-senbei to be more correct, I guess. I read about them."

"I see." Getting up, Drifter took the uneaten Vollan and rolled them in strips of the white cloth from the back of the car. These, with the little provisions left in the package Loran had given him, he rolled together to make a larger bundle. He set it outside, picking up Bard's sack from the seat.

"What's in here, other than food?"

"My other shirt. And, well...a book." Bard looked up out of the corner of his eyes, expecting Drifter to laugh at him or scold him for carrying something so impractical. Instead, the loner reached into the car and brought out a worn, rectangular object.

"Would you mind if another joined it?"

Bard got up and came over to him. "No. What sort of book do you have?"

Handing it to him, Drifter went back to digging through the rear of the car.

"A dictionary." The boy turned it over in his hands, thinking that it was an odd piece of writing for the taciturn wanderer to carry with him.

"It helps keep the mind clear." Drifter pulled out a few objects to stuff in his pockets, including what looked like a flashlight. "One of the things that saved me from insanity, just after the disaster."

"Oh." Bard tucked it abruptly into his sack.

"I'll show you how to play the game with it, later." Drifter shot him a look over his shoulder, adding, "you'd be good at it."

After that he asked if the boy wanted to take some of the white cloth as a cape, to keep warm on the cold nights ahead. But Bard shook his head, not wanting the extra weight. He was already wearing a good shirt, thick jeans and a brown jacket of clumsy make that he had once tailored for himself, using a pattern from a book and an old pair of curtains to make it. With that and the sack, he felt that he would have enough to carry.

Drifter locked the car behind them, taking the keys. He seemed to hesitate for a minute with his hand over an odd switch on the dash, but then shook his head and closed the door without touching it. Picking up his own bundle, he took a reading of the sun and sky with his pale eyes.

"This way."

They set off walking along the sidewalk, grit from the destroyed buildings crunching under their feet. It was only then that Bard realized he had little idea of why they were trying so ardently to reach the locked gate. But he was working too hard keeping up with Drifter to voice his questions at the moment. Despite his thin and weak appearance, Bard was used to walking all over the Academy sector, including the pilgrimages he and his guardian made to the ocean. But Drifter walked with a swift, long stride which soon had Bard panting. It was strange to watch him move along, as he limped without it slowing him.

They walked for a few hours down cracked sidewalks and across littered streets, the silence intensified now that they were out in it instead of traveling through it in the enclosed car. There were no engine sounds from the vehicle to break the eerie quiet, only their footsteps and breathing. At one point, they came to a great chasm opened up across the road, ten paces wide and disappearing into the rubble of structures on either side. Bard knelt beside it, peering down into a subterranean world of broken cement, packed earth and dangling wires. A few metal pipes spanned the gaps, or hung broken off at violent angles. Far down, the crack terminated in a span of darkness he could not pierce with his gaze.

After a brief rest they circumnavigated this crack and continued, finally arriving at a huge sign built of steel pipes painted to look like logs and sheet metal striped to be planks. The paint was starting to come off of the sheets in ugly, rusty patches but the words on it could still be read; 'Native Sector'.

"I read about this sector," Bard said as they stood looking at the sign, "a long, long time ago it was open prairie inhabited by tribal people. 'Natives' so to speak. They were granted this land to live on 'as long as the grass grew and the sky stood above'. But eventually they were assimilated into the rest of the country and spread out, leaving this land for the city to be built across. That's how it got its name."

Drifter regarded him curiously for a moment, before reaching into a pocket and taking out Dick Chelsea's scroll. "Here. You're good with words. Find out what steps we're supposed to take next to find the gate."

Bard set his sack of goods down to accept the scroll. Opening it with care, he read over everything silently. Then he chose a piece to recite aloud, "*'Take the path between the great oaks marked by death and the rocks that reach towards the sky. Follow it northwards for the first quarter of a mile.'*"

He looked up with a shrug. "That's the original. Dick's notes say *'These archaic trees and rocks are long since gone. But I think if you follow the main street north for the same length it should get you to the next landmark, which still stands.'*"

"Simple." Drifter accepted the scroll back. "What is the landmark?"

"A tall rock, like a column of stone, with ancient carvings on it," Bard explained, "it was encased in glass to protect it when the city was built."

"It is back to its natural exposure, now." Drifter switched his bundle from one arm to the other. "It should only take a few minutes to reach it. Come on."

With a sigh too soft for his companion to hear, Bard picked up his own sack and slung it over his shoulder. When Drifter moved off he plodded after, wishing that something would happen to stop them for a longer rest. And, only a few minutes later, it did.

On their right-hand side was a long strip of buildings, all small businesses broken up by the disaster. The other side had larger, more separate structures which might have been hotels, personal palaces and the like. The two travelers had just come up even with a mostly-intact garage on the right when they were hailed by a sound from within it. It was a voice, high and scratchy like that of an angry cat.

"Hey, hold on there, friends. Don't walk past so quickly!"

Drifter froze, head whipping around to fix the speaker with his gaze. Half-hidden in the shadows of the garage was a rickety table, propped up on one end by rubber tires stacked in a heap. Seated on a cut in half barrel behind it was a man so bony he reminded one instantly of a praying mantis or other famished insect. His face was crooked, sheltered by a broad-brimmed hat decorated with hanging shards of metal. The mouth grinned awkwardly, missing teeth leaving dark gaps throughout it. His clothes barely clung to his narrow, drumstick shoulders and his hands spread to each side were like claws. In front of him on the table were a variety of minute objects. Peering closely at them, Bard thought they were cards and dice.

"I said, don't walk away so fast!" the shriveled figure repeated, "come join me for a few minutes, pass the time in delightful games of chance. Relax! Enjoy yourselves!"

Drifter shook his head. "Thanks. Life is enough of a gamble without."

"But there are prizes to be won as well." The man leaned over his table, distorted face taking on a cunning look. Bard noticed for the first time that his hands were both burnt almost black with the scars of the Greenspark.

With another shake of his head, Drifter started to move off.

"My prizes are not to be taken lightly," the cardshark insisted, standing up, "come play against me before I make you!"

Drifter just kept striding steadily along, not even looking back. Bard trailed behind him hesitantly. Suddenly there was a crash and a screech behind them, followed by the sound of running feet. Bard stopped in his tracks, spinning around to see the crazy, thin character dashing towards them, a knife held in each hand and his mouth open in a maddened snarl. He ran with surprising speed, chest thrown out and long, gangling legs swinging. It only took a heartbeat for him to overtake the boy, upon which he swung one of his blades at him with an insane scream of rage. Bard stumbled aside, swinging his sack up to protect himself.

One of the knives slashed through it, ripping open the bottom. The other blade was stopped mid-air when Drifter caught the gambler's wrist.

"Leave the boy alone."

"Aghn! You wouldn't play with me!"

The thin man flailed out with his free hand, taking a stab at Drifter. In a move almost too fast for Bard to follow, Drifter twisted the cardshark's wrist, forcing the knife from it, and struck out with a flattened hand at his free arm. Both knives dropped clattering to the ground, while Drifter kneed the man in the stomach, struck him on the neck and forced him to his knees. Another blow and the bony figure was sprawled across the pavement, groaning distantly. It had all happened within a minute, so quick Bard was left blinking.

Drifter rubbed one hand with the other, giving a shake of his head. "The scorch bit that one deep."

"But, you..." Bard couldn't find the words for a moment. Collecting himself, he said, "that was some sort of martial arts, wasn't it? What sort? Karate, Kung Fu, Jiu Jitsu?"

Stooping to pick up one of the knives, Drifter returned, "I don't know. I made it up. Another of those things that kept me sane after the Greenspark fell."

Straightening, he held out the blade hilt-first to the boy. "Here, you need a knife. Might as well take this one. Unless you prefer the other?"

Bard hardly glanced at the blade as he took it. It was formed in a dagger-shape with a brown handle, tiny cross hilt and long blade. He was still staring at Drifter through his round glasses. "You just *made* that *up*?"

"That's what I said." Drifter turned away from the downed man to start walking again. "Didn't you hear me?"

Bard was forced to hurry to keep up, juggling the new knife and his torn sack all the while. "Yeah, but...it sounds pretty incredible."

"Incredible:" Drifter began, "not credible; surpassing belief; too extraordinary and improbable to admit of belief; unlikely."

The boy blinked at his back. "That's right."

"What is unlikely about it? People had to make up every type of fighting at some point. The quiet of a destroyed world, the pain of a fresh wound and the cracked cement at the edge of your mind all act as focusing elements. Especially when what neighbors you still have are literally trying to eat you alive. So I learned to concentrate. On learning things. On living. Whatever I put my mind to, it ate up to fill the void of what had been. Including inventing a new form of martial arts to protect myself."

Drifter finally paused, whipping around to fix the boy in the burning light of his gaze. "Do you understand now?"

Startled, Bard stopped in his tracks and leaned away from him, clutching the sack like a shield. "Y-yes sir."

"You know." Drifter gave him one of his dead smiles. "You're a terrible liar."

He turned back to walking, leaving Bard feeling like he had just been raked over hot coals and out onto the hearthstone, confused about where he had come from and why he had been allowed to live. More than ever he did not understand this terse, enigmatic personage he had been forced to go on pilgrimage with. But he found himself oddly wishing, for the first time, to understand more.

Drifter frightened him. But his hints at a terrible past made Bard wonder if he had always been so difficult to understand, or if it was his rights of passage into a brutal world which created his taciturn exterior.

"Do you want me to teach you?" Drifter broke in on his thoughts.

"What?" Bard looked up from the darkened pavement they were traversing.

"My fighting skills. Whatever you want to call them." Drifter glanced over his shoulder. "It isn't hard to learn, since I simply made it up."

"Well, I...I'm not as strong as you."

"It doesn't take strength to learn. To learn is to gain strength. Besides the fact that fighting by that method is more about focus and precision than brute strength."

"Maybe..." Bard stopped to point at a large object over on their right. "Wait, is that the rock pillar?"

The buildings on the right-hand side of the road had given way to an open area, circular and about a hundred yards in circumference. In the center was a splintered shell of glass. The broken glass ringed one half of a large column of rock, a finger-shaped boulder, standing pale and jagged. On one side the other half of the pillar had broken away to crash through the glass and smash into the tiled ground, cracks running all thorough the stone. Ancient scribbles, animals and figures like a child would draw, could still be seen marked on the two halves of the pillar.

After inspecting the stone both from a distance and close up, Drifter asked the boy to interpret the next stage of the journey. This was a longer and more vague section of the map, which Dick's notes could only partially translate. It told them to go towards the setting of the sun until they came to a mineral springs (fancy spa, Dick wrote) where they would then turn north again and travel for 'two day's walk'. After that they should come to what Dick's notes described as a great park of science and nature, where the Gate stood. Dick was unsure what would be left of the park, but there should be signs of scientific buildings, fences directly around the Gate and a thicket of conifer trees near the entrance to the whole place.

"Two or three days still before us, hm?" Drifter put a hand to his chin. "At least we seem to have lost that monster."

Bard agreed heartily with this. He had been afraid of seeing the griffin appear over the horizon ever since they left the car. So far, there had been no sign of the great scaled beast. But he worried that it would still follow their trail and overtake them with its great wings.

They stopped and rested for a few moments beside the shattered monument, before continuing in a westward direction down a side-street. They wound their way between buildings, walking in cold, damp shadows or in the bland reddish light of the open streets. The empty buildings with pools of melted metals or dripping glass at their feet watched the travelers go by. The sun glared off of the fractured bones of society, exposing its shame to the world.

At some points the travelers were forced, even on foot, to find new routes or climb over heaps of rubble on their way. Bard noticed that Drifter's limp became more pronounced as the day drew on. Late in the afternoon, when the sun had not yet set but was dripping towards the horizon, Drifter called a halt.

They were in a courtyard paved in white and gray tiles. It stood on a slight incline, the buildings along the lower half of it all knocked down to such a degree that the street below and beyond could easily be seen from where they stood. On all other sides of the tiled area the buildings were crumpled, but still formed a high wall of masonry. A row of pillars stood intact on one side, sheltered by an overhanging roof. This is where Drifter directed their camp to be laid.

Once again Bard was sent to get fire wood. This time no incidents occurred and he brought back an armful to add to the few twigs Drifter was already starting. Soon they had a little blaze hidden from outside view by a row of cracked bricks, which also reflected the heat back towards the travelers. Left-over roast rodents were their meal.

After eating Drifter stretched out in the shadows, away from the fire, and apparently fell asleep, head pillowed on one arm. He was more weary than usual, his wound paining him from the strain that had been put on it. Bard, not as tired as the night before and more nervous, stayed awake for some time, watching the blurred stars come out in the dark sky and listening. Just listening for anything flying or stalking towards them.

Chapter 10: Sco-Ber

Eventually, chilled and frightened as the fire burned down, Bard fell into a light sleep. He was awakened a few times when he thought he heard heavy breathing in the shadows around him. Drawing closer to Drifter, he fell into a deeper slumber. When he was awakened suddenly, the sky was still dark and the hard ground cold. For a minute he did not know what had shattered his dreams, until he saw a nearby movement blacker than the surroundings.

A small, slim shape was bending over Drifter. It moved with such silent softness, like a cobweb hovering in the air, that for a moment he did not believe it could be anything but a shadow. But when it jerked up suddenly and began to move away, still drifting like a dream, Bard cried out. He had seen, outlined against the faintly lighter sky, the image of a small human head.

Drifter came up as if pulled on the strings of his cry. Without waiting for an explanation he took off after the shape, which was now running across the courtyard with small foot-slapping sounds. Drifter's boots made a heavier noise as he ran after, something glinting silver in his hand as he drew it away from his cape. Bewildered, Bard heaved himself up and hurried after them. What had he seen bending over Drifter? And what had it been doing, poised there?

With a rustle and crumble of rubble sliding together the slim shape climbed agilely over the heap of stonework at the bottom of the courtyard. A second later the flapping of Drifter's cloak could be seen on top, before he plunged over the far side. Bard followed with the feeling that he was caught in a nightmare. The broken stones were rough on his hands as he climbed over the low heap. His feet seemed to be continually getting trapped in cracks or stumbling over pieces of rebar. It was with a struggle that he reached the top and slid down over the other side. A brief space of burnt, bare ground and he was standing on the peeling pavement of a road. If it wasn't for the ringing of Drifter's footsteps on the hard surface he would have lost the chase in the dark.

Shivering with the harsh cold of night, he turned to the left and followed the sound of pursuit. On the open street he was able to pick up his pace and gain on Drifter and the mysterious stranger, who were dashing towards a dark shape which rose ahead of them, tangled with the cracked structures to either side. Bard could not guess what the deep shadows ahead of them were until they came right up to the entrance of a tunnel. The fleet figure before them dashed into the shadows. Drifter slowed and paused at the entrance.

A great arc of cement rose above them, forming a maw of darkness deeper than any shadow outside. Cool, damp air exhaled from this opening, smelling of moisture and places that only rats, two- or four-legged, dwelt. The sound of light, slapping footsteps could still be heard retreating down it.

"Wha—?" Bard gasped.

"The key!" Drifter told him with short, panting fury. Without waiting to give more of an explanation he started running again, jerking into the gaping entrance fearlessly. Bard was scared of the heavy cement above them, afraid of what might be lurking in this giant lair built by man to ferry vehicles below the city. But he still followed, not wanting to lose his only companion.

Their breathing and footsteps echoed down the cement tube, creating weird effects of sound ahead of them. After a few dozen yards Bard was shocked to see a bluish light appear before him, flashing suddenly into life. He stumbled, but then recovered when he saw that it was something in Drifter's hand making the light. He remembered the flashlight his companion had earlier slipped into his pocket. Evidently Drifter had a electronic light that had not been destroyed by the Greenspark, one that had somehow survived the strange electromagnetic blast that had accompanied the disaster.

In fact, Bard realized as he ran, Drifter's car had carried working electronics in it as well. It must have a force shield, he thought, that had protected everything within.

But they were still dashing down a tunnel hidden almost entirely in deep shade. The light Drifter carried threw strange shapes against the wall, dancing and flickering as they ran. Far ahead, a small figure could just be seen in the light, thin limbs pumping and long hair flapping. Its ragged clothes also flapped back in the pale light, seeming to wave mockingly at the pursuers.

The tunnel's ceiling suddenly came down in a tumble of broken stone slabs and dusty rubble. A small passage was all that was left cleared, curving past the blockage on one side. The figure ahead of them squirted down it, disappearing from sight.

Panting, Drifter stopped to peer through. Once again, Bard came up with him. This time he was too out of breath to say anything. He just stood shivering from a mixture of cold air hitting his warmed skin and fright at the huge space of echoing tunnel around them.

"Well, only one way to go." Drifter's voice was harsh with running and fury. Holding the flashlight ahead of him, he squeezed into the crack and disappeared, taking the light with him. Bard glanced around wildly, trying to decide what to do. But if he didn't want to lose his companion there was, as Drifter had said, only one way to go. Taking a deep breath of air, Bard started into the narrow passage. Cold stone grabbed at his arms, dust brushed off against his head. His feet stumbled around rough jags on the smooth floor.

It was only a few minutes, but seemed like forever, until he was able to straighten up and see the light Drifter carried once again. It was immobile, not advancing, and there was no sound of moving footsteps. Bard blinked in the sudden light, trying to take in what was happening.

They were standing in a sort of wide, round chamber made by the intersection of one tunnel with another. Ahead of them the space was blocked off by another heap of rubble, this one honeycombed with dark holes like a wasp's nest. To each side the intersection was collapsed into more heaps, full of dark holes . In the center of the intersection, on top of a metal grating leading down into darkness, stood a ragged child. At first Bard could not tell if it was a girl or boy, its hair was so long and face so dirty. After a minute he decided it was a boy, by the squareness of its shoulders and face. The boy was not more than twelve, though his limbs were so browned and expression so toughened he could have been twice that age.

But the thing which made both Bard and Drifter pause was not the one lone child. It was that more than a dozen of them were jumping, wiggling and crawling out of the honeycombed rock and skipping up to stand ringed in aggressive defense around the boy in the center.

They were all dressed in ragged clothes held on by ratty strings and armed in a peculiar fashion. Each youngster carried a long whip-like section of stiff wire in one hand, mounted to a wooden handle. In the other hand they had a variety of smaller weapons from kitchen knives to hammers, all painted or carved in personalized symbols. One of them, a girl with a cape of pink carpet and a crown of dead Christmas lights bound to her forehead, stepped up beside the boy. The only weapon she carried was a table leg carved into a heavy club.

Drifter looked at all of them sharply. "Give me back the key."

The boy in the center tilted his head to one side, smirking. "Why should I? We're the Sco-Ber and do as we like."

"Yeah!" the crowned girl put in right on to of him, "Scotia-Bernie gang. An' he's Bernie, while I'm Scotia, so we're the bosses."

Closing his eyes for a moment, Drifter seemed to collect his wits and push his anger down.

"Look," he said, opening them again, blazing with repressed emotion. "I need that key. It's important to me. I'll trade you this light for it if you will give it to me right now."

He held out the flashlight on the palm of his hand. Bernie seemed to consider, looking at the flashlight with one eye like a bird. His hair hung down in his face, until he pushed it back with a gnarled little hand.

"No." He shrugged. "I don't like you. We won't trade."

As soon as he had pronounced the words, Drifter made his move. He darted towards the boy, grabbing for the hand that had the key sparkling in it. But as he moved the children realized what he was doing and also darted forward, surrounding their leader with a guard of wire swords and short weapons. Drifter's knife seemed to appear magically in one hand as he slashed out at the nearest ones, parrying their blows. Wires hissed and the light flickered wildly, confusing the whole scene. Bard was paralyzed with fear and uncertainty on the edges of it.

Suddenly the swarming mass, including Drifter, was halted at a word from Bernie, "wait!"

Everything paused. Drifter fell back, his arms sporting a number of thin slashes from the sharp-edged wires. The Sco-Ber looked back and forth uncertainly between their leader and the interloper.

"You want this key that bad, huh?" The boy held it up, bronze sparkling in the light. His face suggested that he might give it up for the right price.

"Yes," Drifter grated, panting.

"Well, here's for your precious key, then!" With a sneer, the boy threw the key between his feet, where it clanked on the grating and disappeared into the darkness below.

"No!" Drifter jumped forward, knocking children away left and right. They began to press back, blocking him. For a moment it looked like they would swarm him, but then Scotia gave a strange, high cry as a signal and the whole mass of the Sco-Ber fell apart. Bare feet flapping and little limbs scrambling, they scuttled away into their dozens of holes. The only one who did not escape was Bernie, whom Drifter pounced on as he tried to escape and struck down with a blow from the knife. The young boy fell to the ground with a gasp, life's fluid leaving him in a red tide.

Bard's mouth drooped open and he stared at the scene in shocked horror. No matter what the young gang members had done, he had not thought that Drifter would kill one of them. Not even in revenge. But the man stood grimly wiping off his knife before turning around to fix Bard with his pale eyes, flashlight pointed at the grate.

"He threw the key down there."

Bard felt transfixed, fear bubbling through him in waves. Would this terrible man stop at nothing if someone got in his way?

"Y-yes." Bard agreed with a dry mouth.

"Could you fit down there to get it?"

"I—well—I..."

Drifter knelt beside the grating, prying at its edges. Soon it came up and he flopped it heavily to the side. It fell beside the dead gang leader with a clang, bars reddening. Pointing the flashlight downwards, Drifter exposed a narrow hole surrounded by cement, leading down to a depth of perhaps twelve feet. There it opened out and water could be seen glinting inkily in a paved gutter.

"You'll have to be the one to do it," Drifter explained, looking up, "I might get stuck and you are not strong enough to pull me out."

Bard's mind was still spinning with the happenings of the night. He could hardly grasp reality or form words to describe it.

"But, how...?"

"My cloak will make a rope." Drifter reached up and undid the ties that held it on at his throat, shedding the dark blue cloth. With a few deft twists and a knot he made a sort of rope, something that could be held onto and was strong enough to bear Bard's slim weight.

"Here." Drifter held out the flashlight. "Take this. Go down there and find the key. It's important."

When the boy still hesitated Drifter looked at him, his expression holding a surprising bit of pleading. "Trust me. I'll pull you back up. Just find the key."

Acting mechanically, as if the words had wound him up and set him going, Bard took the flashlight and moved over to sit on the edge of the hole. Drifter knelt across from him, seeming smaller and less imposing without his blue hood and cape. It was dangling down the hole, gripped tight in his hands. The drop was not a long one. Bard gazed down at the sparkle of water for a moment, wondering where it came from and went to. Then he put the light between his teeth and wrapped an arm around the cloak, sliding gently off of the cold cement floor.

It took his weight. He hoped that the seams would not part as he grappled his way down it. The slick wall went past him in a blur and he dropped off onto the floor beside the wet gutter. His feet hit solidly, sending a shock through his heels. Looking up, he saw the cloak still hanging down, knot inviting him to climb back. All he had to do was find the key. And it could not have gone far.

Up above, Drifter sat in darkness, listening to the sounds of scurrying feet and crawling knees, whispering little voices. The Sco-Ber were still nearby and active in their holes. He braced himself for them to creep out and hunt for vengeance, come for him with their whips and knives. He had his own blade to defend him, but he did not dare let go of the cloak with even one hand or move from his place. Bard might try climbing back at any time, requiring Drifter to be gripping the improvised ladder solidly. Drifter could only sit and hope they did not emerge until his companion came back.

In the subterranean tunnel, Bard did not think of those dangers. He glanced up and down, pointing the flashlight both ways. The tunnel was small and cylindrical, branching in many directions to his right and running steadily away on the left. Wires and pipes clung to the wall, safe from Greenspark, yet melting under the rust of age. Recalling himself to his mission, the boy pointed the flashlight down at the gutter. The key was too heavy to have been washed away. Looking down through the oily glint of water he saw something shining bronze under its surface. His fingers slid into the black liquid, curling at the cold sliminess. The key jerked out in a shower of drops, each one gleaming pale gold in the light.

Bard tucked it into a pocket of his jacket, before reinserting the light's metallic body in his mouth. Moving over to the cape dangling down, he grumbled around the flashlight, "coming up!"

Wrapping his hands in the coarse fabric he began to climb. At the same time Drifter hauled on it, pulling him scraping up through the damp cement of the hole. Bard flopped panting onto the floor beside him, getting wearily to his knees.

"Here."

He held out the key.

Drifter took it as if he had been starving and it was a scrap of meat. "Thank you."

"Now maybe you can tell me," Bard said, standing up and readjusting his glasses, "why it's so important to you? Why are we going to the Gate of Eternity? What will happen if you use the key on it!"

The last words were almost shouted. Tired and shocked by the night's activity, weary of the mystery Drifter surrounded his quest with, Bard was close to breaking.

"Dick never told you about the Gate?" Drifter was polishing the key between his fingers. He stuck it in his belt.

Bard shook his head mutely, waiting for an answer.

"I'll tell you. I'll explain everything." Drifter stood up, limping towards the exit through the hole in the wall of rubble. "But let's get out of here first."

Bard followed after him, giving him the flashlight when he held his hand out for it. Its light was starting to dim, the battery running low. Drifter held it high as they navigated the tight passage and began to traverse the long tunnel. Somewhere behind them rang a high, mocking laugh muffled by the rubble walls.

THEY MADE IT OUT OF the tunnel into the darkness of the night. Though Bard thought that he had slept a long space before awaking, and it seemed to have taken hours to retrieve the key, in reality there was still an hour left until dawn began to break.

As the flashlight went out, Drifter led them around the wall of rubble, back up onto the hill where their camp had been laid. A few red coals still peeked out of the ashes, glowing like feral eyes hoping for a good feed. Drifter rummaged around and pulled up a few twigs and slices of moss to throw on it, making flames flicker once again. The flashlight, turned off, went back into his pocket. With a sigh he sat down on one side of the fire. Bard crouched across from him, shivering with a mixture of cold and fear. He did not know what he was afraid of. But the picture of Bernie laying dead with a red pool spreading around him kept reappearing in his mind. A dread anticipation was on him.

Before saying anything, Drifter reached down and rolled up the left leg of his pants. Bard drew in a tight breath when he saw the burn scar underneath. Cracked and blackened, it appeared damp in the firelight. Drifter lay a hand against it and then drew the hand away, staring at the moistness on it laconically.

"It's getting worse." He wiped his hand off on the cloak, which he had somehow put back on while they traveled, and jerked his pants back into place. "No matter. It won't be long until I don't have to worry about it anymore."

Looking up, he met Bard's horrified gaze. "A direct hit."

The boy made a slight noise but did not reply.

"Now, the key," Drifter leaned forward, speaking slowly and carefully, "this might be hard for someone of your age to understand. I'll try to be concise."

Bard made a dismissive gesture, drawing up his knees.

"You can see how the world has been going. Pain, starvation, fighting all around. The abomination of desolation. It's not just that something bad happened and we've got to get over it. Not like all of the other wars and destruction of the past. It's this. We're nearing the end of the world. This is the apocalypse."

With a motion, Bard made as if to interrupt. But Drifter held him back with a raised hand. "Wait. I've seen angels dancing in the darkness. Demons flying in the sky. The world has been destroyed. Not just this city, this continent. I've heard tales from travelers of other lands as well. They are all gone. It is time to end the suffering that the remnant, the elect, have been going through. It is time for the end to come."

He stood up, looking down at Bard solemnly. "The Gate of Eternity will bring about the end of this world and we will be at peace. This key is the only thing that can open it."

He looked like a prophet of old standing there, face picked out by the flames while the rest of him faded into the surrounding darkness. Bard's mouth slowly dropped open, staring up at him. It took a moment for him to process everything Drifter had just said. Once he had, a flash of anger ran through Bard like a hot wire.

"No!" He jumped to his feet, fists curling into balls. "You can't end the world just like that, on a whim! I don't want everything to end. I want to rebuild it, to fix the world, not destroy it! I'm not *ready* to end yet."

He stood panting, shocked at himself for having spoken some of his deepest-held secrets. Yet he was determined to defend them until the end.

"It's time, kid. The world can't last forever and someone will end with it."

"No!" Bard repeated again, all of his frustration with the companion he had been imposed on flashing to the for. "It doesn't have to end. You're just scorch-mad! I won't let you end it."

Drifter's gaze sparked perilously. "You can't stop me."

"Oh, yes I can!" Bard jumped forward around the fire, reaching for the key. With a smooth precision, Drifter struck him on the jaw when he came close. For a moment he was filled with rage at the boy's impudence, which put strength into the blow. It connected with a solid cracking noise and Bard fell to the ground, laying in a crumpled position, his glasses fallen beside him.

Drifter blinked and looked down at the still form, feeling the anger give way to remorse. Bard was just a weak boy, too young and foolish to know any better. Kneeling beside him, Drifter felt to see if he was still breathing. A faint movement under his hand reassured him.

At that moment he heard a heavier, wetter breathing from across the boy. Looking up, he saw a pair of red bulbous eyes glittering at him from the dark. Firelight flickered off a set of white teeth. A large mouth gaped open.

"This one's not for you." Drifter grated softly, sliding his arms under the boy to pick him up. Gently, he laid Bard by the fire, using one of their packs as a pillow to rest his head on. Sitting beside Bard, Drifter drew his knees up and rested his elbows on them, bowing his head inside the arc they made. In silence, he watched as the sky turned gray and then flushed pink, steel giving way to peaches. The sun rolled up in the sky with an inexorable gradualness, conquering the night.

When the sun had come up about a hand's length from the horizon of ruins, Bard began to stir. Drifter leaned over him, eyebrows contracting as the boy's eyes came open. Without his glasses on, his face looked smaller, more in proportion. But his eyes also looked more tired, ringed in shadows.

"Drink." Drifter took the flask of water and held it to the boy's mouth, supporting his head. Still groggy, Bard sipped what water was in it. But the flask was soon empty.

"I'm...I'm still thirsty," he muttered, flinging an arm across his eyes to protect them from the sun.

"I'll find more water." Drifter arose, nodding at the dagger in Bard's belt. "Lay here until I come back. Protect yourself with the knife if you need it."

With that he was gone, disappearing into the shadows of a nearby building. Bard lay still for a few minutes, breathing lightly. Once he was sure Drifter was gone he rolled to his knees and stood up. For a moment dizziness overcame him.

But once his head cleared he was even more sure of what he wanted to do. Everything was a little blurry until he picked up his glasses and fit them back to his nose. That done, he snatched up his sack and hoisted it over one shoulder. There was still a bit of hard bread and the like in it. He would have to care for himself from now on out.

"I memorized the whole scroll," he muttered to himself in determination, "I can get to the gate ahead of Drifter and stop him."

Leaving no time for hesitation or to become frightened at himself, he walked over to the low wall of rubble, climbed over it and started trotting down the road. After a bit he turned off to the side at a random location and climbed over a pair of fallen marble pillars, starting down a side-street.

Meanwhile Drifter was returning with a flask of fairly clean water. He would still have to heat it it before it was safe to drink, but the boy could always have it hot, as a sort of tea. A flavorless tea. Unless there was something in his pack to spice it with...

Drifter's mind registered something missing before his eyes realized what was gone. Bard no longer lay beside the camp fire. He was not even in the area. His pack was gone and his glasses disappeared from the ground. Bard was gone.

If someone had kidnapped the boy they might have taken the pack. But no one would have stopped to pick up the glasses while struggling to subdue the boy and drag him off. The only person who would have picked up Bard's glasses...was Bard himself.

Intuitively Drifter knew what had happened even before his mind formed this conclusion. The boy had run away on him. Dick's last wish had been for Drifter to watch the boy and now Bard was gone.

Drifter's shoulders slumped as he looked around the empty courtyard one more time. There was no point in going after Bard. Even if he could have tracked the boy, Bard would not want to come with him when he caught up. It was best to continue his mission in the hope that he could finish it before anything truly terrible happened to the foolish runaway.

Chapter 11: Loneliness in Two Volumes

Taking his own bundle and hiding the remains of the fire, Drifter set out towards the west. He still had to find the ancient springs that had once become a spa, and were now probably ruins. After that, he would turn north and walk for however many days it took him to reach the park in which the Gate was kept. He wished, as he walked, that his car had not betrayed him. It would have been only a few hour's drive to reach the park, if the roads had been fairly clear. Not only that, but the chance of getting mugged by an unknown gang on the way would have been greatly decreased. As it was he was an open target, plodding across the plains of the wrecked city like a flea on a dog's back.

But Drifter did not take the open road when he could help it. Instead, he kept to the shadows, slipping around the edges of buildings and walking down marble colonnades. A he walked, he past by buildings that would have housed every sort of store and business. Markets, stripped out inside, general stores fallen in, places that sold tools and small machines full of crushed, rusting junk...

Near noon he stopped on the edge of a low hill, where the road coasted down below him and rolled out across a wide flat. This flat was sparsely filled with structures, wide spaces glaring around the buildings where there had once been lawns and private groves. The installations themselves were large mansions, the palaces and play pens of the rich. Through the middle of the flat land ran a narrow river, water shrunk to a muddy trickle. A highly ornamented bridge had once crossed it, spanning the waters with pride. Now the buttresses hung empty, pillars stuck up from the river bottom like jagged teeth and the waters were clogged with fallen bits of stone and rebar.

There was no good shelter from prying eyes anywhere nearby, so Drifter began to walk down the road into the valley. He hunched forward so that his hood would shield his eyes from the sun, which seemed brighter and warmer on the dead world today than it had been for the last few weeks. His feet thumped in their own peculiar pattern on the pavement. Slowly, the hill spooled away behind him and the flat road came up, stretching before him to the bridge. Cracked statues, often of lions or mermaids, rested beside gaping gate posts on each side of the road. The gates were fallen down or hanging at odd angles, broken arms that would not swing. At a distance of a few hundred yards, the mansions watched Drifter pass, arched windows peering at him coyly or trickling tears of bubbled glass.

Nothing seemed to move in the great buildings. Even the wind was still, leaving the gates to hang in silence. A Rabiter crossed the road ahead of Drifter, making him pause. But the creature just snarled and kept on its path.

After what seemed like a long walk, Drifter came to the broken bridge. There was a steep bank beside it, leading down to the gravel and mud of the river bottom. Someone had worn a path down one part of the bank, perhaps creatures going to drink from the water. The side of the bridge, what was left of it, had been uglified by the personal marks and remarks of the humans who passed by. In chalk, charcoal and paint, words or just symbols like nasty faces had been scrawled on the pale stone.

Drifter paused to look at them, trying to figure what the most recent were. He had been standing for a few minutes gazing at them when he heard a step behind him. Tensed, he turned to see what was coming his way. It was a much more peculiar spectacle than he had been expecting.

A man and woman walked arm in arm down the road towards him, looking like a scene from a faded photograph. Both were dressed in clothes so old-fashioned they might have been called historical. The woman had a long dress, with puffed sleeves and a wide skirt, the waist uncomfortably tight. Over one shoulder an umbrella hung indolently. The man was wearing a top-hat, swallow-tailed coat and tight waistcoat underneath, while a walking cane hung over his unoccupied arm. All the fabric on the couple's clothes was faded, odd colors that ranged from dusty plum to old mango. It was ripped and torn from use, sometimes hanging in strands where it should have been complete. Their shoes were tight old models with the heels flapping and toes worn.

"Top of the morning to you!" the man called out in salutation as they approached, "wonderfully temperate air today, 'ey?"

Drifter narrowed his eyes without replying.

The couple came to a halt a few yards from him, inspecting him with cocked heads. Both had light burn scars on their hands and face.

"Sullen type, isn't he my dear?" the man said to his companion.

"Oh, quite." The woman shrugged, a bit of lace pulling apart on one shoulder. "Do you think he talks?"

"I really don't know."

The woman smiled shyly. "Do you think he knows who we are?"

"He should." The man stared at Drifter with wide eyes. "But it is possible he does not."

Jerking forward suddenly, leaving his companion behind, the man held out a hand gloved in torn white kid. "I'm Caesarius, King of the Palaces. And this is my delightful wife, Queen Ambrosia."

Drifter gazed at his hand until it faltered. When it was withdrawn, he returned, "they call me Drifter."

The man drew himself up straight. "Ah. Well. Welcome to our realm. It runs from this bridge eastward to the edge of that hill. All the mansions and grand palaces you have past belong to us, as our rightful realm. Land bequeathed us by the green fire from the sky, an act of the Lord's to denote our ascendancy."

"Nice." Drifter shrugged. "I'm happy to finally know the reason for the Greenspark fire."

"Quite." They both smiled at him in complacent idiocy.

"Is it fine with you if I leave your realm now?"

The man bowed his head magnificently. "Of course, sir. My country has open borders for all. I am no petty tyrant to keep you here against your will."

"Thanks." Still at his most ironic, Drifter turned and started down the bank towards the river. Behind him he could hear the 'king' and 'queen' continue to discuss him in naive sentences.

The river was low and sluggish, but the bed thick in mud. Drifter picked his way across gravel-bars, trying to find a solid crossing. Finally, he was forced to wade right out into the brown water, feeling river-muck ooze up into his boots. Every step became a fight, and the water soaked into the legs of his pants. It was with an effort that he dragged his feet up out of the mud on the far side and climbed the bank. Panting, feeling the sting of the wetness against his old burn scar, he glanced over his shoulder towards the bank he had left behind. The wonky couple still stood there in their torn finery, apparently discussing him, the weather or whatever else filled their scorched minds. Seeing him pause, the woman waved and the man touched his cap.

Drifter raised a hand to them fractionally, before heading on his way.

That evening he camped in the shell of a building, on the opposite side of the valley, where the town became thicker. The mud had dried and caked onto his boots and pants. He flaked it off idly, sitting against part of the cold brick wall. He had not started a fire, as there were recent signs of inhabitants in this part of town.

"Not much further to the spa, if luck is with me," he muttered to himself.

Drifter had re-read the scroll in the last of the day's light and found no clue as to how far away his next way point was, only that he had to turn north at it and walk two days before reaching the park where the Gate stood. Now, he leaned wearily against the wall, thinking again of the comforts of his car. And trying not to think of Bard, out alone in the city for perhaps the first time in his life.

IT WAS BARD'S FIRST time alone in the city at night. Even when traveling to the ocean in the Academy sector, it had always been with Dick. Somehow the lank, tall scholar had seemed to hold the night at bay with his words of wisdom and stories of relics that had been found. Bard wished that Dick were there. Were not dying. Had not betrayed him.

Because Bard felt betrayed by Dick, to some extent. Not enough to hate him. Only enough to wish that Dick had never sent him away. Why had his guardian told him to travel with Drifter to the Gate of Eternity? He had evidently not opposed Drifter's project to end the world and every life on it. But why not let Bard stay with him in his last moments...?

The boy threw a twig angrily into the dark. He was camping not far from Drifter, though he did not know it. He had followed his own path through the structures on the hill, crossing the valley at some distance from the main road, out behind the great mansions. There had been a little footbridge of steel there, still intact across the river. He had crossed it with some hesitation as it creaked and clanged at his every step. After that, he had crossed the rest of the valley without incident and come to a place where the buildings became thicker once again.

At that point, he was to the north of Drifter by a few miles. But there was fresh graffiti on the walls of the buildings and he had heard the sound of loud voices in the distance, laughing and shouting in a frighteningly mocking manner. Veering away from the sounds, he traveled south until the graffiti became less and the voices had long died away. By that time, the sun was sinking in a trail of blood towards the horizon. He decided to make camp.

Even that idea, finding a camp site alone, was thrillingly new to him. On one hand, he was frightened about the gang he had heard finding him or getting too cold to sleep. On the other hand, the taste of freedom was exciting.

Searching around the immediate area, the boy found a place where one building had collapsed beside two others, making a hollow in the space between. After clearing a few small slabs of stone, it had become a perfect little fortress, walled in on one side by the rubble and the others almost entirely blocked off by the standing structures. The only avenue that was left was a tiny alley between the buildings, mostly clogged by melted trashcans and other debris.

With a handful of twigs and the flint from his pack to light them, Bard soon had a cozy nest inside. He sat staring at the fire, thinking back on the last few days.

Drifter was not unnaturally cruel. But Bard thought that nature had made him cruel after the disaster. He was a survivor, someone who would follow his own aims and fight for his life to the end. Someone almost unstoppable once he chose a goal.

"How to stop him?" Bard murmured angrily, "I have to stop him."

But short of killing the loner, the thought of which made his stomach quirk, he could not think of a way to halt Drifter's progress. Perhaps he could sabotage the gate when he reached it. If he destroyed the keyhole, would it make the gate unlocked, or break it so that it was stuck shut? And what could he destroy it with, anyway?

Throwing another twig into the shadows, Bard let out a sigh. He had never really been prepared for something like this. He had been raised as a scholar, both before and even after the Greenspark disaster. Reading old manuscripts, translating texts and fashioning experiments out of what he read were his specialties. That and identifying relics by what he read. Not hunting through the ruined city in a race against one of its toughest inhabitants.

"I wish Dick were here," he sighed. Then, angry at himself for his weakness and mad at the whole world for setting him in this situation, he curled up to go to sleep.

With the shadows at his back and the whole broken world around him, it took some time for him to fall unconscious. When he did, his sleep was strung with beads of vision, dreams reflecting his life.

He saw himself as a little boy again, going to school in the academy sector for the first time. Then, visions of the Greenspark made him shudder and cringe, before fading to a dream about a recent time, when he had taken leave of Dick Chelsea.

"Why do I have to go? I want to stay here, with you."

"Drifter will care for you now. My time is near, young Bard...I don't want to leave you alone."

Alone...

Alone...

Bard woke to a sharp pain in one foot. With a scream he sat up to see what looked like a white rabbit crouching over his shoe, teeth working steadily. Another sharp pain struck through his foot and he realized that the creature was a Rabiter and that it was gnawing at his toe through the shoe. With a gasp he kicked out, sending the creature flying. It thumped against the wall of a nearby building and slid down to scowl at him through red eyes, a drop of blood hanging from its jaw.

"Go away!" Bard shouted, picking up a stone and flinging it at the beast. The Rabiter hopped nimbly out of the way, letting out a growl like a miniature rabid dog. But when Bard reached for another stone it scampered off, disappearing down the alley.

"My foot..." Bard drew up his foot and cradled it, feeling a hole bitten clean through the tough fabric of the shoe. Inside, his big toe had two sets of lacerations on the side of it, places where the Rabiter had bit him. Luckily it had not had time to make a big enough hole in the shoe to bite the toe clean off.

Bard felt the wounds and tears welled in his eyes at the pain. They were nasty little incisions, welling blood rapidly. Afraid of infection, Bard cast around for something to clean the wounds with. But he did not have any water with him. The last time he had drank had been at the muddy river, where he had tried to take only the cleanest water he could find. But he had nothing to carry it in or boil it for safety. Nothing to bathe his wounds with now.

Tearing open his pack, Bard searched for something to stem the bleeding, at least. He had a small hunk of dry bread, a few raisins, his spare shirt and the two books. Snatching the shirt, he wadded it into his shoe against the cuts, wincing as it pressed against them. He hoped the blood had washed out whatever infection was carried on a Rabiter's teeth. But rodents were known to carry sicknesses that affected men more than themselves. Bard bit his lower lip, frowning with worry. He had never been gnawed by a Rabiter before, though he had heard of it happening.

Would his toe swell up, turn blue, fall off?

Bard choked down a sob and forced himself to be calm. He had to stay focused and deal with whatever came up, not waste his time borrowing trouble. Peeling the shirt back off, he found that the bleeding had already slowed to a tiny trickle. Using the knife Drifter had given him, he cut a wide strip from the bottom of the shirt and wrapped it awkwardly around the toe. Then, he wadded another strip into the shoe, blocking off the hole that had been bitten in it.

He had not looked closely at the knife before. Now he saw that it had a hefty blade, sharpened on both sides of the point. The handle was firmly attached and neatly made, brass rivets holding together strips of smooth, reddish-brown wood. A tiny cross guard, more ornamental than useful, protected the connection between blade and handle on the outside. It was a fine knife, from he little Bard knew of them.

He used it to hack up his bread and eat it with the raisins for breakfast. It was early morning, with the sun growing red over the horizon. He stood up, ready to go on. The dry crumbs of breakfast made Bard thirsty after he had gone only a few yards. He realized that he would have to find water soon, hopefully some clean enough to drink unboiled. Perhaps he could even scavenge for a pot or metal flask from a building nearby. But whatever else he did, he had to keep moving towards the Gate of Eternity as quickly as possible.

Drifter could have wasted a little time looking for him, but he knew that the loner would push himself afterwards to reach the Gate quickly. And when Drifter pushed himself it was hard for anyone to keep up with him.

Bard stuck to the edges of buildings and side-alleys as he made his way north.

His thirst got worse as he traveled until it reached the point that he decided to scout around the nearby buildings for a vessel and a supply. It would detract from his traveling speed, but he had to have water to keep going. And Drifter would have to find supplies of his own as he traveled, slowing him down a little. At least, Bard hoped it would.

He wandered through a few half-ruined structures without finding anything of use, before reaching a building that had once been a private home. It had a second story, still mostly intact. As he came in the front door, he immediately heard the sound of dripping water. Following it down a musty, scorched hall he reached a room littered with dusty furniture, surprisingly unmarred by fire. The stone construction of the house had saved the furnishings, though one wall of it bulged out dangerously where it had been hit by the earthquakes.

The ceiling above had a long, jagged crack running across it from one side to the other. A chandelier with a few of its crystals and bulbs unharmed hung askew next to the crack. Slowly, a drop of water ran down the crack, hit a jag and dripped off onto the chandelier. From there, it undulated down the hanging strings of crystals to fall with a *plink* on a broken platter laying on the floor, as if put there for that very purpose. The platter was too cracked to hold the liquid and it ran away into the carpet, creating a rotten marsh of plush.

Bard stared at the white plate for a minute, eyes fixed by a blue pattern around the rim, being marred with water like teardrops. With a shake of his head he hurried across the floor, pile squishing at every step. He had no time for day dreaming.

On the other side of the room was a wide staircase of marble leading up to the next story. The floor there was unstable, groaning at his light treads. Multiple ways led off of the landing. Two doors were jammed in their frames so that he could not open them. The third door led to a wide room which was missing half of its roof. Pigeons roosted in the joists, fluttering away with guttural cooing noises as he entered. They left the building like phantoms, or white shawls thrown into the sky.

The long crack ran through this chamber's floor. The left-hand half of it was shaded by what remained of the ceiling.

A bathtub sat moldering with yellow rings in its stomach, silver chipping off the shower head and feet. A toilet without a lid snuggled against the far wall, dry as desert sand. Over on the right there was a fancy porcelain washbasin, sitting on a gray marble stand. The stand had once been white, but joists falling and burning around it had changed its color forever. The washbasin was, amazingly, just barely cracked on the near side. Because of the open roof above it, the vessel had filled with rain water, which was now oozing from the seam. It was only half full. The water had been trickling away, down to he floor and across I before dripping into the room below. As he looked across at the basin, Bard estimated it to be about a gallon of water left in the container, enough to quench his thirst for more than a day.

He stepped out onto the floor and felt it sway under him. Walking lightly, he avoided the large crack below as much as possible. Slowly, the boy inched his way over to his target. The basin.

He reached it and stood upon slightly firmer flooring. The basin was too large for him to carry far, especially on his journey. The marble stand around it had a few pigeon droppings encrusting its sides. But the water inside he bowl appeared pure, much cleaner than what he had taken from the river. Leaning over, he took a long slurp. Cool and refreshing, it slid down his throat. It was only when he raised his eyes in silent gratitude towards the sky that he noticed what spanned the gap on the stones above his head. A sort of iron trellis had once been placed on the roof for vines to grow up, as there was a platform which could be reached from another room. Flowers had bloomed on the vine, its green leaves had reached for the sky. But when the Greenspark struck, it was all withered away to nothing and, in the ensuing disturbances, the long iron trellis had been knocked across the gap in the roof. Someone had been on the roof when the disaster hit. In the last throes of death the owner of the house had fallen onto the searing trellis. Now a blackened skeleton lay sprawled across it, hideous skull staring down at the basin directly below as if pleading for a drink of water.

Bard choked down a scream, fixated by revulsion. The skull stared at him, jaw gaping and eyes empty holes. It was right above the basin. Bard tasted the water in his mouth turn to ashes. Every drop had run over that weary skull.

Unable to contain himself, Bard turned and dashed out of the room. His footsteps echoed on the unstable floor, setting up a deadly reverberation. As the boy crossed the living room below, he heard an ominous cracking and creaking above. Slamming out of the front door, the sound turned to a steady rumble of falling stone.

Bard did not stop running until he was across the street and behind another building. Then he leaned, panting, against the wall and peeked back with one eye. The house had imploded, crumbling into a heap of huge, jagged chunks covering a crushed lower story. Rock was still sliding and falling, dust rising in streamers like smoke.

He had drunk water from a dead man's head.

As he gasped in fresh air and tried to fight off the horror that had taken over his mind, Bard saw a figure walk slowly into view down the street. It moved with a slight hitch, making the gray-blue cape hanging down its back swing from side to side irregularly. There was something distinctly familiar about that irregularity. It was Drifter.

The man stopped a few yards from the recently collapsed building, bright eyes sweeping the scene. After a moment he turned, slowly taking in the surrounding area. Bard jerked away from that searching gaze, hiding behind the building. He thought he must have been seen, and waited every second to hear those slightly uneven steps coming towards him down the alley. But after what seemed like a long time, there was no sound of approach and the boy dared peer out at the street again.

Drifter was disappearing up it, bundle tucked under one arm. He skirted the fallen ruins of the house and turned down a side-street, escaping the boy's gaze. With a quickly in-drawn breath, Bard finally moved from his place. Not knowing why he did it, drawn like a magnet to a blade, he followed Drifter's path. Not too closely, not enough to overrun him around a corner. But when he reached the turning in the road he looked down it, seeing ahead the flicker of blue-gray and tan as Drifter rounded another corner. Fearing that he would be seen if he tailed him directly, Bard began to ghost haunt Drifter's path from one street over, checking down alleys until he saw the silent figure pass.

Eventually he lost the man around a corner. Not seeing him appear down the next side street, Bard determined to climb the tallest building he could find and see if he could spot Drifter from there. He did not dare continue on his way without knowing where the loner was, as he might accidentally run into him around any turning.

Choosing a building with steps up the outside leading to a platform on top (much more stable and empty than the last one) he quickly mounted the steps and had a view of the nearby streets. Shading his eyes with a hand, he peered all around. In no direction could he see a moving figure. The only living thing he could make out was a bloated red lizard of some sort resting on a stone nearby. It had huge bubbles of reddish material on its back legs like inflated rubber floating devices, and a head with a jaw too deep for its snout.

But after a moment of scanning the area, Bard noticed a building directly to the east which was set a little apart from the rest and surrounded by a rusty chain-link fence. It was a large, low building made of alternating white and blue stone, most of it still intact. A huge dome had once protected the central chamber of the place. Now it was smashed in and its broken shell screamed at the sky. The thing which attracted Bard's attention was a large slab of granite set up vertically outside the building, just on the inside of the fence. It was worn and scorched from the disaster but still bore three large letters in faded blue. 'SPA'.

"The ancient springs!" Bard whispered, thumping his fist on the curb of the roof. "I've found it!"

Chapter 12: Monster and Man

Drifter stopped before the entrance of the abandoned building. At one time it would have been the retreat of rich folks and the chronically ill. Now pigeons roosted on its gutters and fluttered through the gaping doorway. Not so different than the rich folk, with their billing and cooing, strutting themselves for the others to see. In fact, they directly inherited the position, as there were no celebrities left in all of Civitas Apex. None that could be recognized as such.

In front of the spa, a dozen low steps radiated out in tiers, making access easy. At the top of them a doorway stood, wide and arched at the top. Its glass doors were shattered, laying across the top steps in glittering fragments. Inside was dim, struck through with shafts of light from the broken dome on top. Drifter took in the building from a few feet distant of the lowest step. He had found the spa that used to be ancient springs. Now all he had to do was turn north, to his right, and keep walking. Within the next few days, he should reach the park of science and the end of his self-imposed mission.

But he hesitated in front of the rounded steps. There might still be water inside somewhere, fresh spring water that would be untainted. If not all of it was mineral-water, that was. He did not yet need more himself, as he had filled the flask the morning before and drank little since, but Bard was still out there somewhere. And if the boy was, for some reason, trying to come in contact with Drifter again he would have known to go to the spa and wait for him. Especially as he could get clean drinking water there, something he would have a difficult time doing elsewhere.

Besides which, the mineral water might be good for the wound on Drifter's leg. It continued to ache and weep, from the combined evils of the harsh use it had been put to (especially in fighting the griffin), the lack of care he had given the scar and more recently the river mud that had caked it. Drifter disliked putting any part of himself before his mission, but he had to be in one piece to complete it. After that, it would cease to matter.

Stalking warily up the steps, he slid into the arched door. A band of shadows enveloped him just inside, while ahead the tiled floor was lit from above. The tiles were cracked and scorched, the chairs that had once ringed this large waiting room burnt to spidery lines of black. A pair of pillars held up each corner of the room, white, with skirts of charcoal gray. A desk curved around one edge of the chamber, made of some sort of dark, impermeable stone. The few bones laying on the floor about it, cracked and gnawed, showed where some terrified citizen had attempted to hide.

To the left and right, doors led off of the main chamber. One had a metal plaque above it carrying the word, 'Massage'. The door across from it was missing its sign, but Drifter guessed it had once pointed the way to the springs.

He stuck to the shadows as much as possible, gliding around the outside of the glass-strewn room to reach the right-hand door. It led into a long, wide hall stained with amorphous yellow splotches on floor and roof. A damp and moldy odor began to permeate the air.

After trying various doors which led nowhere, to shattered rooms or ones with furnishings that did not interest him, Drifter found a set of stairs leading down into a low, wide and dimly lit chamber. The sinuous drip of water wound its way up the stairs, suggesting grottoes of cool liquid.

In the dim light of the wide room Drifter found a set of three partitioned chambers within it. He looked in the nearest one and discovered a huge, set-in pool rimmed in green tiles. He was underground now, where the Greenspark could not hit directly. The floor was damp and muddy, the tiles still in their places. The pool brimmed with lapping liquid, which came in through a piping system in the wall and ran out again through one hidden below the surface. A soft ripple spread over the pool as a drop fell from the roof. The edges of it were encrusted in a thin, whitish powder like salt.

At one time a sign had been affixed to the wall, explaining rules and perhaps the uses of the pool. Now the sign hung down, face against the wall, as if ashamed of an existence with no masters. Drifter cast a glance at the sign before walking to the edge of the pool and dipping his fingers in. It was cool, almost cold, with a slight thickness to it unlike pure water. When he drew his fingers out and touched them to the tip of his tongue it left a tingling sensation behind. With one more glance around to make sure that he was alone, Drifter rolled up the left leg of his pants and unlaced his boot. The leather was still a little damp from crossing the river, but that was no reason to get it any wetter. Underneath, his sock was stiff with dirt and mud. Drifter gazed at it dispassionately for a minute before deciding that he would leave it on. That way, it would get washed in the water at the same time. Holding his breath, he dipped first his foot and then his leg into the lapping liquid.

The mineral water was cold on instep and calf, stinging on his scorched shin. He let his breath out in a hiss and waited for the sensation to fade away. It was good that it stung. That meant it was accomplishing something.

Mud swirled away into the water, making dirt patterns before being drawn down and refreshed. After a short time, Drifter peeled his sock off and wrung it out, flopping it over the boot. It was odd to see his own foot splashing down in the water like some sort of dank fish. He counted the toes to make sure that they were still there.

After a few more moments of soaking, Drifter pulled his leg out and began to rearrange his gear. He was just drawing on the boot, when he heard a faint noise echoing towards him from the direction of the staircase. Footsteps clicked on the floor, followed by a pair of voices.

"He went this way, c'mon."

"Hee hee, we'll get him now!"

Coarse voices, adult but childish in their glee. Drifter finished tying his boot and slunk over to press himself against the wall. Had someone seen him come down the steps?

"He's a tough one. Be careful."

"Are you sure he's still here?"

"He went in early this morning. And you know they don't move in the day time."

Drifter saw two men come into view, both raggedly dressed and carrying improvised spears. They gave the pool room hardly a glance, passing by with the whispered words,

"the Chardog's probably hiding back further, where it's darker."

It was not Drifter they were hunting for. He stayed hidden in the shadows, unseen as they passed by. He noticed that one of the men was also carrying a lantern, as yet unlit, while the other bore a heavy club in his right hand as well as a spear. Both had lengths of rope wrapped around their middles.

As quiet as the dark Drifter began to shadow them. He did not dare come up too close, in case they lit the lantern or made a sudden turn. Instead, he followed at a distance, cautiously. He passed another partitioned-off pool, this one filled with a darker, more greenish liquid. Ahead, the two men turned into the third compartment, pausing just inside to light their lantern. Yellow light pooled out of it, gleaming off of the tiles on the floor with a sickly radiance.

Drifter paused, wary of the light. Inside the partition, he heard a shuffling noise, a growl and a startled yelp followed by the unpleasant laughter of the two men. There was another growl, a series of short shouts and laughs from the men and then the clearly-spoken words;

"He's bound now! Hah, he's ours."

Mockingly, the other spoke to their victim, "poor doggy can't move, can he? Now doggy's at our mercy!"

"We'll make him pay for the trouble him and his brethren cause us!"

The deep, rumbling growl of a Chardog was turned abruptly into a pained yelp. The men laughed, the dog whined and then cried out again. Drifter's expression became hard and sharp-edged as obsidian.

Stalking forward, he looked around the edge of the partition. This one held a pool that had gone dry, the edge stained but clear of encrustation. Down at the bottom of it was a few bones and scraps of fur, as well as a torn cushion from a couch that must have been dragged there at some point. It was a Chardog's lair, where it hid from the light and devoured its prey.

The lantern was set on the edge of the basin, just above a set of steps leading down into it. On the floor next to the steps a large Chardog lay, paws bound and huge eyes flaming. It writhed and snapped but could not get up. Blood ran from a wound in its flank, while its head had a large, lacerated bruise above one eye. The two men stood on the step above it, faces twisted in evil leers as they brandished their spears and jabbed at it mercilessly. Every time the beast cried out in pain, its tormentors laughed.

Drifter descended unseen and lay a hand on the shoulder of one tormentor. The man gave a start and turned, gripping his weapon.

"Why torture the beast?" Drifter grated, "it suffers from the destruction no less than we do. If it kills to eat, it is only acting naturally. You could try doing the same."

The man jerked free of his grip and whirled the spear around between them, while his companion drew up his club threateningly. They were both hardened and tough, corded muscle standing out on their thin arms. Both bore light burns from the disaster, but no blackened scars. They were men of the ruins, survivors no less than Drifter.

"What business is it of yours?" the first man returned, baring his teeth. "This is a *Chardog*, can't you see? They're our enemies and we make them pay for the pain they have caused us. You got a problem with that, you can join it!"

Drifter regarded them both calmly, stepping back up onto the step above. "Nothing deserves to suffer extra in this broken world. Kill it or let it go free."

"You gonna' make us?"

The Chardog whined hopefully, as if recognizing a friend in Drifter.

"If need be."

"Just you *try!*" The first man drew back his spear for a throw. He was not slow, used to quick decisions and the actions which followed. One had to be quick to survive in Apex as it was.

But Drifter was faster. He leaped from the higher step, kicking the spear out of his way mid-air. All his weight came down on the man's chest, knocking him from the last shallow step to the floor with Drifter on top of him. There was a crack of breaking bones and the man's head slammed against the stone. He moaned, but did not move. Drifter jumped from him to land on the tiles near the dog, just as the second fellow's spear whizzed by. It clattered off of the pool's wall, falling uselessly to the floor. The thrower did not waste a second, raising his club and coming after Drifter with set, burning eyes.

Drifter waited for him, hands empty. It seemed that he was relaxed, not even prepared for an attack. But when his adversary approached, he moved like winged fire. Stepping aside from the club's blow he brought his hand down on the man's wrist, shocking the weapon loose. A second strike to his adversary's chin made him stagger to the side, losing his balance and impetus. Drifter came after him, striking to midrift and head until the second man also lay still on the cold, echoing floor.

Drifter looked down at the two unconscious men, one of which would probably never move again, before turning to the beast which lay bound nearby. A few expert slices of his knife set the dog free. It scrambled to its feet, staring at Drifter with its huge, red eyes as if trying to decide between attacking him or bowing to his will.

Drifter was on one knee on the floor, an easy target. With a quiet gentleness, he spoke to the creature, "your wounds are mine, our freedom shared. Depart, beast of the night, depart in peace."

The Chardog tilted its head to one side, stepped forward to nuzzle the man's shoulder with its large, damp nose, and then padded away up the stairs. Drifter followed it with his eyes, stiffening as it passed a figure standing silently at the rim of the pool. It was Bard, his eyes wide behind the glimmering glasses as he stared down at Drifter and the two pummeled men. He did not even shy from the beast as it padded by, his gaze was so intent with shock and horror.

Drifter stood up, seeing a monster reflected in Bard's gaze. The monster that Bard saw in him.

Frustration filled Drifter. The boy beheld him with pure horror, as something insane and evil. Without a word, Drifter strode up the steps and brushed past him, stalking down the chamber through the dim light. He went up the steps at the far side. Drifter did not wait for the boy to follow and did not want him to. He knew that the boy would either shy away from him in terror or treat him like a beast to be pitied and cautiously led out of its terrible ways. The boy's fear bit into him as a sharp pain, striking to his heart.

Blindly, he chose paths through the doors and halls of the abandoned building until he found himself coming up yet another set of steps, which led out onto a balcony at the rear of the building. It was cracked and broken on one end, stone sticking out in jagged teeth. The banister was partially wrecked, hanging down towards the ground in steel strands. What was left of it, Drifter gripped until it furrowed his skin, leaving white marks behind.

Why should he care what the boy thought?

Bard had left him. The boy was just another denizen of the ruined city, to be avoided or dealt with cautiously, careless of his emotions. But Drifter had promised Dick to watch the boy, give him one last fling in life before it all ended. And in Bard he recognized some of the last sparks of humanity, a will to live and see life with delighted wonder. While in his native environment of garden and books, machines and relics the boy was not merely existing. He was living with an interest in life.

Drifter slid down to sit on the broken balcony, closing his eyes and calming himself with deep breaths. His whirling thoughts slowly stilled to a leaden sea. It was not a time for anger, nor for hesitation. There were other people like Bard, a few of them at least, living in Apex Haven. There was also Loran, untouched by the scorch that had come with the Greenspark fire. Those people, a handful out of all Apex perhaps, a few hundred maybe in the world, deserved a better life. But there was only one way Drifter could give it to them. Only one way he could find peace from the scorch.

He had to complete his mission.

Standing up, he gripped the railing and swung himself over the edge. Hand-over-hand he climbed down the hanging steel rail. It was a drop of perhaps six feet to the ground at the bottom. He took it easily before looking about him. His pack of goods had been left behind in the spa, set beside the first pool where he had bathed his leg.

But he did not care. The key was still in its cylinder, the scroll tucked in his uniform shirt. It would only take a few days to reach the Gate of Eternity. He did not need to eat in that time. Only drink a little, and he had his flask of water with him. In a forced march, he could make the distance quite quickly. Then everything evil would be at an end.

He turned towards the north, using the sun as a guide, and began to walk. It was not the dogged plod of earlier that day. Nor a trot or wasteful dash. It was a long, striding march that ate up the ground without expending too much energy. It was a walk that could not be stopped.

BARD STOOD ASIDE AS Drifter passed him, feeling as if he had just seen a dark phantom brush by. Down below, the two men that Drifter had either incapacitated or killed lay still, faces pale in the lantern light. As the loner's footsteps echoed away Bard shifted his gaze from the pool to the hall and back again. He did not move for some time, rooted to the spot by the scene replaying in his mind, the scene of Drifter striking down a man mercilessly and then gently letting a Chardog go.

Chardogs, Bard knew, were beasts of the night. They raided human camps when they could, killed and ate people, devoured any bodies they found and were said to walk with phantoms like pets. Bard had never seen a phantom. He had only heard Dick's description of seeing one. But he imagined them to be pitiless wraiths of evil, the spirits of bad people come back to life. And now he began to wonder if Drifter was one of them.

After a few minutes of standing still in the echoing, damp chamber Bard shivered and began to walk out of it. He did not want to meet Drifter on the way back out. He was scared of the man, yet somehow, his fear had turned to determination. Bard decided that he needed to stop Drifter on his quest, no matter what it took. Even if, he shivered at the thought, he had to kill the man to do it. In his mind Drifter ceased to be truly human. He was now allied with the Chardogs, a beast to be destroyed before it devoured the world.

Bard had already found a clear, cold spring of water in the abandoned place and drank from it, filling a glass bottle he had also found there and capping it with a bit of wood. After filling the bottle, he had heard voices further down in the building and followed them until he came to the spot where Drifter was fighting the other men. Now he left the spa altogether and turned north, steps speeding up until he was hurrying on his way. Now and then, he felt a twinge of hunger and unrest in his stomach, but he ignored it for the moment. His toe also was paining him at every step. Bard set his teeth and drew on a reserve of strength he had not known he possessed. It was time for action like he had never known it before.

Later that day, he began to hear footsteps ahead of him down streets, or stalking between buildings. Peering down an alley cautiously, he saw Drifter. Pausing, the boy leaned against a chunk of cracked stone to catch his breath. He had caught up. Should he try to pass Drifter and reach the Gate first, or make some attempt to slow the loner on his course?

Bard knew better than to attempt a direct attack on the loner. He decided to follow for now, and see what happened, wait for an opportunity to present itself. Carefully, with a cunning he had never used before, Bard began to stalk Drifter. He watched him from between buildings, followed him at a distance down streets and waited for him to pass between fallen heaps of masonry.

Drifter was not looking around himself. He had set his course to the north and followed it without deviating. If he knew Bard was there, he gave no sign of it. He was locked on a distant target.

By afternoon, Bard was flagging. His hunger and the pain in his foot slowed him. He could not keep up much longer and he knew it. If he wanted to slow Drifter down, now was the time.

They were traveling through what had once been tall buildings, many of them broken off now in jagged stubs not more than a story high. Piles of rubble and stones lay beside the streets or spilling out into them, making a jungle of ruin to be crossed. A few avenues were still mostly intact, though buildings leaned over them precariously. Bard and Drifter were both traversing one of these, perhaps two hundred feet apart, when the boy looked up to see an opportunity at the end of the avenue.

There, a building had been broken off above the second story, its top mostly laying in crumbles around it. But a section of wall, made up of bricks and stones, still stood on the roof of the second story, poised dangerously over the edge of the street.

Summoning all of his energy, the boy turned off the avenue and scrambled over heaped-up broken buildings, or ran behind ones that were still intact. Pushing himself, he made it to the two-story structure at the end of the street. A metal sign hung from the front of it, held out on weakened iron arms. The sign was blank, white metal bent and peeling. Bard entered a side-door and found himself in what had once been a laundromat. The tall, square machines stood in ranks up and down the room, doors hanging open as if still waiting for dirty clothes to be shoved in. The machines closest to the stairs at the back were singed, cords melted and paint chipping off.

The next story was completely burnt out, whatever sort of mini mart or restaurant it had been blotted from the room. The steps up from there, to what was now an open roof space, were rickety. Bard dashed up them recklessly, heedless of their tortured groans. He came out not far from the heap of masonry on the roof. Panting, he threw himself down beside the stacked bricks and looked off of the edge. Down below, Drifter was just approaching the building, shoulders hunched as he strode forward. He did not look up or appear to notice the boy.

Bard didn't give himself time to consider the enormity of what he was doing. He had never taken a person's life before, or even considered it. Now he set his thin shoulders to the wall of bricks and pushed. It took more effort than he had expected. But once it started going, the heap was poised so delicately that it all slid off at once and plummeted towards the earth. In a rain of dust and clattering stone the stack fell and struck the pavement. Bricks bounced away and cracked on the hard surface. Bard gasped at the noise, suddenly afraid to see what he had done. Timidly, he crept up and craned his neck to look over the edge.

The pile of bricks had become a dusty heap in the middle of the road. They hit so hard that some had rolled away or scattered to end up near the curb. Others were cracked, bits and corners laying at odd angles. Bard expected to see a blue cloak laying crumpled underneath the pile, a hand reaching out terribly or a leg twitching. Some sign that his plan had succeeded. But the heap did not seem to cover anything except for the road.

"Didn't manage to kill me, did you?"

A voice rang up from the side of the street a little further on. Bard raised his horrified eyes to see Drifter standing in the shadows of the building across the way. He had his slingshot on one wrist, the hand on the sling as if about to shoot.

Instead, he shrugged and continued on his way down the street. Bard sat back, still panting from his run and the excitement. He had tried to kill Drifter. The thought sunk its fangs into him. Perhaps worse, he had failed and Drifter knew it.

Slowly, the boy made his way down from the top of the building. He couldn't fall behind. He had too keep up. But all of a sudden he was feeling very weary and even ill.

"Maybe it was the river water." He mumbled to himself, leaning against the building. "Or that water that had gone over the skull..."

Gradually, he sunk to the ground and rested his head on one up-drawn knee. Waves of nausea, hunger and tiredness slowly overcame him and he sunk into a restless sleep.

He was awoken by a touch, sometime in the gray of twilight. Frightened, he groaned as he straightened his back. Bard felt cold, stiff and utterly sick. Not only that, but he was terrified about what might have touched his arm. It lessened his fear not at all when he saw a hooded figure leaning over him.

"Please! I didn't mean it!"

A woman's voice came out of the dark, cool and calm. "I will not hurt you. Sit still."

Bard subsided, obeying the gentle command in her voice. Tilting his head back, he could just make out a pale face and dark brows. It wasn't Drifter, that was certain.

"Who...who are you?"

"My name is Loran." The woman came to sit in front of him, back straight in dim profile. "Did Drifter mention me to you?"

"No. I—Do you know him?"

"We traveled together, briefly." Loran shrugged. "I don't know him well."

Bard shook his head wearily. "We've been traveling together for a few days. I don't know him at all." His mind felt fuzzy and incapable. "Drifter says that's he's going to end the world. I've got to stop him...I've just got to..."

Darkness swirled around Bard again, making him feel sick. Loran reached out suddenly and lay a cool hand against his forehead.

"You're ill."

"I know...it was the mud, or maybe the skull..."

And total darkness came over the boy once again.

IT WAS NOT LONG AFTER that he awoke to the soft, comforting sound of a fire crackling. As soon as he had made a move, someone's hand slid under his head and Loran's voice ordered, "drink this."

A bowl was put to Bard's lips and he drank in a warm broth with some sort of dusty aftertaste like herbs. Looking up, he saw that a few lengths of white cloth had been put around him as a bed and a fire was burning cheerfully nearby. Loran knelt beside him, the hood of her purple robe pushed back. Deep black hair like watered silk ran over her shoulders. Her expression was one of concentration, lightened by a touch of pity.

"You've had a hard time recently," she said when Bard took the bowl from her and sat up a little more, propping himself against the wall. "An infected bite on your toe, illness and starvation. Did Drifter treat you so poorly?"

Bard held the bowl close to absorb its warmth, shaking his head. "I ran away from him. I don't understand...he wants to end the world."

After these words he took a few more sips of the broth. The ill feeling slowly receded from his stomach and hunger replaced it.

Loran sat back on her heels, sharp features expressing interest. "So I guessed right. He does think that Eternity for All lies beyond that gate."

"Doesn't it?" Bard looked up in surprise.

The woman shook her head slowly from side to side. "Not necessarily. Not how he thinks of it at least. Drifter believes that we are in the apocalypse, the great battle before the end of the world. He theorizes that by opening the gate he can end our suffering and bring about endless peace. But his ideas aren't built so much on fact or true prophecy as they are on vague rumors and hope."

"He doesn't seem like the sort of man to believe in hope," Bard muttered bitterly. After a few more slurps he added, "then what *is* beyond the gate?"

"I'm not sure. But I wonder...perhaps a clue as to why the Greenspark fell and what it was."

Bard sat forward a little, narrow face intent. "I always thought it must have been some sort of meteor that hit into the moon and fragmented, spewing space rock mixed with strange chemicals across the world."

"Many people think something like that." Loran nodded to show respect for his idea. "But there are two problems with that theory that I know, even though I am no astronomer."

She held up a slim hand to count them off on her fingers. "First: if that were so, the Greenspark would only have affected one side of the world as strongly as it did. The other side would have been turned away and only experienced nominal effects. Second: the relics and phantoms."

"You mean, that they didn't appear until after the fall?"

"Yes. Even if the phantoms were 'ghosts' or spirits of some sort caused by the intense loss of life, it doesn't explain the relics—"

Bard held up a hand. "But wait, the relics *did* appear a few hundred years before the fall, right?"

Loran smiled. "Good, you know your history. But why? Isn't it odd that 'ancient relics' should just appear in the world? Including a gate which no one can open, no one can move and had not been seen before. Also, I don't believe that phantoms are the spirits of dead people. And they did appear just after the fall. So what links these three things together?"

Bard stared into the almost-empty bowl. After a long pause he shook his head. "I don't know."

"As of yet, no one I have spoken to does," Loran said softly, "but I wish to find out. I was in the Academy sector researching relics in the library when I came across mention of the gate. Reading the legends about it, I realized what Drifter must be intending, as I had already seen his key. I left my studies and began following his path. I thought at first I would be too late, as he had the car and I did not know how far ahead of me he was. But luckily, I ran across a friendly stranger with a truck that he had somehow kept safe and still working. A beat-up old thing, still running just enough to convey me and my things with the driver. Then, after just a day and a half of driving, we came across Drifter's car. I decided to go by foot towards the gate so as not to be spotted as easily."

"Then you saw me laying here and just decided to help?" Bard gave her a glance full of gratitude. "Thank you."

Loran brushed it away with a gesture. "I would have for anyone. But, actually, I saw you trying to drop the bricks on Drifter and what followed. If you had been a cannibal looking for meat or another enemy, Drifter would have shot at you with the sling. As it was, I guessed you must know him. And a little of his intent."

"I see." Bard gulped down the last of the soup. "But it was still kind of you. Now what are you going to do about Drifter?"

"Follow him." Loran nodded her head firmly. "And see what is beyond these 'Gates of Eternity'. If it is the end of the world...well, I'm ready to meet our Maker. I simply do not believe that it is true."

"I'm—I'm glad." Bard's face turned a little pink with shyness. "I don't want the world to end yet. I still want to live and do things. Maybe even make it a better place."

"Good." Loran lay a hand on his shoulder, pressing down gently but firmly as she took the bowl. "But for now you must rest. We will continue together in the morning."

"Won't Drifter get ahead?"

"He'll have to rest at some point. He can't walk forever."

"Can't he?"

Loran's face became surprisingly cold and hard. "We'll just have to hope not."

Chapter 13: The Gate of Eternity

Drifter marched on through the night, avoiding a courtyard speckled with campfires and torches on the way. Inside it, a group of men crouched around the fires, eating some roast meat larger than pigeons or Vollans. Drifter did not stay long enough to count feet or look for fur. He circumnavigated the courtyard in the dark and journeyed forward.

As dawn was breaking he was making his way through a strip of town playing on the 'Native sector' theme. Stone statues of natives with feathers in their hair stood at street corners, faces broken and limbs missing from the Greenspark fall. Many of the buildings had been framed in heavy timbers to add to the ambiance. Those had burned the hottest and converted into heaps of charcoal with crumbly, burnt bricks inside of it. Ironically, those with cement logs painted to look realistic had survived better, the false trumping the real.

Drifter walked on until noon, when the sector's style was fading from tourist traps to research labs and large, office buildings with tiny, fancy cafes between them. By now, Drifter's leg was starting to pain him again and he was feeling the edges of weariness. He could have eaten, but he was not yet truly hungry. He had gone days before without finding anything much to eat. It was part of his survival skills to travel on little for many miles. But he did not want to push himself so far that it slowed his progress. Better to take small rests now than collapse later on.

Finding a place where a building had half-fallen and created a sheltered nook, Drifter sunk down with his back against the stone. Pulling his flask from his side, he took small sips of the tepid water. Except for a Redflash lizard disappearing into a crack, nothing moved nearby.

He scanned the rooftops and alleys carefully, wondering if Bard was still following him. Above him, a slab of overhanging stone protected his head from any 'accidents' coming down. It had been surprisingly audacious of the boy to attempt his death with the pile of bricks. Crude, but enterprising. He had almost decided to stun the boy with a stone in return. But something turned him away. Bard didn't know any better. And he would probably be far behind Drifter now, having to find food and water to survive.

Capping the flask, Drifter leaned back and let his eyes fall half shut. He floated for a time in between sleep and wakefulness, letting his body rest. While it rested, his mind roamed free, turning on memories new and old. He tried to avoid the older remembrances, but they kept reappearing in his thoughts unbidden.

Images of people he had known before the Greenspark, places he had been and things he had done. It had none of the pain or suddenness of the memories the phantom had forced upon him. They drifted through his mind easily, mixed with thoughts and ideas from his immediate situation in life. But they still made him feel uncomfortable when they became sharp or personal.

Finally he broke the thread of waking dreams by shaking his head and standing up. All the images slid away down a dark funnel to where he kept such things hidden. It was time to continue on.

Evening came on as he traveled through the ruined city. Red stains touched the edges of toppled pillars and arches, creating illusions of blood and roses. Shadows lengthened out, taking the shapes of long-dead gunfighters and natives with their hair in the wind. As the night came on, Drifter found memories resurfacing even as he walked, forcing themselves on his mind.

"Do you want a son or a daughter?"

"Whatever makes you happiest."

"I think it will be a boy. He kicks so hard. But I am happy with whichever we are given."

"We're so lucky..."

"Life has been good to us..."

The voices became a sort of hallucination, played over the sharp reality of night in the broken sector. Drifter watched for lights, heard the scuttles of rats and other creatures and walked with his normal level of alert wariness. At the same time, images and sound played lightly over his subconscious. His mind wavered between the worlds.

The boy that lived next door, a happy lad of fourteen, had been riding back from the park on his bicycle. He had a slingshot on his wrist. He had been throwing stones at birds with it all morning. None had been hit, but he was still happy with the day's fun. His bicycle broke down half-way home, the chain coming apart with a stick in it. Leith slowed in his car and asked if the boy would like a ride...

The slingshot got left behind, on the seat, in a rush to get up into the house for dinner...

The boy never had a chance to come back for it.

The cityscape closed around Drifter, hanging over him in darkness. No sound of voices or light of fire broke its solemn procession of standing and fallen shadows. He was forced to climb over a heap of rubble at one point, then cross a wide crack in the pavement on a slab of stone like a narrow bridge. His feet were sure on the slick material, even with a slight halt in one leg.

He worked at a garage, patching tires, fitting new wheels and fixing damage on wrecked cars. His boss liked the work, made sure that he was comfortably paid. The only person there who didn't like him was the secretary. He would hear her high-heeled shoes tapping on the cement floor and scoot further under the malfunctioning vehicle, hoping the sound would pass on by...

One day he smashed his thumb, working with heavy tools. Smashed it so hard that it broke the knuckle. The secretary walked by just a second later and gave him a hard look, as if he had done it on purpose. He could almost hear her chiding him 'clumsy, clumsy!'

Dawn was breaking, yellow fluid floating on the edge of a cement horizon. Drifter saw a break in the buildings ahead of him. He walked out on the edge of a great, open area which rose in a low slope towards the sky. Scraggly trees burnt into black twigs curled up out of the scorched ground like skeleton hands. Blackened stubs indicated where bushes used to stand. A cement path wound up towards the peak of the hill from somewhere far over to Drifter's right. It was patched with black, where hedges had overhung it.

Up at the top of the long, low rise were the frames of a few buildings. A faint line showed where a fence circled around them. Drifter could not make out the Gate from this distance. But he felt it up there, waiting, as if it were a friend beckoning him to a long-awaited tryst.

Bowing his head, he started up the dusty slope. He seemed like part of the desiccated scenery, another shape that blended in with the tree trunks and earth. The visions had left him and he felt empty, until he stood at the edge of the hill.

A fence was still intact in places, but the aluminum staples had often melted where trees grew close, allowing the webbing to fall down. The buildings had hedged the clearing in on the right, frames and rubble indicating their position. In the center of a place that had been clear of bushes and trees before the disaster stood the Gate.

It was taller than Drifter, perhaps ten foot at the peak. Arched and wide enough for two people to have walked in side-by-side. The stone the arch was made of was silky black, smooth and hard as glass. The door was also solid black, set smoothly into the frame. Down where a handle or knob would usually have been, there was only a large key hole, like an illustration from a children's book. There was nothing else to mar the flat surface of the door.

Drifter drew a deep breath, moving across the intervening space as if impelled. He stopped in front of the gate, eyes roving over it carefully. There was nothing around the gate and frame, no wall it was set into. The arch was perhaps a foot thick, maybe a little more. When he walked around it, the back side looked just like the front, except for that there was no key hole in it. When he fixed his gaze on the key hole he could not see through it. It was dark inside, impenetrable.

"I've made it," he told himself, splaying a hand on the cold, smooth door. "The Gate of Eternity."

He straightened up and drew the bronze key from the cylinder in his belt.

BARD FELT MUCH BETTER when he awoke, even when Loran made him get up early in the cold morning. She had bundles of food with her, wrapped in white cloth like Drifter's had been. Loran made Bard eat some bread and cheese, drinking more of the medicated broth with it. She ate little herself, impatient to be on the way.

With a bandage and salve on his bitten toe and his stomach finally satisfied in every way, Bard was ready to move on. They started walking, the bundles split between them for easy carrying. The boy soon found that Loran was just as difficult to keep up with as Drifter, despite her more delicate build. Her strides were long and steady, not slowing even after an hour of walking. The pair moved on through the morning, then into the afternoon. Though Bard kept his eyes open, he did not see Drifter ahead of them at any point in the day. They rested, briefly, at noon and ate from the packages of supplies. Loran had bottles of water in one package, heavy to carry but pure for drinking. As they traveled, Bard and Loran shared their stories, the woman explaining about her gift of prophecy and how it had saved a handful of people from the scorch, while the boy told her about Dick Chelsea and his own upbringing in the Academy sector.

That night, they rested and slept for a short time, but then pressed on in the darkness. Loran seemed to have an internal compass guiding her around the worst obstructions and on the straightest paths. Bard was not sure if they were on the same trail as Drifter had followed, but the woman inspired him with a mixture of confidence and awe that he could not argue with. He felt that she was special, a sort of sorceress sent to help him out of his troubles. Loran was beautiful, confident and had a mysterious energy hovering around her. The boy appreciated her kindness as much as he felt overshadowed by her ascendancy.

When they reached the destroyed park of science it was with a suddenness that startled Bard. They were coming through a narrow pathway left between two piles of wreckage, Loran in front and the boy behind. When they got to the end of the alley, Loran made a small noise of satisfaction. Bard came around her and found himself looking up the slope of a low, empty hill with the dead trunks of burnt trees standing across it. At the top, the frames of a group of buildings stood facing them. They had come out on the edge of a parking lot in front of the hill, with a scorched cement path leading from the lot up towards the peak.

Bard stood staring at the top of the slope for a long moment, breathing hard as he realized that they were finally at the end of their journey. Loran touched him on his arm, directing his gaze up the hill towards their left.

A shape hooded in dark blue was most of the way up the hill, making its way towards something in front of the buildings. Bard gave a little start as he recognized Drifter.

"It's him! But he's still ahead of us."

"Come." Loran began walking quickly towards the path. "We don't want to miss the opening."

They hurried over to the cement path and half-ran up it, Bard panting heavily by the time they reached the top. Loran was also breathing hard, but did not flag as they came to the top. Raising a hand, she cautioned her companion to go carefully. After crossing a sagging bit of fence, they moved around the ruined scientific buildings until the Gate came into view. Bard peeked around the edge of one structure cautiously, though Drifter was so intent on the Gate that he would not have noticed them if they had stepped out boldly. He was standing in front of the dark arch, in profile to the watching pair, key held ready in one hand.

"Shouldn't we stop him?" Bard whispered timidly.

Loran shook her head and pushed back a hank of dark hair, watching with an intense gaze.

Seeming to steel himself, Drifter moved his arm forward and inserted the key in its hole. Bard could hear it clink into place, sliding snugly into the mechanism. With an energetic twist, Drifter turned the key to the side. The door made a deep noise of acceptance. *'Chunk!'*

It began to swing open without any aid. Drifter fit his fingers around the edge and pulled it further. From their angle, Bard and Loran could not see what was inside. But they saw the loner's eyes widen with surprise. A neon blue light glowed from inside the gate, expanding outwards. The bystanders found themselves moving away from the building to get a better angle to see. But before they had gone far, the blue light exploded outwards in a shock wave of electric sparks. Drifter's arm flung up in front of his eyes to shield them as the shock hit him. Sparks danced over him in a random pattern of intense blue. Without a sound, he collapsed to the ground as the sparks and light faded away. A moment later, the doorway seemed to be empty, gate hanging open without a sign of light behind it. A small, black object tumbled out onto the ground. Then everything was still.

"Drifter..." Bard gasped, making an involuntary movement forward. Loran put her purple-clad arm out to slow him.

"Wait." Her voice was icy. Instead of going directly towards the gate, she began to lead the boy around it in a half-circle. When they reached a point behind the inert form of Drifter, they could both see into the portal. Neither of them had been expecting what was inside.

It seemed to be the entrance to a wide, dark hall running from left to right. The hill was bare of anything but the lone doorway. But there was a heavily tiled floor and black stone walls surrounding the passageway inside it. Built onto the open door, on the inside surface, was a set of shiny silver rails, arranged into what looked almost like the barrel of some fantastic gun. These led back to a machine set to the right of the entrance, in the center of the hall. It was made of silver metal, black tubes and gleaming rails. Bigger than a person, it hulked there like some sort of ancient monster reimagined in steel. On one side of it was a huge storage bin of black plastic, taking up the rest of the path so that a person could have barely squeezed past to traverse the mysterious hall. The bin and the machine were coupled with a short, flexible tube.

The object which had tumbled out onto the ground was a cube of black material, perhaps six inches on each side. From the angle of its fall angle, it looked to have been sitting on the rails and been somehow dislodged when Drifter swung the gate open. What had created the blue shock wave was a mystery. The whole gate was a mystery, with things inside of it which were not reflected in the world around it.

"It's a gate to somewhere else. Somewhere not on this plane of existence," Loran murmured, dark eyes narrowed as she inspected the machine and doorway. "Some sort of teleporter...or portal."

After staring at the machine open-mouthed, Bard's gaze had reverted to the figure lying prone before them.

"But what about Drifter?"

"Ah, yes." Loran seemed to come back to the immediate world with a shock. Moving forward cautiously, she came up to the still form. No flash of light jumped out to meet her as she neared the gate. Bending down, she lay a hand on Drifter's chest for a moment. Frowning, she knelt to listen at the same spot. After a moment Loran arose with a shake of her head.

"He's...dead?" Bard whispered.

"I can detect no life," Loran said sadly, shaking her head so that the black hair tumbled down around her face. But after a moment she pushed it back and went over to stand just before the gate, peering in.

"Be careful!" Bard warned, still hanging back. He did not want to see another person destroyed by the power from within. Though he had tried, halfheartedly perhaps, to kill Drifter himself just a few days before, he found himself strangely shocked that the loner was dead now. It had seemed to impossible to destroy him, as if he was a part of the land and the air that could move through any danger unmolested. Now he lay there on the ground like a broken doll, inert.

"I think that it was a trap of some sort." Loran bent to look in the passage, before pulling back out. "A one-time trap, for whoever opened the door. Well, he got what he was looking for. Eternity. Even if he did not spread it as generously as he wished."

Bard shook his head, brain whirling. "But...who built this? How can there be a passage inside and nothing out here? What does it all mean!"

"Perhaps..." Loran stooped to pick up the black box which had fallen to the ground from within, gingerly at first and then holding it in both hands. "This little thing can tell us."

Blinking, Bard looked from the cube to the machine it appeared to have come from, then down at Drifter on the ground. Everything had happened too fast for him to fully grasp yet. He felt like a layer of the world had just been torn away to reveal a second skin beyond, one he had never suspected was there.

The woman moved over to lay a hand on his shoulder, looking into his face. Hers was lit with an inner light. The glow of an inventor on the edge of discovery or a detective about to solve the crime.

"We'll find out the truth now, Bard. Everything. I have a feeling that this gate and its contents somehow tie together with the Greenspark fall, the phantoms and everything that has been happening. But we must have patience and go carefully. We are dealing with forces far out of our control."

The boy nodded, numb to the point where he wished everything was just over and he could sit still somewhere to think it all out. Looking past Loran, he pointed at the ground.

"And Drifter? I mean...shouldn't we...?"

The woman looked up suddenly, gazing around them. At the same time Bard became conscious of the sound of deep breathing and the soft flapping of wings.

"I think his friends have come for him."

Half a dozen Chardogs and at least as many Charwings had come up without Bard or Loran noticing. The birds glided around in the air, watching with their beady eyes. The beasts sat on their haunches, waiting patiently. It was daylight, not their favored element, so they were not going to push an attack on the humans. But they wanted past and would wait until night if necessary to get there.

"What about the gate?" Bard turned to look at it. "Should we go through it and see what is down the passage?"

Loran shook her head, already wrapping the black cube in a length of white cloth from her robe. "No. We must leave now, before the creatures press us. Come."

She grasped his arm gently and towed him away, cradling the cube under one arm. They avoided the night creatures by going around the buildings again, before descending the path. Behind them, they heard the flap of descending wings and the heavy pad of paws.

THE CREATURES GATHERED around the inert form, birds landing on the baked ground and dogs crouching nearby. For a time they did nothing, just stood and looked at him with bulging red eyes or cocked heads. One Charwing hopped forward, perching on Drifter's chest to look into his face. They seemed to be waiting for something, expecting him to sit up and speak to them as he would have before.

As they stood in this manner there was a movement inside the gate. A hatch opened on the bottom of the machine and something crawled out. Shiny, silver with many little arms around the outer edge, it looked like a crab made of steel.

It had no features, nothing but a round plate as a body and the six arms ending in half-formed claws. A second followed it a moment later, with dozens more pouring out afterwards. Like ants they strung out across the ground in a steady stream towards the still body. The beasts of the night saw them coming and took fright, the Charwing flapping noisily off to land a few yards away while the rest drew back the same distance on the ground. They turned and watched as the crab-like forms crawled over Drifter and around him, enveloping him in small, shining shapes like a swarm. The body heaved and lifted, carried on two dozen tiny bodies of steel. With minute clicking noises they made their way towards the gate and disappeared inside.

Disappointed, the creatures of the night faded away.

BARD RAN A HAND OVER the smooth, featureless black box. It seemed to be made of metal, though what sort he could not tell. If it was tapped with the point of a knife it gave off a hollow resonance. But it weighed more than appearances would dictate. When he hefted it in one hand it soon tired him and he had to set it down again.

"What could it be?"

They sat on the edge of a courtyard surrounded on all sides by rubble and ruin, white pillars and iron rebar sticking up from the crumbled tide at random intervals. Loran had the skirt of her robe flattened around her and the box set on the edge of it.

"I'm not sure." She touched it delicately, with the tip of a finger. "But I know someone who might be able to find out better than we could."

"Oh?" Bard looked up hopefully. The shock of the scene on top of the hill had not yet worn off and he felt lonely, as if the city were tangibly more empty without Drifter in it. Finding another person, almost anyone else, would help alleviate the feeling.

"Yes." Loran nodded. "Unfortunately, he is far from here—"

Bard's shoulders drooped and he made a small noise of disappointment.

"But. I have a way to summon him and we can go to meet him half way. In fact." She scooted the box aside onto the ground and stood up. "I think it would be wise if I called in more than one friend. Many of us are seeking answers and I believe we have come very close to the core of the riddle."

"How will you summon them?" The boy asked, peering up through his round glasses with the noon sun glinting off of them.

Loran clasped her hands together and bowed her head. "I have my ways."

Not waiting for him to ask further questions, she turned and strode away through the heaps of rubble until she disappeared from view. Bard knew that he was not supposed to follow her. He sat staring at the black box, wondering what sort of secrets it held. They were still not far from the hill with the Gate on top of it. But he did not want to think of what had happened on top of the hill or what the creatures might be doing there now. Instead, he concentrated on the box, considering who could have built it and why. The machine it had come from looked like a dispenser, or something which the box would shoot out of. Could it be a sort of signal flare?

But Loran believed that the gate had something to do with the Greenspark fire. Something clicked in Bard's mind. It was such an enormous thought, such a leap of logic that he was almost afraid to complete it. When he did, one word came to his mind, burning bright.

Greenspark.

What if the Greenspark fire had not been a natural anomaly? It could be a weapon instead, something made by man to destroy wide swaths of civilization. But who on earth would build such a thing and use it against the whole world? It would take a person extremely embittered and cruel to create a weapon like that, someone who loved destruction and pain. And then to launch it against most of the world, as far as Bard new, make it sweep over all large continents and countries. The boy stared with glazed eyes at the box, picturing the huge area of ruined Apex and the many other countries that must have suffered. Then the people, individual people who had their families destroyed, minds driven to the edge of sanity by the Greenspark fall. Like Drifter. So pained by the effects of the weapon that he had sought to end the world as it was known.

Loran came back as Bard stared at the box. Crouching across from him, she looked into his eyes.

"So, you've come to the same conclusion as I."

The boy met her gaze slowly, voice trembling as he spoke, "but who? What person would try to blot out all life in a terror of pain and flames?"

"We'll find out," Loran promised, "Elisha is on his way. We must go to meet him. But there is more to this than first meets the eye, Bard..."

"What do you mean?"

"That gate is not merely a room holding a machine to spit fire. It's a portal of some sort. Whoever built it has powers beyond our understanding. Not only that, but we still have another mystery mixed up with it. The relics."

Bard blinked, seeing a side of the question he had not considered before. "The key. It's a relic, but it fits the lock of the gate...which means whoever built the machine either used relics for his scheme, or—"

With a nod, Loran stood up. "Created them."

"But...but, how could the gate have opened from the inside? How could this box, this tiny cube, make something like Greenspark fire fall from the sky? And why is it still here, why did it fall out of the gate?" Bard jumped to his feet, hands clamped into fists. "I don't understand! There are too many questions. What if our idea isn't right at all and this box doesn't have anything to do with the Greenspark?"

Loran touched him lightly on the shoulder and he felt calmness flow from her like a reviving stream. No matter the madness of the questions, she was staying focused.

"That is what we are going to learn. And you are right, it might have nothing to do with the Greenspark. But that is not what intuition tells me."

The boy bowed his head, fitting his glasses back into place with a gentle push of his finger. He wished, intensely, that Dick were there to explain things to him and lead him through the arguments logically to a conclusion. His guardian had always been good at making complicated things obvious to him.

"So what's our next step?"

"We travel back west," Loran explained, "Elisha, one of my friends, was still over in the Arc sector where we built our bunker. He'll be coming to meet us."

"And he can tell us what the box is for?"

"I'm hoping that he can open it safely. He is a sort of tinkerer, an expert in all things mechanical, electrical...and explosive."

Bard sighed and picked up his sack from the ground, along with a few of the bundles that could not fit in it. "I see. In case it does have Greenspark fire in it. Okay. But it will take days to meet him if he's coming from the Arc sector."

"As to that," Loran said with a small smile, "he has transportation. And I have a plan."

She gathered up the few bundles left and tucked the black box carefully into one of them, before cradling it on her arm. Then she began to lead the way towards the west, striding with apparent ease around the rubble of society.

Chapter 14: The Car

They walked all that day, angling both south and west through the Native sector. Bard did not recognize the individual streets after the first small section of city, as they had come almost directly north when going towards the gate. But by now, all of Apex was starting to blend together in his mind. Not used to traveling further than from Dick's tower to the sea, all on Terminal Point, he could not clearly picture the places they seen. Not as if it were on a map. One street faded into the next, the groups of ruined or standing buildings began to look alike.

The next morning Loran seemed to be sunk deep in thought as they crouched over her little cooking fire. Eventually she asked Bard, "do you know what was wrong with Drifter's car when he left it? Did you run out of fuel again?"

The boy shook his head and explained that the fuel had been impure, causing it to plug up.

Loran's dark eyes narrowed. "Then it might be worth our time to make a small detour and get it running."

"Drifter said that it could take days to clean all of the parts well enough."

"Yes." Loran rubbed her hands together speculatively. "But I have an idea for that as well. It would save us a lot of footwork, danger and even time in the long run."

Bard shrugged. She was in command, as far as he was concerned. That day they turned their march to the south, angling back a little towards the east even. They did not meet anybody, hardly even saw a living thing. By the end of the day the food in their bundles was starting to get low, but this did not seem to concern Loran greatly. She remarked that they would last a day or two more before having to rely on other incomes of supply.

The next day, they were crossing a shadowed area under a leaning structure when Bard surprised a Vollan scurrying out of its hole in a crack of the pavement. Acting on reflex, he snatched it up and whacked its head against a slab of stone, stunning it. A moment later he was sorry he had hurt such a soft, delicate little creature. But it was food and went into Loran's tiny stew pot that evening.

They made two batches of soup from it and picked the bones clean before throwing them away.

Spurred on by his success, despite loathing having to hurt creatures, Bard kept his eyes open for Vollans as they traveled on. After a few misses, he was able to hit one on the head with a flung rock, knocking it over long enough for him to pick up. After that he also caught a pigeon in the same manner. He was more used to catching and eating the fat birds and felt less compunction about it. Though before, he and Dick had used such contrivances as birdlime, a sticky substance pigeons got stuck in, or nets to procure them.

Throwing rocks was inaccurate and took a lot of strength to stun something. He wished that he had a slingshot like Drifter's to hunt with. Or even a bow and arrows, so that the beasts would be dead when he picked them up. But he knew that such things took time to make. Time they didn't have to waste.

Finally they reached the part of town where the car was parked. Bard recognized the ruined buildings with the tree growing up through them, where he had met the griffin before. He warned Loran about it and they came cautiously to where the car was keeping an eye on the heap of rubble and the sky.

It was strange to see the gray car sitting there unharmed, as if waiting for them. It was even more odd to see it while Drifter was not there. It was like they were creeping up on a private part of someone's life without permission, or as if they should find Drifter there ahead of them, smiling bitterly with his light eyes. But he was not waiting for them and the car was easy to reach. It sat in the shade of the nearby buildings, hood shining a little in one stripe of sunlight. Bard walked up and touched it gingerly, then ran a hand down the cold smoothness. He hoped that Loran would be able to get it going again. It would mean a place of safety against the emptiness of the dark nights.

Loran walked to the door and tried it, then frowned. "Did he lock it when he left?"

Recalling the scene with a start, Bard nodded. "That's right. He took the key."

The woman rolled her eyes. "Miserly man. He thought he was going to end the world and he still didn't want anyone getting into his car."

She lay a hand to the lock and closed her eyes for a moment. Bard shuffled his feet, wondering what they were going to do. He began thinking about breaking the window and hotwiring it to start, when Loran stepped back and the door came open with a click.

"What?" Bard came closer. "I thought that it was locked."

"It was." Loran waved a hand. "But I unlocked it."

She pulled the door open and popped the hood, moving around the awestruck boy to get to the front of the car. The hood opened up above her on oiled hinges, creating a roof she leaned under.

"Do you know about vehicle engines?" Bard asked curiously.

"Not beyond the basics." Loran ran a hand over the components inside, following tubes and wires to their termination. "I can name most of the parts I see. Not all."

Grease and dust were left on her sleeve as she pulled her hand back, putting a smudged finger to her chin.

"Then how will you fix it?"

She gave him a long, cool look. "The same way I opened the door."

"Magic," Bard breathed, eyes widening in his glasses.

"Not how most imagine it." She leaned back over the engine, eyes drooping half shut. "While I work, look for a spare key in the car. It will make things easier, later."

The boy wanted to stay and see what she was doing. But he obeyed her, moving around to climb inside the open door. It felt odd, getting in the car again. He had not thought that he would see it after they left it the first time. The air inside seemed to hold an impression of its master, lingering after he was gone. It felt like Drifter inside, smelled of campfire smoke and the mustiness of abandoned buildings, as he did.

After searching the glove compartment and looking through some of the rubbish in the back, the rags and tags of a nomadic life, Bard found a key taped under the dash at one point. When he peeled it off and had it in his hand it looked like the key Drifter had used for the car. Elated, he bounced out to find Loran standing in front of the hood, rolling her sleeve back down over dusty hands.

"It's done." She seemed a little weary, though her straight back and shoulders did not show it. "And you have the key."

"You mean, the fuel system is cleaned out?" Bard looked from her to the components under the hood. "Already?"

In reply the woman pointed at a little heap of blackish-tan dust laying in front of the car on the pavement. "I just hope that the rest of the fuel is better."

Made solemn by the acts he had witnessed, Bard gave her the key. She took it with a matter-of-fact tilt of her head, carrying it back around to the open door of the car. Sliding into the seat, she stuck the key in its place before straightening her robes around her. With a pause as if to prepare herself, Loran turned it.

The engine grumbled, then roared into life. At first it ran hesitatingly, but once it got clean fuel to burn everything steadied out.

"Shut the hood," Loran told him, speaking over its noise. "Then get inside."

She slammed her own door, waiting for him. Bard used both hands to close the hood, picking up their bundles and tossing them into the back before jumping in himself. Acting slowly, with a frown of concentration, Loran put the car into gear. It jerked forward, before evening off into a steady roll.

"It's been some time since I've driven," she explained demurely, "even before the disaster it wasn't my favorite mode of transportation."

But it wasn't long before she had mastered the way of driving it, slim foot pressed on the pedal and delicate hands grasping the wheel. She seemed to apply the same almost mystic concentration to steering the car as she did studying relics. Bard gripped the edge of the chair until the ride became smoother, afraid they would smash up on some protruding bit of wreckage. After Loran evened out, he relaxed with a sigh of long-held breath.

The black box Loran had set on the chair between them, tucked carefully back against the seat like a baby. Bard ran a finger over it now and then, mind turning over the problem of what was in it and what it would mean.

"The car seems to be running fine," he said after a while.

Loran nodded once, before asking, "do we still have fuel to put in it?"

"Yeah, a little." Bard gestured with his head towards the back. "Wrapped up back there."

"Good. We may need it."

The city faded past them outside, the sky shifting from pale, dusty blue to red and gray as the sun began to set. While it still hung over the horizon Loran slowed the car. They had entered a section of city with shorter, sharper hills and more of them. The buildings ran up and down the slopes, dug in or tumbled down. Sometimes it appeared as if the structures had acted like dominoes. When the first fell over, it hit the next, toppling them in a long line. One place they passed had two buildings collapsed sideways onto a third, which was bulging but holding the weight. It was like a bizarre, giant lean-to with everything balanced so that it was just about to fall.

The car slowed down at the peak of one of these hills, where there was the remains of a gazebo made of white stone, surrounded by the cobwebs of burnt bushes. Loran stopped there, pulling over beside the cracked structure. A pair of iron benches, painted dark green, still sat inside. Loran shut off the car and got out, stretching like a cat.

"I need to get my legs moving again. You may start camp, if you like," she told Bard. He got out and stood by the car as she strode off, then wandered over by the gazebo. The twigs of bushes were a little less burnt than in many places he had been, as the hill had been mostly bare even before the Greenspark. He began harvesting branches for firewood, breaking them off as close to the ground as he had strength to. He had moved part way around the little building when a flash of color in the hedge caught his eyes. Leaning down, he looked closer at the stripe of bright green. An inarticulate noise of joy escaped him.

It was a few sprouts, growing up out of the gnarled roots of the charred bush. Young, supple and deliciously vibrant, they were a promise of life under the scorch. Bard touched the little stalks with reverent fingers, remembering the plants he used to grow in the shielded dome. Without his watering, many of those would be struggling to survive. But out here in the world, where it mattered, there was a bush coming back, sending up the first sprouts in years.

If they were unmolested they would grow, first as a cluster of thin stalks and then branching out into a bush like the parent hedge. Leaves would unfurl, twigs bud...there would be blossoms. And if they were pollinated there might even be seeds.

"The world doesn't have to end yet," Bard whispered to the sprouts, "it can still regrow."

As he crouched there Loran returned, coming to bend down next to him. Silently, they shared the positive energy of the green stalks.

Later, they sat on the floor of the gazebo, backs against the hard metal tubes of the benches. A cold wind had sprung up outside, finding its way through cracks in the structure and making the fire flicker. They had a little meat and dry bread roasting on sticks over the fire, a mixture of Bard's scavenging and the last supplies. Tomorrow he would have to hunt more, better, perhaps search abandoned buildings for leftover provisions. For now, they had a small meal, just enough to take the edge off their hunger.

The wind outside seemed to make the night darker, more full of menace. Bard put his arms around his knees and shivered, from loneliness more than cold. Loran sat with her robes spread out over her legs, chin propped on fist as she stared at the flames. The light flickered across her face with the wind, creating weird shadows on it.

Bard looked up, suddenly feeling that they were being watched. A sound like breathing, deeper than the wind, reached his ears. A pair of huge red eyes gleamed in at the doorway, smoldering brighter than the coals. He sucked in a breath of air, feeling himself go cold and stiff. Loran also stiffened, eyes fixing on it darkly. The shape of a half-open jaw loomed into the light, large nose twitching under its load of slime. Webbed claws clicked on the hard stone floor. A low growl filled the gazebo.

Bard reached slowly for his knife, mind racing. Could he strike at at the Chardog before it could get its jaws on him? Out of the corner of his eyes, he saw Loran raise her pale hand towards the beast. Her voice wavered in the flickering light.

"Beast of the night, dark's delight, leave us until the morn..."

The Chardog blinked slowly, like an eclipse of the moon. Its growling had stopped and it snuffed towards Loran's hand as if taking her scent in. Bard was still tensed, ready to spring if it moved towards her. But to his surprise, it turned softly on clicking claws and walked away into the night.

"How...how did you...?"

Loran's head bowed forward, hair falling over her face and she laughed, half-sobbing. "Drifter. He could talk to the beasts. I didn't know if it would work, but I learned it from him."

"That's right." Bard let go of the knife, remembering. "He tried to talk to the griffin. And he said...the beasts of the night obeyed him. That's why he saved the Chardog from those men. It was his friend."

Shaking back her hair, face composed now, Loran said solemnly, "I don't know why those words work. They aren't exactly the ones he used, but he seemed to just make up poems to speak to them. And the animals listen."

They sat for a few minutes without a word, fire dying lower. Eventually Bard threw a handful of sticks onto the flames and asked hesitantly, "Loran, do you think that, well...he's happy now?"

For a few minutes the woman did not reply, staring into the embers as she had before. When she answered, her voice was low and dark but clear, like water running under a bridge at night.

"I don't know what his beliefs were, Bard. Perhaps before the disaster he had more fixed ones, as he seemed to have a solid idea about the end of the world. But I do know that he was not naturally cruel or evil." Looking up, Loran met his gaze. "He followed his mission through a sense of compassion for the people of the world, not for personal gain. And I think that will be taken into account."

Bard twirled a stick in his fingers, coming to an unexpected conclusion. "I hope so."

DRIFTER STOOD IN A field of wheat, the stalks reaching up beyond his knees. The golden heads were ripe and full. He ran a hand over them, feeling the rough awns and the bulge of the grain. It was a rich harvest, reaching onto the horizon on every side. A warm breeze bowed the grain over so that the stalks flashed golden in the sun. A young, warm sun more yellow than any bar of men's gold. It rode in a sky so blue it was pain and joy at once to gaze into it. He could have spent all day, weeks, just looking into the azure depths of that sky.

And the growing field, full of life and hope. Down below the golden straw, green sprouts were coming up from the rich earth. He could see them all around his boots. He did not move for fear of crushing one little plantlife off of the earth.

But when Drifter looked up again there was a cloud on the horizon. It was not a normal cloud, the harbinger of clean rain. It was shaped like a cylinder, huge and fat on the edge of the sky. Dark too, almost black except for where its edges faded into gray softness.

As he watched it, the wind picked up, whipping towards him over the grain. The cloud started to move, coming over the sky with a huge shadow. It loomed towards him and he threw up an arm to block out the wind, enveloped in terror. The darkness moved over the field and blotted Drifter out.

THE NEXT MORNING LORAN and Bard drove on for a short time, coming to a valley in the hills where a huge structure stood. At one time, it had been a mall, stretching from one side of the glen to the other. Its roofs had fallen in at various places, smashed down by the falling Greenspark. Shattered and melted domes stood up above the roof space. It was only one story tall at most places, a tall story, with a second level at a few chosen points. Courtyards and walkways opened up in the center of the walls, giving a glimpse of tiled floor or shadowed hall. It was a huge, rambling building laying dead between the hills.

"Perhaps we should stop and look for provisions here," Loran suggested, eyes narrowing as she looked down at the place. "It's so large that there might be things in it others have missed."

"Alright." Bard gripped the knife at his belt. "I can hunt for Vollans, too."

The parking lot of the mall was a shattered, black expanse of pavement on the southern side. Its buffers and islands were barren, cracked with heat. The gray car rolled out onto it and came to a halt in front of the main entrance. Loran ignored the lines painted on the lot. What other cars were there would never move again.

A great dome stood over the double doors, shading the tiled floor underneath with jagged shadows. Broken glass glittered across it in a wide swath. The pillars upholding the dome were yellowed with grime and rain, a few of them cracked. Bard felt a sense of looming danger as they passed under the dome, as if it were about to fall on them.

The doors of the mall had been glass, with miniature trees and shrubs potted beside them. The heat of the branches burning had melted the thin metal door frames, cracked and started to melt portions of the glass. They stood open, a gaping maw with echoing shadows beyond.

Bard paused before the doorway. "Do you think it's safe inside?"

"What is safe anymore?" Loran returned with a shrug.

She led the way over the lintel, into a wide hall made dim by the overhanging roof. But after a moment Bard found that it was not truly dark inside. Just gloomy, with odd gleams of light reflecting off of the walls from sun rays ahead and behind. Their footsteps rang on the glossy floor, startling echos which disappeared like imps down diverse ways. The hall ran straight for a long ways, the shadows sometimes broken by a skylight overhead. Here, earth-filled boxes showed where domesticated plants had been grown indoors. In between, hard-cushioned benches and chairs lined the ways.

On either side were the store fronts, usually paneled in glass or thin, dark walling. Bard found himself jumping when they passed clothing outlets, imagining that the mannequins were living people staring out at him. He did not like the empty stores much better, as the shadows seemed to be concealing more than should be there.

Loran led them to a great intersection of the walkway, an open courtyard sprinkled with broken pillars and shattered glass. The floor was tiled white and black, many of the neat squares broken. One of the halls leading from it, straight ahead, was partially collapsed in a pile of dusty fallen stones. Bard lifted his head when he heard a scuffling noise and saw the dart of some creature going beneath the heap. There were Vollan to hunt here, and broken jags of marble to hunt them with.

"You seem to have found some game," Loran commented, noticing him stiffen. "stay here and hunt. I believe there will be food courts down here, to our left—"

She indicated the hallway, which had posters peeling off of its walls which had depicted sandwiches, fried potatoes and other food for sale. "I will search those for edible leftovers. I may wander some distance looking, so I will meet you back here in an hour. Will that suit you?"

Bard nodded, proud to be asked and given the respect of a man instead of a boy. "An hour. I'll be here."

She smiled slightly and moved away down the passage. Stopping just under its overhang, Loran called back, "I don't think anyone is here, but be careful."

Bard waved to let her know he had heard. Bending over, he began to pick up shards of marble to use as ammunition. He wished once again that he had some sort of projectile weapon to aid his hunting. It was slow and frustrating using rocks, just hoping they would be enough to slow a creature for him to catch.

Once he had a good handful of medium-weight shards, a little smaller than his fist and jagged all around, he began stalking towards the heap of rubble down the hall. As he stepped into the shadow of the overhang the memory of the Sco-Ber made him pause for a moment. But they were left far behind, deep in the tunnel underground. There were no holes large enough for people in this heap of stone, except for one larger gap near the lower corner. Bard shook the thought of wild children away and went back to his hunt. There were many fat Vollans living in the heap, as well as a few ugly, greenish-gray rats of a large size. Bard knew better than to try eating a rat. There was no telling what one had been living off of. He only threw stones at the Vollans, which scrambled about from hole to hole carrying tiny bits of nesting in their mouths or looking for food of their own.

He missed until he had only a few stones left. Forcing down his frustration, he took his time with the next shot and knocked a creature down. Feeling a brutal satisfaction, the boy drew his knife and jumped forward, pinning the creature down before it could move. At the same time a second Vollan popped up near him and darted towards the largest gap in the ruins. Bard shot his last rock after it on reflex, crouching over his kill. The stone struck the rodent a glancing blow, making it squeak and stumble. Bard came after it in an instant, but the creature scrambled painfully out of his way down the large gap. It left a few tiny drops of blood behind, showing that it had been injured, just not stunned.

Angry at losing so many of his shots, and knowing that the rest would be frightened into silence anyway, Bard hurried after the injured Vollan with a cry. It had disappeared down the large hole into deep shadows. He followed, squeezing his shoulders in and stooping to wiggle after it. It was a surprisingly short tunnel through the collapsed roof. He came to the other side in just a moment. It was darker here, but not enough to blind him. Ahead of him, the walls bulged and crumbled out into the path, blocking half of the hall. The other half was open, leading to what looked like some sort of open cafe strewn with light metal tables. The Vollan had vanished from sight, apparently diving into a pocket in the rubble Bard could not see.

Frowning, he slammed his knife back in his belt. He still had time to go back and hunt before Loran returned, but the creatures would all be hiding in their holes now. He only had one Vollan for all of the trouble of hunting.

Peering down the dim hall, he inspected the tables and chairs sitting around in tight groups. If there was a cafe here, there might be a food storage place somewhere in the back. He might as while scavenge for dry goods the rest of his time. It could possibly turn up more than hunting did.

Careful not to trip or knock into anything in the shadows, Bard walked down the hall. It felt close inside, the air moist and stuffy. When it widened out into a cafe, the air lightened a little, thanks to the small, cracked skylights set at an angle in the roof. They sent streamers of golden light down onto the floor at places, or onto the round tables.

One of the lighted tables appeared to have an object on it. Bard moved closer to take a look. It was a wide, flat box with a red pattern on the lid and a golden hasp. It looked like something that would be used to hold cigars, not food, but curiosity prompted him to open it anyway. The hasp clicked open easily under his thumb and he peeled back the lid.

Inside, something gleamed and glittered on red velvet lining. Set snugly in an indent was a weapon, a pistol. But one unlike any Bard had seen before. It was of a very old make, with a wooden stock, polished honey brown, and gleaming double barrels. All over, from the butt to half way up the barrels, it was chased in gold. The pattern swirled and spread like climbing leaves, catching the beam of light from above. Chiseled deeply into the stock was a familiar branching mark.

"A relic." Bard bent over the table, touching the weapon as if afraid that it would melt away under his fingers. "A pistol that is a relic. Dick never mentioned one like this."

Beside the gun, in the case, was a set of smaller indents, each containing a brass and lead bullet, sticking upright for easy removal. Bard blinked at them, suddenly realizing that he had found the projectile weapon he needed. He lay a hand on the gun, starting to take it out of the case.

A movement in the shadows forestalled him. A white blur coalesced from a nearby hall, forming into a swirling shape. No features but big, empty, dark eyes on a delicate human head, long hair that floated around it without a gust of wind. A body and form almost human, but not quite.

Bard had never seen a phantom before, but he knew that was what it was. He stood bent over the table, face paling as it neared until his features had hardly any more color than the wraith's.

The white form slid to a stop in front of him, though its hair continued to billow out and around in mad waves. A thin robe, like silk worn to gauze, appeared to hang on its angular, delicate body. A hand reached out towards the boy. When it passed through the sunlight, the radiant beams went straight through it, making the apparition of flesh glow.

Bard could not move. He tried and was rooted to the spot. The hand touched him gently on he forehead, making cold shivers run all through him. It was like being touched by the foam of an ocean wave.

"*Take the weapon and go.*" A tinkling voice ran through his mind, played on invisible harp strings. "*She is in danger. You must hurry.*"

"Who?" Bard thought the question more than said it. The words barely formed on his lips.

"Your companion. Do not ask questions. Go!"

The phantom stood back and started vaporizing into the shadows. Bard picked up the gun, found that it was already loaded when he broke the barrels open to check and picked up the case. He did these things as if he always had, though he had never seen a weapon like it in real life. Whether it was memories of something he had read or seen before, or something the phantom put in his mind, he was not sure.

Bard found himself running back the way he had come, squeezing through the tunnel and coming out into the light of the open courtyard. It was as if a compulsion were pushing him forward. He glanced around the courtyard and, seeing no one, hurried down the left-hand hall, which Loran had taken. It soon became dim inside, the way lined by various candy, sandwich and popcorn shops. They went by swiftly as Bard strode down the hall, gun clasped in one hand and case tucked under his arm.

He came to a split of ways and paused, about to call out. But then he heard a harsh voice echoing from down one hall.

"Your magic can't effect me, witch woman. C'mere. What have you got in that bag?"

Loran's voice was too low and controlled to be made out. The man's voice grated something and the sounds of a struggle came to Bard. Turning down the hall, he ran as quietly as possible until he saw a slice of light falling from above across the passage. Just outside of it, a tall man stood dressed in a sort of armor, made up of leather pieces sewn with bits of steel or lengths of narrow chain strung together.

He was big, powerful, and had Loran by the arm, drawing her nearer. There was already a red mark like a bruise on her face and wrist. Her eyes flashed dark fire as she reached for something at her belt. A cloth bag lay sprawled at their feet.

"Now, none of that!" the man growled, grasping her other hand at the wrist as she tried to draw a knife. He twisted it and she cried out, dropping the blade to the floor.

Bard dropped the gun's case with a bang, raising both hands to hold the gun trembling, pointing at the armored giant.

His voice was hoarse as he cried out, "let her go!"

Still twisting Loran's wrist as she struggled and kicked at him, the giant swiveled his large, bearded head to stare at Bard. His teeth flashed and he laughed. "Put your toy down, kid. You ain't going to do nothin' with it."

At the same time, with a casual gesture, he let go of Loran with one hand and raised it to give her a blow across the head with the armor on his upper arm, knocking her to the floor. He turned towards the boy, grasping at a long knife in his own belt.

The pistol's trigger seemed to take a terrible pressure to pull. Bard wasn't sure where he was aiming, except for at the huge man. The gun went off with a loud report and a recoil which made his arms tingle, the barrels jumping up as it went off. There was a clang like a struck barrel and the man looked down at a hole in his homemade chestplate.

"You hit me!" He seemed surprised and angered more than pained. Looking up, he took a few steps forward as if to rush the boy. Bard pulled the trigger again and the other barrel unloaded into the giant. This time he cried out and stumbled, blood oozing from the holes in his chest. He gripped them, coughing and staggering towards Bard, who stood watching in horror. Finally, the man fell at full length on the tiled floor, armor clinking around him. His hand stretched out once more, threateningly, before he went still.

The boy looked from his gun to the man in shock. It had done something big. He had done something big. Suddenly, he remembered Loran and hurried around the fallen giant to where she lay.

"Loran?"

She stirred and sat up painfully with his help, wincing. "I'm alright."

Loran ran a hand over her face, frowning at the marks on her wrists. Then she looked over at the fallen man. "You killed him."

"I had to."

Her eyes took him in thoughtfully. "Thank you."

Bard flushed red and helped her to her feet, finding to his irritation that he stuttered as he replied, "o-of course. It was the ph-phantom that warned me. And gave me this weapon!"

Looking at it as he held it out, Loran's expression became darker. "Another relic."

"What do you mean, *another* one?"

As an answer Loran went over to the dead man and stooped down, pulling something from around his neck. "He jumped me suddenly and I tried to...well, influence him to let me go. But I could not do anything to him. Here's why."

She held out a chain with a pendant dangling on the end of it. The pendant was shaped like a skull with red jeweled eyes. On its brow was etched the branching mark.

"It blocked me." She held it out for him to see. "A magic relic. Or anti-magic perhaps, you would say."

Bard shook his head, amazed and shaken from killing his first man. Seeing that he was pale and trembling, Loran picked up her cloth sack and the case, putting a hand on his shoulder to steer him back out through the halls to the open courtyard.

"Now tell me, did you say something about a phantom?"

Bard nodded, trying not to see the round wounds with blood leaking out of them, crimson life leaving the body. "I found this pistol in its case, back there."

He indicated the hole in the heap of rubble. "It was on a cafe table. When I opened the case a phantom appeared. At least, I guess it was a phantom. I've never seen one before!"

He was shaking all over now from the shock of the incident. Though Loran bore the bruises, she was coldly alert.

"Calm down. Be at peace, Bard," she told him firmly, soothingly, "Explain what it looked like."

The boy sat down and took a deep breath, looking up to explain what he had seen and how the apparition had acted. When he was through, he took a deep breath of air and felt much better about the whole thing.

"That was, indeed, a phantom," Loran said, laying a finger to her chin in thought. She stood still for a few minutes, so still it almost seemed she had turned to stone. Eventually she spoke, "I've never heard of one taking interest in human affairs before. It's as if something has changed...perhaps opening the Gate did effect the world in some way."

"I don't know." Bard put his head in his hands. "Everything is so confusing now."

"Come." Loran pulled him to his feet. "Don't give in to moping. I have some food and you have a dead Vollan over there, I see. Let's return to the car and continue on our path. It's the only way we'll find the truth."

They collected the Vollan, before making their way through the dim halls back out into the sunlight where the car was parked.

"Loran, how does your magic work?" Bard asked, realizing that she had indicated it could be blocked.

She gave him one of her long, cool looks. "It's just a gift I was given."

And she would not say anything more.

Chapter 15: The Halls of Sanity

Days passed one into the next as they traveled. Except for giving alms to a few children monks living in a ruined library, they did not interact with anyone but each other. They saw a few inhabitants, one a woman picking her way with animal-like caution and grace through the ruins, a bow in hand and arrows in a quiver on her back. Another time they came across a man, freshly dead and recently picked at by scavenging birds. What had killed him was not evident. Most likely starvation or illness.

Bard used his gun to hunt from time to time, though he only had two dozen rounds to work with and no sure place to get more. One day, he found a very rare creature while hunting, one which gave them meat for many days of traveling. A deer, its antlers gleaming an eerie green color as it stood on a slab of stone staring at him. It was skinny, tough and Bard was sorry to destroy it when there was so few around. He knew that it must have had a hard life, hunting for mosses and sprouts in a city where most of those things were dead. It made its meat tough. But it was a great windfall for the travelers, who could cover more ground when they did not have to stop to hunt every day. It also saved on bullets.

Bard pressed Loran from time to time about the unusual skills she had exhibited, but she would not give him more of an answer than that it was a gift. He knew that she had foreseen the Greenspark, and he accepted that more easily as clairvoyance or prophesy, but the things she had accomplished more recently were a deeper mystery to him.

Finally, they reached a place where the buildings opened out into a large courtyard. Dry, broken fountains lay in each corner of it. The empty pedestal of a statue stood in the center. Whatever had been on the pedestal was destroyed, laying in fist-sized chunks of stone around the middle of the courtyard. The buildings which ringed the place were tight-packed, most of them fronted by covered colonnades. Some of the pillars were upright, others lay at odd angles on the ground or tipped against their brethren.

Loran pulled the car to a halt on the outer edge of the courtyard, in the shade, giving the steering wheel a small caress of satisfaction. "We've made it. His car has done well for us."

Bard nodded. "Is this the place we'll meet your friends?"

"Elisha should be here soon." Loran frowned up at the sky for a moment, where the sun hung a little past noon. "I don't know if Jerome will be able to make it for a few days. No one else was willing to come."

Secretly excited by the idea of new people to meet, ones that were not scorch-mad or cruel, Bard simply nodded a second time at her words. He was learning to be more serious and calm, more grave, as time went on. As the hunter of their little group and, he sometimes like to think, the main protector, he felt a weight of responsibility. Out from under the kindly but indulgent guardianship of Dick Chelsea he was growing up fast.

Bard got out to scout around the area, peering into moldering buildings and charred corners to make sure they were not being observed by man or beast. Loran sat in the car with the door open, watching the sun and a few wispy clouds moving through the sky. Her face was impenetrable, expression a gently closed book.

When he was satisfied that they were alone, Bard returned and reached into the back to take out his old sack of provisions. There was nothing to eat left in it and the shirt was both torn and soiled from use on the Rabiter wound on his toe. That was well healed now, under Loran's ministrations. She seemed to have tins of salve and bandages hidden in her robe like thorns on a rose bush.

But there was still the two books in the sack. Drifter's dictionary and Bard's own book. Taking out the former, he weighed in in his hand for a moment. He felt Loran's eyes on him as he leaned down to shove it back in the glove compartment, where it belonged.

"He never did show me how to play his game," he commented as he straightened up.

Loran snorted lightly. "It was simple. He had memorized almost the whole book and would have a second person quiz him on the meanings of words. Strange amusement for a loner."

With a shrug, Bard moved over to sit in the sun against a car tire, pulling out his book. It was wide and thick, but when he opened it, only half of the pages were filled in. A simple pen lay clasped in its leaves, ink half gone. One page beside it was blank, but the other had a poem scrawled down it in neat, flowing script.

'Where river meets the apple tree,
Darkness waits and grapples me.
Flowing water, endless hair,
Takes me down to death's dark lair.
Sweet scent of autumn fruit awaits,
Down beyond the water's gates.'

The poem was unfinished. As he had a few times before, Bard lifted the pen, held it for a moment and then sighed and lay it back.

"Did you write that?" Loran's voice broke in on his quiet thoughts. He jumped and looked up to find her standing beside him. He hadn't heard her moving. The book was shut quickly and firmly by his hands.

"No, it's Dick's. A book of poems. He didn't finish it."

"But asked you to?" Loran raised an eyebrow.

Bard shrugged, returning, "he said that I could write in it whatever I wanted to. I guess...yes, I thought I could finish it for him. But I'm just not much of a poet."

"You could try prose," Loran suggested, "it is easier to start and has it's own merits."

"Maybe." Bard stood up, putting the book back in the sack. He didn't really want to discuss it. Loran seemed to know this, but she added one more sentence.

"If nothing else, you can always write what you see around you, for others to read one day."

Bard cast his eyes over the broken structures, void of life, and the sky with its dust-enshrined sun. He did not see anything that was worthy of note, anything that he would want to remember.

To pass the time, waiting for Loran's friend to arrive, Bard started a small fire and began to dry strips of the last deer meat over it. It had stayed good for a surprising amount of time in the cool air, but they had begun to taste a touch of oddness in the pieces that had not been smoked before. Especially where it was fattiest.

He was spitting the thin strips on a stick when he heard a discordant noise in the distance. At first, he paid little attention to it, because it was so far away. But after a few moments he noticed that the sound was coming nearer. Bard jumped to his feet. It was a sort of chugging, clanging noise, echoing eerily through the city. He could distinctly hear light crashes and slides coming after it, from walls that could not withstand the resonance of the sound. It was like a giant monster growling through the streets, advancing towards them invisibly.

The noise began to reverberate around the courtyard, bouncing off of the buildings around them. Bard grasped his knife tightly, looking wildly towards Loran for an explanation. She stood calm, hands tucked in sleeves.

"What is it?" he shouted, pictures of griffins and dragons swirling around his head.

"Elisha." Loran stepped closer so that he could hear her over the noise. "I told you he has a conveyance, remember? But it is steam-powered, not crystal fuel."

At that moment a vehicle came into view down a narrow alley, filling it with steam, smoke and its own gleaming body. Bard had never seen anything like it, except for perhaps pictures in old manuscripts of inventor's wild ideas. It was built like a long, low truck with a huge, round boiler for a nose and a tall cab perched up above it. Behind the cab, a pair of stacks reached towards the sky, smoke billowing up from them and soot falling down in a soft snow. Gleaming rods turned around at the wheels, steam whistled from between them and the back of the truck seemed to be taken up with a tiny house. It was a shack made of grimy rags, sheets of half-rusted metal and corrugated roofing, but a house nonetheless.

The sides of the house swayed and clanked as the truck rolled roughly to a stop a few yards away. One of the stacks was loose, also clanging and shaking wildly on its stem. The windows of the truck were grimy with soot and cracked, one of them missing a small triangle piece. Bard did not know how the whole thing stayed together as it went over bumps in the road.

It sighed to a stop and puffs of steamy air shot out as some sort of brake was set. One of the doors opened and a man hopped nimbly to the ground. He was not tall, nor large, but his arms were well-muscled and slick with sweat. He wore a sort of leather apron, tied around at the waist with a greasy belt containing a set of instruments and tools. Large leather gloves encased his hands until he shucked them off as he drew nearer. Red hair waved above his head in an unruly tuft. Stubble the same color covered his narrow chin.

"Loran!" he had a surprisingly high voice, with a touch of foreign accent to it. "And ye have a friend as well. I'm Elisha, boy, Elisha McDon."

He pronounced the last name with a peculiar drawl to it, so that it sounded more like 'McDoon'.

Bard found his hand being squeezed inside one worked and scarred until it was almost thick leather itself. Then the newcomer turned back to Loran quickly.

"You're looking none the worse for travelin' in this ruined world. No one's spitted ye for 'longpig' or taken you captive yet, 'ay?"

"Actually, I was taken captive once, by the Falel gang," Loran's tone was at odds with his, chilly and liquid. "But I was rescued by a most...interesting man. His story is caught up with that of the box. I'll explain more, later. This is Bard. He's also protected me from capture, recently. There are things in this world becoming stranger than ever, Elisha."

"Well, it never was quite a straight path, was it?" The man smiled, his eyes squinted back in folds of leathery skin so that one could hardly see the green twinkling out. "Good job, young'un, for watching her. She's a lady with some talent and a will of her own, 'ay?"

Loran raised one eyebrow in a mixture of disapproval and amusement. "Come, dispense with your pleasantries, my friend. We have serious business at hand. Let me show you the object we found."

"Bring it into the shack." Elisha nodded towards the house on the back of his rig. His tone was graver now, meeting her request. "It's where serious, quiet-like business belongs."

As she went to fetch the cube, he showed Bard the steps at the back of his truck, leading up into the shack. There was a vehicle door hung at the top of the steps, giving entrance into the place.

"My big steamy doesn't mind the weight," he explained, "and it saves me havin' to find a safe place to sleep every night."

But when Bard went into the structure, he was surprised Elisha could sleep in it at all. There were tools on hangers and benches around all of the walls, metal bins shoved under the benches and an intact wooden table set in the center of the floor, with bar-stools bolted down around it. Everything was a little greasy, grimy and dusty, with the polished look of well-used objects. Other than the table, the only thing which looked like it belonged in a normal house was a sort of wood stove set up against the wall, with a chimney connecting into the main stacks through a window. But as it was made of a small metal drum cut down in size, with a door inserted in the front, it did not appear very homey, either. A pile of split wood and kindling lay next to it, all with charred edges. Bard wondered how many dead trees the inventor must go through to keep his truck running, let alone cook his meals.

Loran came in then and they each took a stool, perching around the table. Loran lay the cube on the heavy wooden slab, putting a hand on top to forestall the man from touching it.

"This has an odd story," she said carefully, "one which you should hear before trying to find out what it is made of or take it apart. Because, if my theory is correct, it may contain something dangerous. Even explosive."

"Oh, 'ay?" Elisha was leaning forward, looking at the black cube curiously. "I'm all ears, m'dear. But it doesn't look like it's meant to be opened. What might it contain that is so dangerous?"

Loran bowed her head, face shaded by the hood. "If my idea is right, then this might just be a form of projectile. One to be shot high into the atmosphere before exploding outwards in either many or a single falling form of destruction. The Greenspark."

Elisha leaned back in is chair and looked at her through his squinted eyes. "That's a tall statement, Loran. If it's true, then the Greenspark fire disaster was due to human malice. But I see one problem already. It would take millions of these projectiles, nay, billions, to cause Greenspark all over the world."

"That is true." Loran agreed with a nod of her head. "I don't know if there would be other launchers or if the machine this came from was the only one. It might be nothing but a wild leap of the imagination. Hear the story and you may judge for yourself what to do next."

While Bard and Elisha listened, she began to sketch briefly her journey with Drifter, what she had learned in the library and what happened afterwards.

THE BED WAS HARD AND cold. Drifter came to a consciousness of it gradually. Sometime in the near past there had been a period of intense pain and odd sensations, all of it blurred by a sense of semi-wakefulness. He had not been able to see and his mind had not worked properly. Everything had been like a mad dream. Now, he realized with growing consciousness that he was laying on something firmly padded, his eyes were closed and he was very tired. Weariness pervaded his whole being like a malignant ghost.

Prying his eyes open, he found his vision grainy and blurred. A white surface was somewhere high above him, lit flatly as if by electricity. He blinked and things cleared slowly until he could make out that he was lying close to a wall of hard, gray material. It was not a shade of gray that could be given any name. Descriptions slid away from it. The pale surface above was a ceiling, perhaps ten feet up. A bar of white light gave out a soft, ambient glow.

He raised a hand with some effort and ran it over the smooth wall. It felt like metal, or maybe polished stone. He let the hand fall on his chest wearily and closed his eyes for a moment. He was too disoriented to untangle the mess at the time. It was only a sense of wrongness that came to him when he tried, as if he had made a plan and it turned out less cohesive than anyone alive had intended.

A clicking sound, very soft, made Drifter open his eyes again. Tiny noises like leaves skating on cement came to his ears. When he turned his head it was to see that a door had come open in the wall of the bare room he lay in. Three figures were entering, none of them with the appearance of humans. All were tall, angular and had skin that was truly, purely white. Their faces lacked any features but dark eyes and the light seemed to trickle right through them. Masses of snowy hair swirled around them, alive without a breeze. The only color they bore was that each wore a sort of stiff vest, trimmed in metallic tape. These were made in bright colors, green, crimson and golden-brown.

Drifter stared at them and a word impacted in his brain. Phantoms. He drew away from them against the wall, without the strength to react in any other way.

The wraiths lined up in front of his bed, staring emptily with their dark eyes. Slowly, each fell to its knees and bowed to him. Their hair waved over their inclined heads, seaweed in the ocean.

"Human"

"Human"

"Human"

Three voices, notes on a harp, rang in his head. With a vicious suddenness Drifter remembered everything. His mission, the opening of the gate, the blue energy that had struck him...

"Are...you...angels?" His voice was distant, harsh in his own ears. He sat up a tiny distance, holding out a hand towards them. It was a helpless gesture. It wasn't until he made it that he noticed his right hand was different. The wrist glittered silver, coarsely shaped like flesh, made of hard metal. His hand was flexible metal fingers, set around a dot of glowing blue material in the palm. It seemed to be a glass lens, lit from behind. He was not sure. At first he was uncertain that it could even be his own hand. But when he curled his fingers the dark metal replicas followed the motion. He bent his elbow to hold the hand close, staring at it in disbelief. Something dark and cold tore at the edge of his mind. They had changed him.

As he sat trying to take in the appendage that was now his own, the three wraiths rose and left him, door closing with a soft hiss.

It seemed all a dream, something on the verge of insanity.

BARD LISTENED TO MOST of the story, but he did leave at one point to pick up his skewers of meat and set them in the car for later cooking. When he returned, Loran was almost at the end of her recital. Elisha had a large mug of something steaming in front of him, which he sipped contemplatively as he listened. Loran had a small teacup of herbal tea. Bard was offered another as he came in.

"Well, this is all most puzzling," Elisha said when Loran was through her story. "But it seems to me there is only one thing to do until Jeroam gets here."

He lay his big hands on the black cube of metal. "Take it apart!"

Loran nodded. "Carefully. Then once our friend comes?"

"Go back to the gate of course, m'dear." Elisha said gravely. "And find out what that machine is all about. Not to mention the portal, passageway, whatever it is sitting in, that is in this world but not of this world."

Immediately, he began to run his fingers over the box, looking for crack or joint. But every corner was sealed, every edge a smooth, rounded line. After establishing this fact, he tapped the object with his fingers, leaning over to listen closely to it. One long arm reached out and grasped a hammer from the bench, which he used to tap on it as well.

"It's definitely hollow," he declared, "though not empty."

"How can you tell?" Bard asked, leaning forward over the table with interest.

"Resonance." Elisha hit it a little harder with the hammer. It made a ringing sound, but it was dampened as if something were touching the walls on the inside.

The tinkerer shrugged. "Besides the fact that it is too heavy for its size, if the metal is thin and the inside hollow. I'm not sure what sort of material this is, it doesn't feel like anything I've seen before, ye see, but I don't think the metal itself weighs more than steel or is thicker than about so much."

He indicated about a third of an inch with his fingers. "But it is very stiff for its thickness, ye understand. And strong."

Loran nodded to all of these suppositions and bits of information. "Can you open it?"

"Oh, 'ay." Elisha's expression became surprised. "Of course I can. The thing is to do it without harmin' or settin' off anything inside."

"Well." Loran gave a dry smile. "Can you do that, then?"

With a promise to try his best, the inventor picked up the box and set it on the bench which ran around the room. But before he would work on the object, he insisted that they all sit and have dinner with him. At the mention of 'dinner' Bard looked up through a gap in the flapping fabric of the roof and saw that the sky beyond was starting to darken. He went to get the last of their venison, looking up again at the sky turning bruised purple with the black shades of buildings standing against it. He saw a star appear, twinkling in the misty haze, and wondered if there really were other worlds out there at all like their own. Not nearby, perhaps, but so far off that the most powerful space craft constructed before the disaster would take years and years to reach it.

With a sigh, he went to fetch the meat. Whoever lived on those worlds was lucky to be so far away from this one.

When he returned, Elisha was cutting up potatoes to put in a pot and boil. Bard's eyes lit up and he swallowed hungrily. It had been months since he had potatoes, the last being when he and Dick had harvested the few small ones growing in the shielded dome, carefully saving the best to replant. Before that, he had vague remembrances of eating them regularly before the Greenspark. But, though he had been a dozen years old when the disaster struck, everything from the time before the fires was somewhat blurred in his memories.

The venison, they roasted over the open fire in the stove, which radiated heat until the little shack was more than cozy. A smell of scorching oil and dust came with it, but the passengers did not care too much. It was nice to sit on the faded bar stools around the heavy table and smell dinner cooking, talking quietly about things past and to come. It was homey.

Elisha told them a little about his time in ruined Apex. Like Loran, he had been seeking answers about why the Greenspark had fallen and the phantoms appeared. He had not learned much new having to do with the former, but phantoms he had run across multiple times.

"Once I saw one, just in the shades of evenin' like this," he said, knotting his worn knuckles together in a double fist. "Sitting in the middle of the road it was, legs crossed like a child. In front of it were a series of pebbles, lined up on the ground. It seemed to be playing a game with them, or counting them over like a miser. Its strange shape seemed to waver in the twilight and its hair billowed around it without a breeze. When I got nearer—"

"You went towards it?" Bard interrupted with surprise.

"Aye. I wanted to know what it was, you see. Maybe if I got closer to it I could ask it some questions. No one has ever tried that before, as far as I know." With a quirked smile Elisha went on. "Before I could get near enough the white being just jumped to its feet and made a loud, ringing noise like a bell. Then it ran off, or perhaps 'glided' is a better word. Floated away faster than I could follow and disappeared into a bunch of old buildings."

"They act very strangely," Loran murmured, dark eyes reflecting things far away and unseen.

Soon the dinner of salted, boiled potatoes, toasted bread hunks and venison was ready. They ate it on the table as darkness fell outside, Elisha lighting a bright oil lamp which was suspended from the ceiling. The yellow light, walls (no matter how flimsy they were) and presence of multiple people made Bard feel safer and more cozy in the little shack than he had since leaving the Academy sector.

After supper Elisha began getting out various cutting tools from drawers under his bench. Everything from a cold chisel to a hacksaw was laid out on the work surface as neatly as a surgeon's tools. Bard leaned on the bench nearby, watching with a growing interest in not only the box itself, but the tools used to work on it. Elisha started out by simply scraping at the surface of the box with the sharp, angled blade of a knife. Though it left a faint scrape mark, he could not raise any shavings, even from the corners.

"This would rather shatter than peel," the workman remarked.

Next he took the hacksaw to it. It made a small groove after much hard sawing, but the teeth skated instead of digging in. It was a very brittle, hard material, which Elisha vowed again that he had never seen nor heard of before. He did not wish to use the cold chisel on it, for fear that it would puncture through and strike what was within, or simply fragment the whole cube into small pieces.

"Time for the crystal torch," he decided, "though we must tread carefully. I don't want to heat whatever is inside."

Opening another drawer he removed an instrument that Bard had never seen before. It was a pair of small cylinders on one side, with tubes running from it to a nozzle with various controls on it, such as a pair of valves and trigger. Elisha also took out a sparker, for lighting it.

"What if you set the cube in a bowl of water while cutting one side?" Bard suggested, "it might help it stay cool."

"'ay, it might." Elisha nodded at him. "Though it won't cool whatever is directly under the surface I'm cuttin'. Still, we can try it. Fill that little pan there from the reservoir."

The 'reservoir' was a small metal tank covered in the general grease and dust of the space, set up on the wall near the stove. It had a tap on one side, which squeaked as Bard turned it to fill the indicated pan with water. He set it on the workbench and Elisha put the black box inside. The water lapped only a third of the way up its edges, but Bard hoped it would serve to keep the whole thing cooler.

"Now, don't be lookin' directly at the flame as I cut." Elisha cautioned, "It's not bright like a welder, but still enough to make ye blink flame light all evenin'."

He fished a pair of darkened goggles from the drawer as he spoke, pushing them down over his bright hair onto his eyes. Then he turned the valves on the cutting instrument and lit the nozzle. It made a sandy, whooshing noise before purple flame jumped out, pale and intense. Bard tried the avoid staring directly at it, though it was difficult when he wanted to be looking at the box to see what it contained.

All this time Loran had been sitting calmly at the table. Now and then she turned her head to watch what they were doing. But much of the time she propped her chin on her knuckles, staring off into some part of space only she could see.

Chapter 16: What's Inside a Riddle

The fingers flexed and bent just as a human hand should. When he touched his cheek he felt their cold hardness on his face, yet also had sensation at the end of his finger tips. Not as fine a feeling as his other hand had, but still a feeling of touching something malleable. Drifter held the hand up over his face, opening and closing it against the whiteness of the ceiling. He had a strange feeling of disconnection to the appendage, as if someone had said *'look, here's a hand, try it out'* and he had put it on for a test-run.

Weary, he let it fall to the bed beside him. After resting for a moment, he heaved himself up into a sitting position, swinging his feet off onto the floor. Though he still had the same brown uniform he had stolen from a soldier's body months ago, someone had taken his cloak away. And his boots. His feet were encased in new socks, stretchy and white. He stared at them with almost as much surprise as he had used on the new hand.

Feeling something odd about his left leg, he reached down and rolled up the pant leg, suddenly wondering how bad the burn scar had become since he had fallen unconscious...or whatever had happened to him. But under the tan pants there was no blackened scar. His leg was smooth and whole, the skin where the scar had been was now unnaturally pale. He stared at it for a minute, before running a finger down the sharp bone of his shin. It was soft, unworn. But it was unblemished skin. They had healed him.

Drifter rolled his eyes and slumped back against the wall. "What sort of game are they playing with me?"

After a moment he added another pressing question, "who are 'they'?"

There was no immediate answer. He was not even sure if this room was anywhere in Apex. It did not feel like his home town. He thought back over what had happened before his awakening and furrowed his brow. The last thing he remembered distinctly was opening the Gate of Eternity.

"The world should have ended." He looked up at the white ceiling and the flat electric light. "Did it? Is this the World to Come?"

It did not feel like a better world. He was tired and felt ill, as if he had been caught in the grasp of a deadly fever for many days and was just recovering. Of course, there had been the phantom-like people who entered the door and bowed to him. A circumstance both bizarre and otherworldly.

"If it didn't end the world," Drifter murmured, eyes narrowing, "what was behind the gate?"

He searched his memory doggedly, hunting down any stray thought from that time. All he could remember was a brilliant flash of blue light, blinding him as it burst out of the gate. And a sensation like sticking one's hand in a light bulb socket but a hundred times stronger. What had happened to the rest of the world when he was struck down? Loran, Bard...the people of Apex Haven.

He sighed and started to brush a hand across his face. But when he felt the cold touch of metal on his cheek he shoved the hand away in exasperation. Drifter was a man of action. He wanted to get up and pace the empty cell, try to find the now-invisible doorway. Beat at it, pry at any crack in the walls or floor. Anything except sit on the bench trying to piece together his memories. But he was still tired by the mere act of sitting up, let alone getting to his feet.

One of the odd things about the room was the complete lack of sound from outside. Except for a faint humming noise from the light and perhaps inside the walls, everything was still. It made it feel as if the cell were deep underground, separated from any passage by a wide thickness of stone.

"Underground," Drifter muttered, "that's where Loran said that she hid during the Greenspark fall. Her and her friends...could I have been taken there?"

He imagined Loran coming to the gate a few minutes after him, looking for it in scholarly interest, finding him laying there...and what? Spiriting him away to a place deep underground?

That did not make any sense. Drifter shook his head and decided to do what an animal would do in such a situation. Sleep until he regained his strength, or at least until something new occurred. He lay down on the hard bed, which had a slight cushion for his head, and closed his eyes. On the verge of sleep he recalled the vision of the wheatfield.

He squinted his light eyes open for a moment, remembering the fullness of the golden heads and blue of the sky. "Was it Heaven?"

There was no way for him to tell now. This world could be a nightmare or another vision on the edge of eternity itself.

Sleep sucked him down in its black whirlpool.

He was awakened later by the first sounds he had heard from outside the cell. It was what must have been a loud shouting, though it only came to him as a passionate whisper. Sitting up again, he found that he was not as weary as he had been before. The bit of rest had done him good. He leaned his head against the wall, moving it around until it was at the end of the bed and he could hear the noises a little louder. Shouting, something thumping on the floor and a clatter...then it all trailed away into silence again.

Drifter drew in a quick breath. Whatever was out there, phantoms, humans or monsters, he was not entirely alone. But why had they left him in this barren cell so long without coming in?

His throat felt dry and he thought sardonically that if they wanted him as a prisoner they would have to bring him provisions at some time. Otherwise, all they would get was a limp corpse.

His head jerked around as he heard a faint clicking and hissing from the wall where the door was concealed. A portion of the smooth, gray surface swung inwards, gradually opening into a rectangular doorway. Beyond it, he caught a glimpse of a hall walled in white. Before he could move, a trolley was thrust in at the doorway, a small wheeled table with what looked like a cup, pitcher and covered plate set on it. There was other small objects on it as well, but his attention was captured by what was pushing the trolley.

It was a young woman. A plain human with dark hair, closed face and downcast eyes. She was dressed in the white uniform of a nurse, even down to a tiny white hat on her head, seeming to hold her tight bun in place. She pushed the trolley in, swung the door shut with a shove of her hip and came over in front of him.

Turning to him with an efficient nod of her head, she said, "good, you're awake. We weren't sure what state you'd be in."

Turning to pick up the pitcher, she poured a gush of sterile water into the cup. She proffered it to him with a pantomime of drinking, as if not sure he would understand her words. Drifter took the little, plastic cup and poured the empty-tasting liquid down his throat.

"It's just terrible, keeping an Othered like you captive, a secret, and doing what they wished with you that way," the young woman chattered on, in the tone of voice one might use for a dog or an imbecile, "it's against all the rules of the Dagor council, you know."

Drifter held out the cup, but when she reached for it he gripped her wrist with the other hand in a swift movement.

"Where am I, girl?"

He looked at her with his sharp gaze and realized that she was not touched by the scorch. Its sign was not on her, in mind or body.

The nurse tried to pull away but, finding his grip unbreakable, put her other hand on her hip. "Now, I would let go of me if I were you. I'll just call a guard in if you cause trouble, and you'll be neutralized. We don't want that, do we?"

Drifter let go of her arm suddenly and pressed the cup into her hands. "I don't know about you. It doesn't sound fun to me. But I want my question answered."

The nurse tossed her head with a shrug, fiddling with some of the other objects on the tray. "In an Akarnan holding cell in their section of the council building. Other than that, I'm not supposed to talk about such things with an Othered like you."

She picked up a device that looked like a remote controller with a small screen as well as one button on it. "Now it's time to take your temperature, so you just sit still and be good."

Deciding that he would get more from patience than violence, Drifter sat still and allowed her to run one end of the object across his forehead. The nurse then insisted on taking his blood pressure with an electronic cuff of sorts, putting it on his left arm, of course. She cast a few glances at his metallic right hand as if she had not expected it, but did not comment. Drifter went through the motions required of him laconically, saying with some roughness afterwards, "what next?"

He had noticed that the instruments were electronic, their cases unmarred and in perfect working order. The woman was dressed and moved in a way he remembered from before the disaster. Wherever this was, it was not the Civitas Apex he knew.

"We're through with that phase," the nurse told him in response to his query, "my job is to make sure that you are well and able to leave this room and be taken to the Volka section of the council building. The only thing left for you to do is eat a little, if you feel able."

"I'm willing." Drifter knew that the food could be drugged, even poisoned, just as the water he had taken could be as well. But he was banking on the fact that they seemed to want him alive, even alert, rather than in a state of stupor. It was a fine game, where he did not know the rules or the goal. All he had were his wits, which had served to keep him alive through difficult situations before. Though he did not yet feel truly hungry, the food would give him strength and perhaps serve to rid him permanently of the weak feeling that had haunted him earlier on.

The plate she proffered him had a few strips of fried meat and a pile of fluffy yellowish bits on it. It took him a moment to recall the names of bacon and scrambled eggs. It had been years since he ate such things.

They tasted flat and salty, inadequate compared to his usual rough, meaty meals. He ate with his fingers rather than the fork, though he felt the nurse watching him and guessed her thoughts. By how she acted, he was an uncouth barbarian in her mind. It didn't matter to Drifter. His strengths were not in being refined or polite.

When he was through eating, the young woman asked him if he thought he could walk some distance. She offered a wheelchair that was outside if he could not. With a contemptuous flicker of his pale eyes Drifter stood up and shoved the paper plate back on the trolley. "Show me the way."

The nurse turned towards the door abruptly. "This way. But remember, there will be a guard just outside who will come behind us. Follow me and do not stray."

Her tone implied that he should be a good animal and heel, even if he had not been taught to it. Drifter fell in behind her in a stalking stride, moving without a limp for the first time in years. He still had a hard time taking in the changes that had been done to him, and the strange unscorched surroundings that he was in. But the feeling of weak dreaminess was leaving him. Everything was becoming hard and cold around Drifter, mostly in a way he did not like or trust. The idea that this was some sort of afterlife had faded in his mind. He was still in his body, this was a real and nonspiritual existence.

Outside of the cell was a hallway of white, smooth walls tinted with just enough cream to keep them from hurting the eyes. The floor was gray, the same inexplicable color as the walls of his cell. Electric lights were fit in the ceiling, small, round disks of flat white.

As soon as they had left the room, a man dressed impressively in slick black armor started following them. He was carrying a long-barreled gun slung in one arm and various other devices in his belt. Drifter did not deign to give him more than a glance. His face was soft even if his armament was strong.

The guard's footsteps echoed down the hall, slightly muffled by the apparent thickness of the walls. Drifter's were soft in his socks, while the nurse shuffled along in odd shoes that made little sound.

On the way they passed little, lit rectangles of red or green in the walls. Drifter guessed that they indicated doors set in the wall, invisible like the one in his cell had been due to the lack of an apparent joint between wall and door. After walking by a few dozen of these, they became less frequent. As they went, Drifter noted a few odd details. Firstly, a small stain on the floor which looked suspiciously like blood. Secondly, there was another trolley like the one the nurse had brought to him. But it was parked against the side of the hall, tray slightly dinged as if it had been through a fight.

Not everything was at ease in the seemingly strict, ordered halls. There had been a riot in the near past, probably the noises Drifter had heard, and two factions were evidently fighting over control of him. Or at least debating it, heatedly. The question was, why was he so important to them? The nurse seemed to think that he was on the level of a wild animal or a captive savage. But if he was so lowly, what made him so important to have in custody?

They came around a gradual corner in the white hall and Drifter got his first clue as to where they were. It was a sight which surprised him into stillness. There, set in the smooth wall, was a rectangular window of clear glass. It had rounded corners and was placed flush in the wall so that there was hardly a joint between it and the glass. But it was not the construction of the window which surprised him. It was what lay beyond it.

The sun was setting, purple and gold, on a wide space of green grass like a lawn. Trees stood in it here and there, leaves brilliant and crisp against the clean sky. In the distance, a series of shining silver buildings rose towards the horizon, lights twinkling on them like a dense constellation of stars. Nearby, the building Drifter stood in curved around in an amorphous wing, culminating in a pinnacle of gleaming stone or metal. Windows glittered on it, streams of light pouring from every one.

Drifter was drawn towards the window as if by a magnetic force. He put his hands on the wall below and looked out, gazing at the flickers of movement and light from the distant city. It was alive. The city had not been slain.

"Move." The guard stepped forward, nudging him with the gun. Drifter twisted his head to look sideways at him for a moment. The guard's eyes and expression were hidden behind dark glasses. But Drifter saw his exposed face, neck and hands. He saw striking points which he could easily use to overcome the guard at this distance without the gun coming into play.

But there would be other guards and he was in strange territory. He turned and followed the nurse as he was expected to do. She had paused when he did, without looking around, and continued when he did in the same manner. He walked a little quicker to come up almost beside her and said quietly, "what city is this?"

It reminded him of Apex before the disaster, with the wide cityscape and constant movements of life within. The architecture was entirely different or else he might have thought that the Greenspark fall was a dream, he a patient in a mental hospital.

"I'm not allowed to talk to you." The nurse returned primly.

"Will someone answer my questions honestly where we are going?"

"You will be told what you need to know in good time."

It was not long before they left that hall and crossed a great, open chamber. Star-shaped patterns of yellow stone were inset smoothly into the dark floor. Banners of blue, gray and gold hung on the walls. To their right stood a huge set of glass double-doors with a pair of giant insignia etched above them. On the left was a raised platform and a podium, indicating that this was a place for speeches to be made. At the moment everything was empty and still.

Across the chamber they entered another hall, this one with reversed colors. The walls and ceiling were gray, the floor white. It seemed to be a mirror image of the other, curving gently back until they reached a door about opposite with the one Drifter had occupied before.

"Is someone waiting in here for us?" He asked suspiciously.

The nurse touched a glowing rectangle on the wall and the inset door swung open. "Please go in."

Drifter gave one last look at the guard with his armor and gun before stepping through the door. He found himself in a room much like the last, except for that the colors were reversed as in the hall and it was slightly larger. There was a little more furniture too, items for general comfort during a long stay. The bed had a thicker cushion. But there was no one in the room.

"Wait—" Drifter spun back towards the door. It was already swinging shut. It sealed with a solid noise and a hiss, leaving him imprisoned inside.

THE ACT OF CUTTING through the cube's wall was long and painstaking. Elisha would cut a little way, then stop and let it cool. They took it out of the water eventually, so that none would leak in when he rotated it. So far nothing had come out of the line they cut and it was far too narrow to see within. The crystal torch was a precise instrument.

Loran stayed sitting at the table, lost in reverie. Bard joined her after awhile, noticing the abstracted look on her face. He touched her on the shoulder shyly.

"Are you okay?"

She started a little and gave him a slow nod, eyes coming back to the present. For a moment it seemed that Loran would say nothing. But then she spoke in a low tone, only for him to hear. "You asked me the other day if I thought Drifter was happy..."

Bard nodded.

"My mind got an impression of him now. Somewhere with gray walls...and electric lighting."

The boy gave her a confused look. "But he's dead."

Loran drew in a sharp breath. "Wherever he is, he is not happy."

Bard's eyes got wide and a disturbed expression came over his face. He was about to say something more when Elisha abruptly shut off the torch and drew the goggles from his head. With a noisy sigh, he set everything aside.

"Ah, well, half way through." He ran a hand over his face wearily. "But my hands are startin' to tremble and I can go no further tonight. Sorry m'dears, but I don't want to make a mistake and I am tired."

Loran arose with a sweep of robe. "Of course. It's late already. Thank you for working so hard on it, Elisha. Tomorrow will be time enough to answer our questions."

"You're welcome, lady." He bowed his head to her. "I'll certainly start early tomorrow, just after brekky."

"Then I am going to bed in the car," Loran said, clasping her hands together, "I'm weary myself, though I haven't been working like you."

She went out of the shack into the night. Bard got a glimpse of the starry sky and ruins through the door before it closed. He looked at Elisha, hesitating a moment before he asked, "Loran has strange powers. I've seen them before. How did she get them?"

Elisha squinted at him, wiping his big, stained hands together. "Well now, lad. It's none of our business, really. But I'll tell you this much. Her gift of prophecy she's always had and it saved my life, or at least my sanity. I was never scorched like so many are, because she warned us weeks before it fell. Otherwise...her intuition and mental powers are also her own. But I think she found a relic that gives her control over other things, if that's what ye mean."

"Yes, that would explain it. She was able to unlock a door with a touch, and I wondered." Bard looked up excitedly.

Elisha did not allow him to ask more. "Like I said, lad, it's none of our business. Get to bed with ye and let the good lady sleep without questions."

Bard blustered and tried to get more from him, but the inventor would not talk. Eventually, the boy left the shack and crossed the distance to the car. As he went, he heard Charwings calling to each other through the night and shivered. Loran's words about Drifter puzzled and chilled him. Before getting in the car, he turned his eyes to the sky and said a little prayer of safekeeping for the dead.

Inside, the woman was apparently fast asleep, curled up in her robe under the steering wheel. Bard took his own corner, as they had for so many nights, and was soon unconscious himself. Neither of them saw the red eyes of a Chardog look in the window. Nor that they faded away peacefully into the night.

In the morning Elisha was already working on the cube when they arose. A personage strange to Bard was waiting in the shack to meet them. Loran introduced him as Jeroam, another of the people who had survived underground during the Greenspark fall.

He was young, in his early twenties, with a fit, tight energy to all of his movements. His hair was dark and long, held back by a bit of leather tied at the nape of his neck. Brown eyes twinkled with life in a quick face, marred by a shallow scar on one temple. His clothes were dark as well, bound by a leather harness holding up a pack and bedroll. A machete hung from the harness on one side, while the other supported a metal flask for water. He greeted Bard by clasping his hand briefly, then whipping away to say a few words to Loran. His speech was swift and vibrant, always getting right to the point. Bard liked him right away.

As Elisha continued to work on the black box, Jeroam explained that he had been wandering the city ever since they left the shelter. He had not learned much about either phantoms or relics, but he had talked to many people and gathered their stories about the Greenspark fire. He had even run into a band of adventurers from another continent, who had crossed by boat hoping to find Apex less ruined than their homeland. In this they had been disappointed, and left for another place across the seas as soon as they re-provisioned.

The scar had come from a fight Jeroam had been in with a gang. He had survived and defeated his enemies, but received a cut from a spear to remember it by. Loran insisted on checking the wound, but it had already healed, leaving only a dark line behind. Jeroam laughed at her for fussing over him and said that it wasn't the only fight he had been in.

"Luckily I was always a fighter, even before the disaster." He grinned. "Growing up on the streets, I had to be."

Breakfast was waiting for them on the table. Elisha had already eaten, so they began without him. As they ate, they talked and the inventor worked, so that all of their stories were understood by the time breakfast was over. It only took another hour for the metal cube to be cut entirely in half.

Elisha had set the two pieces in an empty pan and now moved it carefully over to the table. As they all watched, breathless, he pulled the halves apart.

Inside there was a hard, metal ball set with short metallic wires like spines. It was suspended in the center of the cube by longer, slimmer wires connecting to four of the metal walls. All around this orb was a thin, spongy netting. It filled the rest of the cube. From the gaps in the netting spilled tiny grains of some material, colored green and blue. It poured out into the pan with a musical sound when Elisha lifted the cube and tipped it. The grains built up into a little heap, shimmering peacock colors. Bard touched them gingerly with the tip of his finger and found them hard, almost chalky in texture. Each bit was about half the size of a grain of rice.

"There's hundreds of them!" Bard exclaimed, "but what can they be?"

"I don't know." Elisha set the opened box down and pried the orb from the center loose, breaking the long wires. "But we'll find out, along with what this device is."

It seemed like a difficult job to Bard. Though Elisha evidently came equipped, finding out what the grains were made of would be scientifically tasking.

To begin with, Elisha made sure that all of the grains had come out of the spongy material inside the cube onto the tray. This was not hard, as the netting ripped easily, spilling the bits of chalky material out. Once the box was empty, the tinkerer set it aside on his bench. For now it had no further use for them.

"The thing to do is find out what sort of device this is in the center. If this is a type of bomb, the orb should be its detonator," Elisha explained, carefully picking up the hairy thing and holding it in his hands. He went on to add that finding out more about the orb would not only be the quickest way to start guessing at the grainy material, but the safest. Otherwise he would have to subject it to tests such as dropping it in chemical solutions and crushing it with other powders to find out how it reacted.

"As far as I can tell," he finished, "these grains are something I've never seen before. But there are many chemicals and chemical compounds in the world. We'll see."

As the young men crowded around and Loran waited calmly at the table, playing with the grains, Elisha set the metal ball on his workbench and began inspecting it. It did not take him long to find a small joint running all of the way around it, a sort of crack or line cutting it in half. With some small pliers and a screwdriver he was able to wiggle it so that the crack widened and the object came apart. It fell in two parts reluctantly, a spiderweb of fine wires holding it together on the inside. Elisha peeled it sideways so that they could see the interior without breaking anything. What looked like electronic chips or other electrical parts were fastened to a smaller globe inside, which then had all of the fine wires connecting to it. These went out and fastened to the stiff, short wires bristling on the outside of the orb.

Elisha began to inspect the parts on the inside, tracing out wires and looking at the electronics. After a bit he pulled a device from his drawer which he said was for testing to see if the electronics had power running through them. They did not, though with more poking around and testing Elisha decided that the tiny ball in the center was a sort of battery. The electronics, he guessed to be remote receivers of some sort, as well as a few things he was unfamiliar with. Through this, he came to the conclusion that the short, bristly wires were to convey an electronic spark to the grains of material from the central orb, upon a remote command. But, because of a burnt-out chip or faulty battery, the whole cube had become a dud.

"Which means," Elisha waved a hand at everyone watching him, "that to find out what these grains do, we shall have to hit a small amount of them with an electrical spark. Luckily, I have some batteries and wires around here somewhere..."

"Be careful, friend," Loran said quietly, "this may yet be a device for creating Greenspark."

Jeroam nodded his agreement. "In fact, it's even more likely now! Elisha has proved that it is some sort of bomb."

"Not exactly, lad," The inventor chided, "it could be that these grains do something entirely peaceful when they get sparked. Like...hm—"

"End the world?" Bard suggested.

Everyone paused for a moment, remembering where the box had come from. If the Gate really was something to activate the End of the World, could it have a machine inside to carry out that plan? And if so, could it have malfunctioned?

But Loran dismissed it out of hand. "Nonsense. This cube and machine were made by men. It has nothing mystical about it. Jeroam is right. It must be a sort of bomb."

"Then I'll test a little of the powder outside, where no harm will come if it does burst into Greenspark or explode." Elisha picked up the tray of grains and took it outside. He returned a moment later to have the boys help him gather a handful of various items, including a spool of insulated wire. These they took outside, into the center of the courtyard. After being inside, thinking of wires and electronics so long, it was strange to come out and see the dry fountains, cracked tiles and ruined buildings of Apex. But the city was still all around them, watching with its dead eyes as they delved into its secrets.

Elisha set up a battery, run of wires and a way to activate it with a switch. At the other end of the wires he took a pan and set it on the ground in the center of the courtyard, away from both of the vehicles. He put a small pinch of grains of both colors in it, perhaps three or four of each. They did not know how powerful a shock had been used on the grains in the bomb. Elisha had not discovered what all of the devices in the box did. But this would serve as a first, basic test of the grains. If it did nothing, they would try others alterations until it worked.

Everyone stood back from the pan, over by Elisha's steam truck. He crouched down and lay a hand on the switch.

"Ready?" He glanced up at Loran. She gave a small nod, hands in sleeves and face intent under her hood.

Elisha threw the switch. There was a faint clicking sound from the end of the wires as a spark was generated. It was followed immediately by a peculiar sound, a mixture of fizzing and hissing, with a blast close on its heels.

Whistling like fireworks, something green streaked up from the pan. Four streaks in fact, shooting into the sky. Once they had attained a level far above the buildings around the courtyard, the sparks burst into miniature explosions of their own. There was a sound Bard had heard once before. A terrible noise, which made him shiver and clutch at his arms inadvertently. It was a hissing and crackling, set at a particular pitch which seemed to worm into the ears like a living thing.

Out of the sky four objects came falling. Three of them dropped somewhere beyond the ring of buildings around them, out of sight. The fourth came down just beside the pan where it had started. It was a lump of material like a tiny meteor, about the size of a large man's fist. Green sparks danced around it, flaming with an unholy light. It burned and crackled until it hit the ground. As soon as it struck the hard surface, it seemed to melt, turning into a sort of shockwave moving outwards. Ripples ran through the ground. The buildings around them shook, pieces falling off and dust rising. The battery next to them cracked and bubbled over, acid hissing onto the tiles. The pan was a bent bit of melted metal and the wires blackened for yards.

Bard stood with tears running from his eyes. Everyone else stared in amazement. The boy nodded once, voice pinched. "That's it. That's the Greenspark."

He was the only one there who had seen it before. The brush of scorch in his mind twinged and he started sobbing.

Chapter 17: The Prisoner

Only four grains of each color had gone off to produce the results in the courtyard. There were hundreds in the little cube. No one knew how many cubes there had originally been in the machine or how they had been shot at high enough velocity to reach all of the way around the world. But there was no doubting it now. The gate of Eternity was actually a front for the machine, or one of the machines, which had launched the bombs causing Greenspark to fall. Millions of people killed immediately, many more by the aftereffects. Cities laid to ruin, lives condemned to misery and what was left of nature almost entirely destroyed.

The two questions were:

Who.

And Why.

Because someone had to build the machine. And activate it so that it would launch the infernal bombs across the world. Someone so heedless of their power over mankind that they would use it to wreak havoc and destruction for generations to come. As far as the little band of investigators knew, it was done without provocation. Also, it was done by someone with powers beyond what they had known was possible. Grains of chemical, so small and harmless looking, that could unite to form into Greenspark at a electrical spark. The Gate of Eternity, which went somewhere that was not physically connected to it. And, as Loran had remarked, perhaps the relics themselves, one of which had opened the gate.

A mixture of fear and curiosity weighed on them all. They were up against a power so far beyond them that it might reach out at any moment to blot them out like flies.

The sky felt like an open eye above them. Bard wished that he could crawl into the deepest, darkest cellar of a building and hide forever.

But there was only one thing to do, if they wanted to finish what they had begun. Return to the Gate and discover what made the machine work and what was beyond it.

Elisha left the ruined battery and most of the wires behind. He took what was left of the Greenspark grains and put them in a glass bottle stored carefully in his truck so that it could not tip or rattle around. Loran and Bard made sure that the car was ready to go. Then Elisha built steam in his truck (which took half an hour) and they were on their way.

Loran began to retrace their path with that infallible sense of direction which often surprised Bard. He would begin to think that the buildings all looked the same, that they had made a wrong turn and were heading in a new direction. Then they would pass a building, courtyard or statue so unique in its peculiar state of ruin that he recognized it instantly and know that Loran was leading them straight.

For the first few hours Jeroam rode with Elisha in the steam-powered truck, shack rattling and banging like an iron monster behind them. But after they had paused for a brief lunch and to discuss the trail ahead, the young man decided to move to the car for a time. It was a little more cramped, but he said that the truck was starting to cook him. The firebox was right in the cab, making the whole thing heat up like an oven. Though the outside climate was never truly hot now, even directly under the sun, inside the cab quickly became hard to bear.

At first, Bard felt awkward with the tough, quick young man wedged between him and Loran on the middle seat. But Jeroam was so easy to speak to, chatting about his journeys and the things he had seen as if they were every-day facts, that Bard soon opened out to him. They began talking about ancient devices and engines, the conversation brought on by a comment Bard had made about Elisha's truck. Jeroam did not know very much of engineering, making Bard feel as if he had something to share with him on the subject of ancient feats. Jeroam's enthusiasm was catching and his questions intelligent, so that the conversation didn't lag.

Loran drove quietly, rarely entering a comment. She still seemed preoccupied with some inner vision, as if trying to fit together the meaning behind the appearance of the relics, the Greenspark fall and Drifter's death in front of the Gate.

Eventually, night fell and, after driving by headlight for a time, they stopped to camp. The section of road they were on was wide, though rough with cracks, allowing plenty of room for the truck to pull up side-by-side with the car. The boys were sent to gather firewood for the stove, being warned to look out for each other in the dark. Bard did not feel the night was so empty or terrible with Jeroam as company as they hunted for bushes or trees which were less burnt. After a bit, Bard found a small, ornamental tree standing beside a building and called his friend over to help him break it up.

"Jeroam," he said thoughtfully, after a few moments of branches breaking and twigs cracking. "Do you know anything about Loran's magic?"

"You mean what it can do?" The young man asked, "or about the fact that she has it?"

"I mean, how it works." Bard paused, arms full of broken bits of wood. "I've seen her unlock a car's door and clean its engine of impurities. She also contacted you two somehow, to call you to meet us."

"Oh, that." Jeroam shrugged, tossing his head in the faint, watery moonlight which picked out their forms and that of the tree. "We can all do that. We were all horribly bored while being cooped up underground so long, while the Greenspark fell and for months afterwards for safety. So she taught us telepathy."

Bard blinked. "She *taught* you, just like that?"

Though his face was shadowed, Bard could tell by his tone that Jeroam made a face as he answered, "look, I guess it seems strange to you. I'm used to it by now. But, though the scorch didn't affect us, I think the Greenspark still did, even though we were so far underground. Loran's always had more in her head than most folk. But all of us together down there...well, odd things happened. When the Greenspark was falling we saw visions and heard voices that were not there. Learning telepathy didn't seem so strange after that."

"Oh." Bard furrowed his brow, once again amazed by the mass effect the Greenspark had on all of the world's population. "That makes sense...in a way. But Elisha said she had a relic that was powerful."

"You're mighty curious." Jeroam went back to breaking branches. "If you want to know more, ask her. It's not my secret. Sorry, brother."

As he was not willing to speak any further, Bard was forced to accept his words. They carried the wood back and found the stove already going, with the little that had been left in the shack. Loran and Elisha were getting supper.

DRIFTER TAPPED ON THE walls all around his cell and found no exit that would open to him. It had been a forlorn hope and he knew it. Weary, though he would not have shown it had anyone else been present, he sat on the bed and put his head in his hands. After a few minutes he looked up, noticing something he had not seen before. Hanging on the back of a plain wooden chair in front of a matching desk was his cloak, looking newly washed and neatly folded. He picked it up as if it had been a snake preparing to bite, checking it inside and out. Then, with a shrug, he put it on. It was not cold in the building. But having his cape on with the hood up made him feel a little more like himself.

He had nothing in his pockets and his belt was devoid of objects excepting the loops on his pants. They had taken everything from him, and left him with the strange replacement for his hand. He sat back on the bed, leaning against the wall and flexing the new hand in front of his face. He hardly noticed that it was there, most of the time. Following the flexible, molded metal, he rolled up his sleeve and found were it jointed to his arm right before the elbow. For a moment, he picked at the joint, wondering if it could be a sort of glove rather than a new limb. But the metal blended smoothly in with his skin and did not move when shoved on. It was a robotic hand.

With a sigh he let it fall to the bed. He was a prisoner, there was no doubting that. As one, he had little to do but wait until he found the reasons and a chance of escape or being set free presented itself. It was just as if a large gang, such as the Falel gang run by Steelfist, had captured him in Apex.

With nothing else to do at the moment, Drifter decided that sleep was, again, his best option to pass time and recover strength. He was not yet up to his normal alertness or endurance, something that should be cured before anything of import occurred. Stretching out on the marginally comfortable bed, he pillowed his head on his hands and dropped into darkness.

What felt like hours later he was awakened by a small clicking sound nearby. Looking around, he saw that a narrow flap was just closing in the wall where the door was. A plate had been shoved in, containing food of some sort. Drifter rubbed a hand across his eyes and went to pick it up, finding mashed rootcrops of some sort, perhaps potatoes, a thin slice of cooked meat and some boiled vegetables. Though it was easy food and flavorful, he still found it too salty and flimsy for his tastes. He remembered eating things like them before, even looking forward to eating them, but the only thing he really appreciated was the green taste of the vegetables. Other than that they were so much air and seasoning.

He could not tell whether it was lunch or dinner. Either way, there was nothing to do once it was over. He laid the plate carefully on the ground next to the door and drank a little sterile water from the sink in his room before pacing up and down the floor.

He was in the middle of one of these gyrations when there was a hiss and the door unexpectedly began to open. Drifter paused, tense and alert.

The door swung open inwards and two figures entered. The first was a bent, balding man wearing business clothes and narrow glasses. He carried a briefcase in one hand, clenched as if he might lose it between one step and the next. Behind him followed a guard, in appearance almost exactly like the last one Drifter had seen. The only reason Drifter knew it was not the same one, was that he had brownish-gold hair rather than black.

It was still strange to see people, multiple people at once, who had no touch of the scorch upon them. Drifter stood stiffly, with his arms crossed, eyes glimmering as he waited to find out the reason for his visitor's coming.

The bent man looked up at him and blinked owlishly, jerking his chin at the bed. "Please sit down, sir. I've come to talk to you."

Drifter moved over towards the bed without sitting. "To answer my questions?"

"Not...not exactly." The bent man did not seem scared of him. His hesitation in speaking was due to a wish to be exact, a native vacillation in choosing words, rather than fear. "I've come to ask you a few questions."

"I would like to have a few things cleared up before I have to make answers." Immovable, Drifter looked down at him as he took the one seat and opened his briefcase on the desk. From inside, he withdrew an electronic tablet of some sort, with writing all down its front. Apparently reading from it, the man said:

"What is your name?"

Drifter did not answer and the bald man cocked his head up, still blinking.

"You do have a name of some sort?"

"Drifter."

The man noted something in his tablet with a flick of his smallest finger.

"Now tell me, Mr. Drifter—"

"Just Drifter." The loner gave him one of his flickering, half-dead smiles. "The 'mister' does not apply any more. My name is a title."

"Curious. But on to business. Where do you come from?"

"Civitas Apex. Where do you think? You're the ones who brought me here, not the other way around. I want some questions answered."

The bent man took off his glasses and tapped them impatiently on the desk. "Look here, sir. I am a professional coming to ask you important questions. Your own will be answered by the right people, at the right time."

Sitting himself on the edge of the bed, Drifter looked away.

"I won't answer your questions until I know a few things about where I am and who you people are. If that doesn't suit you—" He clicked his fingers together to finish the sentence.

His questioner raised his chin imperiously, fitting the glasses back on with a shove. "You are being stubborn!"

"Stubborn; Firm as a stub or stump; stiff; unbending; unyielding. Unreasonably obstinate in will or opinion." Drifter's gaze caught the man's like a harpy fastening on a fish. "I think you fit the last description at least as well as I do."

"Sir!" The man stood up, slamming his briefcase closed. For a moment he seemed undecided what to say or do. Finally he leaned forward until their faces were not far apart and hissed in Drifter's face, "I would not be so stubborn, unbending, whatever, if I were you. You are legally a ward of the Volka council. If they want information and you won't give it freely, they may just call in an Extraction Doctor!"

With that, he drew back, tucked his case under his arm and walked awkwardly out of the room. The guard watched Drifter closely as the bent man left, before turning on his heels and following him out. The door shut and sealed. Drifter drew an arm across his face as if to wipe away something the questioner had left there, though it was dry.

"Extraction Doctor." He mused over the words in all of their terrible possibilities and contradictions, murmuring the dictionary meanings to himself.

"Extraction; the action of taking out something, especially using effort or force. Doctor; One. A teacher; one skilled in a profession, or branch of knowledge; a learned man. Two. One duly licensed to practice medicine; a member of the medical profession; a physician."

As always, he used the meanings and their recital to concentrate his mind. It kept panic and madness at bay. Calmly, he turned over the possibilities of his situation, both positive and negative as it applied to himself.

In the end there was not much positive to tally. He was regaining his physical strength and had already reached mental stability. They were feeding him and had not yet resorted to harsh methods in keeping or questioning him. He seemed to be in a place where the people were not touched by the scorch, though that was more of a neutral statement than a positive one. That was all he could think of on one side of the slate.

On the other side, possibilities were almost endless. Concrete negatives were mostly restricted to his lack of information and narrow freedom of movement. Coupled with the fact that he had been physically altered while unconscious, without his consent.

He sat for what felt like hours, turning things over in his mind until they faded gradually away into a gray calmness. Shadows seemed to play across his vision, the shapes of birds and beasts with eyes of red fire. For the first time he felt a sharp longing to be back in Apex. Not as it had been, but as it was. The ruined city was harsh and cold, destroying the careless without compunction. But for one who had learned to live there, survive, it had almost endless freedom. He had chosen where he went, when he awoke or slept, what he ate. Not only that, but the Beasts of the Night were there, the one type of living thing he trusted.

Without warning, his waking dreams were broken by a hiss as the door came open again. He half-rose to his feet, wondering if they had come to question him further so soon. A tall figure glided into the room, white hair waving around it. Drifter stopped and sat back down, staring at it blankly. It was a phantom. But unlike any he had seen before.

Though usually it could not be told whether the phantoms were male or female, this one instantly became a 'she' in his mind. A fine, blank face with angled slits of eyes, long hair floating gracefully around her almost to the floor. Whether she was wearing a wide-skirted gown or that was simply how a phantom was shaped could not be told. The skirt was white, like the skin of her face and hands. So white that snow would have seemed dirty and blue beside it. A wide sash of blue ran from her right shoulder to the opposite hip. A tiny gem of the same color seemed to twinkle in the hair above her brow, though there was nothing there to hold it in place.

She moved into the room with a slow grace, coming to a stop before him. Drifter recalled sharply the phantom who had attempted to touch him in the cafe in Apex, singing so that his memories haunted him all the while.

When she stopped and stood still, or as still as a vibrating phantom could, Drifter noticed that there was a guard outside the door behind her. As the wraith stood without speaking, the door swung closed. The tension in the chamber grew around them in the silence.

Finally it was Drifter who broke it. "Who are you? What do you want?"

At that, the phantom bowed, kneeling down before him. A voice rippled in his thoughts.

"I am Tia, Head Councilor of the Akarnan."

"Akarnan?" Drifter spoke aloud. The nurse had mentioned that name before. She claimed that they, rather than the 'Volka', had been the ones to capture him.

"I have come to tender our official apology to you," The phantom's voice ran on, *"as the rules agreed on in the Council of Dagor demand. And to give at least a slim explanation for our behavior."*

Drifter's gaze focused on her. Now, he might finally come to understand where he was and why. Or even learn what sort of people these 'Akarnan' were, whether spirit, angel or alien being.

The phantom paused, seeming to take breath or order her thoughts before progressing. *"You do not know who we are. To put it briefly, the Akarnan come from the same people as the Volka. We were once humans as well, walking the earth and eating its fruits. But while the Volka studied science and engineering, the Akarnan were people who chose to pursue philosophy and the mystic. Eventually, we came to truths and knowledge that the Volka called madness. We Ascended, leaving our physical bodies behind. Now we walk as pure spirit in the physical realm, never dying, never multiplying."*

Drifter drew back instinctively. "So you are ghosts."

"Not as you know them. We never died. We Ascended."

"That still doesn't explain why you brought me here. Where is this? What happened when I opened the Gate of Eternity?"

The phantom rose to her feet, curling a boneless hand in her long hair. She turned her head so that the dark eyes gazed into nothing near the ceiling.

"I am not supposed to tell you much—"

"But—"

"Wait." The Phantom held out her other hand to forestall him. *"I am not allowed to tell you, because the Volka council is held by the Council of Dagor to explain it themselves, since you have become their ward."*

"When will they?" He clenched his hands, trying to be patient.

"I do not know. Soon. Let me finish my apology, please." Tia gave him a half-bow and he nodded for her to go on, feeling that he was still dreaming.

"When you were struck by the trap that the Volka had built in the gate—"

"So it was them. And it was just a trap."

"Yes. Though it was the Akarnan, not the Volka, who put the relics in your world. So it is partially our fault that you opened the gate at all. My apologies. Also, we secretly built a system into the gate to alert us when it was opened. The Volka's spiderbots dragged you in for them to study, as they thought you dead. But we intercepted the bots and brought you to our medical rooms in the council building. Though your body had died, the mind lives on for many minutes afterward. With our knowledge of mind and body we were able to restore your essence into its physical state."

"Great." Drifter closed his eyes, mouth pulled crooked in an ironic expression. "I've been recycled. No wonder I was so tired. But what about this?"

He held up his right hand, blue glass shining in its center.

"That is our doing as well. We use Volka technology fused with our own when necessary. Your lower left limb was injured deeply. It would have been cruel to restore you with that defect. We cured it. As for the hand...your arm was also injured, by the Volka trap. But not incurably. Now you come to the core of the issue. The one great passion of the Akarnan beyond philosophy."

Drifter regarded the Councilor warily. "Manipulating people?"

"Not exactly. You see, we built the 'relics' and put them into your world because we saw that your world was bland. It was lacking...mystique. The relics, as you Othereds call them, are magical artifacts. They gave your world something greater to strive for, a touch of magic and mystery it was lacking. The greatest wish of the Akarnans was, I am afraid, an arrogant and wild one, but one very close to our hearts."

She paused as he waited, sifting through everything that was being said. When he made no comment she went on. *"We wanted, eventually, to reveal ourselves to a simpler, unascended society in another dimension, and be regarded as powerful spirits to be worshiped. Gods. Or angels at the very least."*

With a sudden show of frustration Drifter slammed a fist into the bed beside him. His voice was low and harsh as he returned, "that's what I thought you were. Angels. I thought that it was the End of Time and I could free the world by opening the Gate. Instead, I find myself captured by power-mad phantoms, annoyingly legal men and a prissy nurse! You lied...with every act and every relic you lied to a whole world...as this seems to be a different world, however that works. Are you aliens on another planet, far away? Nutcases living in a shielded continent away from the rest? What gave you the idea of tricking people into believing in fairy tales like a Gate of Eternity and relics!"

He found that he was trembling with anger and forced himself to be steady. Leaning back against the wall, he crossed his arms on his chest and closed his eyes.

"Finish your apology."

Tia's voice was hesitant now, almost sorrowful. *"Whatever the reasons, it is what we did. I will finish now by stating that we captured you from the Volka in a wish to make you into a sort of hero, a messenger to your people from the gods. We were going to keep you secretly, build on your belief in us as powerful spirits and then release you back into your world to tell the others of us. For that reason we gave you a cybernetic hand, placing in it a relic of great power."*

Her voice sunk to a mental whisper, *"the Volka do not know what it is, yet. They wish to question you and find out, but cannot legally do so until they hold council and inform you of your rights as a ward. Though the Akarnan my have done much harm to you, we have also given you life and a powerful weapon. The Volka would take it from you if they knew. They have already done much harm to your world and wish to keep you as a specimen to study. Beware. This is all the warning I may give you."*

With that, the phantom turned and stood before the door. It opened to let her through, leaving Drifter sitting with his eyes closed behind. The door swung to and sealed. He sat on for many minutes, mind a whirl of confusion and anger. Eventually he raised his right hand and held it, palm-upwards, before him. His eyes opened gradually as an orb of blue power grew above the glass lens in his hand. After staring at it for a long moment, he flung it with a grunt at the wall. The blue orb swished away to splat against the surface, making a small explosion of energy. But it did no harm to the thick, smooth material.

Chapter 17: The Gate Revisited

In the narrow, rubble-ridden streets of Apex a pair of vehicles moved in convoy. The gray car in the lead picked their way, nimbly choosing one road after the other. Behind it rumbled the steam truck, shack rattling and smoke pouring from its stacks. Buildings shook as it passed, knocking already loose masonry to the ground.

They had been traveling for days now, moving through the broken city. A few times Bard rode with Elisha, just to see how the truck felt from inside. It drove with an enjoyable rumble and roll, feeling like it could crush anything in its path. But it was hot and noisy inside. Most of the time the two young men traveled with Loran in the car.

Bard was tired of the constant travel by vehicle, weary of sitting still and watching the buildings of Apex go by. He found some amusement in talking with Jeroam, who was always full of energy and adventure. It also distracted his mind from turning the same questions over repeatedly until it felt ready to catch fire or turn to ashes. But one day, near the end of the journey Jeroam decided to ride with Elisha, just for a change.

There was only two seats in the big truck, so Bard stayed with Loran. The day rolled slowly by from the rising of the red sun to when it stood over them at noon. It had begun to sink past noon when Bard finally got up the courage to look at Loran and ask, "is it a relic that gives you power?"

He expected her to give him cold looks, answer in a round-about way or even just ignore him.

Instead, she raised one eyebrow at him for a moment before saying, "yes. As far as creating orbs of power or manipulating physical objects goes."

Driving with her left, she held out her right hand so that the sleeve fell down her arm away from it. It revealed, tucked far up her right arm, a bracelet shining on the pale skin. It was tarnished gold, with brilliant blue gems set in it, each gleaming as if with their own light. The central piece was a set of tiny gems on a fillet of gold, formed into the branching shape imprinted on all relics.

"It gives me slight powers, reliant on my energy to feed it. You see..." Loran paused, putting both hands on the wheel to jig the car around a fallen stone. "All relics do have power of some sort in them. Many of them just for simple things, such as Drifter's key being able to unlock the Gate of Eternity, when no other key or master locksmith could. Others, like this Band of Trailis, have more generally useful properties for those who have the mind to use them."

Bard sat back, laying a finger to his nose in thought. "You know, I studied relics with Dick for a few years and never really believed in magic. Not until I met you."

Loran shot him a small smile. "It sounds to me as if Dick was more of a scholar, interested in their history and physical appearance, then the sort who would believe in 'magic' either."

With a shake of his head, the boy returned, "I'm not so sure of that. Sometimes I wonder how much he knew that he never told me. He believed in the Gate of Eternity and, I think, knew Drifter's plan for opening it. Dick told me to go with him thinking that the world would end...and approving of it."

"The mind of a human is like the hairs on our heads." Loran said gently after a minute. "Unaccountable to all but the Maker."

They rode on quietly the rest of the day, until the sun set and they made camp. Bard recognized the area they stopped in and realized that one more day's travel, perhaps less, would bring them to the infamous gate. He shivered, wondering if they would find bones still laying before them. Or just scraps of blue and tan cloth blown by the wind.

The night past uneventfully and Jeroam rejoined them in the car for the last leg of the journey. It made the day slip by quicker, until finally they were pulling into a graveled parking lot and Bard was looking up the scorched, tree-pocked hill at the ruined scientific buildings around the Gate.

"Is this the place?" Jeroam was unusually grave as he fixed his gaze on the top of the hill. "I can't make out the gate."

"It's hidden behind the buildings." Bard got out, finding himself reluctant. The image of what they might find at the top of the hill haunted him. Loran stepped briskly from the other side of the car as the steam truck pulled up beside them.

"I'll show you the way, Jeroam. Let's collect Elisha first…"

The inventor parked his truck with a series of steamy hisses and jets of air, before opening the door and jumping out.

"We made it, 'ay?"

"Yes." Loran pointed at the top of the hill. "The gate lies up there. This path will take us to it."

She indicated the scorched cement trail winding up the slope. "But we must be wary. Someone might have come while we were away, now that it is open. Either from outside—"

"Or from in," Jeroam finished for her. Drawing his machete, he started towards the trail. "We came to find out what this gate and machine are about. Meeting the people who built it would probably answer our questions. Even if we didn't like the answer at all."

Steeling himself against anything they might find on top, Bard followed him, fingering his pistol thoughtfully. Loran and Elisha walked together behind them, discussing possibilities in a voice so low Bard could just hear a few words.

"I've looked at it more…" Elisha muttered first.

"…so strange about it?" Loran asked.

"That material…not anything like it here. It's not even natural, ye see…"

But Bard was soon distracted from eavesdropping when Jeroam put his elbow in the boy's side.

"You seem anxious, brother. What are you worried about?"

Bard shrugged, gesturing towards the approaching top of the hill. "What we'll find up there, I guess."

Jeroam put his head on one side as if thinking this over. "Yeah, I guess there might be something dangerous waiting. But I'm excited, not afraid."

With a shake of his head, Bard indicated that he could not share in this excitement right away. Later, maybe, when they were looking at the machine and finding out about it. Not when the Gate was still hidden from sight with whatever might be laying around it.

They crested the hill and moved off of the path around the buildings, crossing the fence where Bard and Loran had before. In just a few paces, they came around the side of the ruined buildings, stepping out beside the Gate.

The door still hung open, blown by rambling winds so that it had wedged against the ground, wider open than it had been before. The tall, smooth arch twinkled darkly, every curve a mystery. The key still stuck out of the hole in the open door, the only ornament to the dark creation. Before it, the ground was bare, not even a mark showing where a body might have lain. Bard had the odd feeling that the Gate was watching them, an open eye gazing sadly on the world. Or that a cold wind might blow out of it, coming from a different part of the land. But nothing was moving in the whole scene except for a single Charwing, who circled in the air above, little head cocked with interest.

Jeroam moved over in front of the door, sizing it up as if he were about to eat it. Cautiously, he moved over to the open arch and peered in, looking up and down the hall inside.

"No one in sight," he remarked, "just a few closed doors further down."

Bard had not actually looked into the doorway before, not daring to cross the space where Drifter had been struck down. Now he moved up beside Jeroam and poked his head in.

To the right, the path was taken up by the big machine and tub, almost entirely blocking the path. But to the left he was looking down a long hall, ceiling arched and floor tiled in huge, black slabs. A sort of dark mist seemed to hang in the passageway, making it difficult to see what was further than forty feet down it. This mist also gave the hall a gloomy, atmospheric ambiance, as if a wraith might pad its way down it at any moment.

In between the Gate and the spot the mist concealed, there was a length of smooth, dark wall broken only by a few doors set into it. Bard counted three, two on the right and one on the left as his Gate was. Each of them had a series of colored stones set into their faces, red, green and even one blue. They appeared to be a sort of code, perhaps an indication of what was within. But if someone dwelt inside those doors, they had not come out to shut the Gate, nor did they open the doors now to see who was invading their hall.

Elisha and Loran had come up to the Gate by now as well. The inventor was running his hand down the four rails suspended on the inner side of the door. They were set in a long box shape, as if to contain one of the Greenspark cubes within them. In fact, the cube would have slid nicely along the inside of the rail, traveling back down past a few wires and tubes connecting from machine to rail, along a flexible joint where the door hinged and into the mouth of the huge machine inside the hall.

Elisha was nodding to himself as he peered into the dark, square mouth of the machine where the rails ended. "Aye, the cube would have been shot from there. I don't yet see how, especially how it could be shot so far as to go 'round the world. But we'll figure it all out with time. Now, what was in this tub?"

He moved around to the big bin at the back, which seemed to be made of normal black plastic, thick and strong. He was actually inside the Gate now, with his feet on the dark floor, but he didn't seem to notice. There was a lid on top of the bin, such as might have been put on a dumpster. He flipped it up and craned his head under it, peering inside.

"'Ay, now that's an odd way to be storing ammo," he muttered, reaching an arm inside, "some sort of thick gelatin. And look'e here, there is another dud still caught in it."

He scooped out a second black box, this one glistening with a thin film from the gel it had been in. He set it on the ground beside the bin, rubbing his arm to get rid of the thin coating on it.

"Noxious stuff, that gelatin."

Bard came over to peer in, wondering what it looked like. The walls were so high he could just stick his head in. Inside, it was almost filled with a thick, clearish-white material about the consistency of stiff gelatin. A rapidly-filling hole could be seen where the cube had been suspended in it. It could have held a few hundred cubes neatly packed inside. Bard guessed that it had been replenished while firing, if all of the Greenspark had come from this one machine.

Jeroam was wandering down the hall, cautiously holding his machete at the ready. He paused in front of one of the other doors, laying his hand on the simple pull-handle it was fitted with.

"Wait." Loran stopped him with a word. "Don't go exploring yet, Jeroam."

The young man looked back with a half-smile. "Why not? We have to open one and see what is beyond at some point."

It was Elisha who answered him, "because we want to take this machine apart and inspect it first, ye young rip! If you open the door there is no tellin' what might come through and hinder us. Do as the good lady says and wait a bit, would ye?"

Jeroam shrugged with a touch of bad nature and returned. "By the time we get that thing apart it will be dark."

And though he said it more from irritation than calculation, he was correct. Elisha had brought a few tools with him, wrench and screwdrivers, but the machine was put together in a way which denied access to both of these things. There was no bolts or screws visible, only gleaming metal press-fit together. The young men were kept busy running back and forth to the truck to fetch him more tools, including his crystal torch and a large hammer. Progress was slow, as Elisha did not want to harm the machine or what was in it more than was possible.

Loran sat watching, helping him hold things when necessary. Her expression was one of concentration, dark eyes seeming to see things or put clues together that the others did not perceive.

By the time the sun was setting, they had not yet taken the whole machine apart. The outer shell had come off, exposing a network of cylinders, pipes, wires, electronic boards and activators of various sorts that Elisha picked through with painstaking slowness. Many of the things they found in it were wholly new to him. Metals, gasses in the cylinders and ways of doings things he had never seen before. At one point, they found a rack holding a single, tiny cylinder with a indent on one end and what looked like an electromagnet on the other. Another time Elisha opened a gas cylinder and yellowish foam bubbled out, smelling strongly of dead fish.

But there were still layers of machinery to pick through by the time it started getting too dark to continue.

"Well, one thing I know for certain," Elisha summed up his findings, "this was used to launch those cubes. But where the people who built it got some of these materials...it escapes me!"

"And there has been no clue as to who built it or why," Loran said thoughtfully.

"That's what we have to find through the doors." Jeroam jerked a hand towards the entrances down the hall, now hidden by gathering gloom.

"Not tonight, lad!" Elisha stood up with a sigh. "Tell ye what. Tomorrow we will drop the taking apart of the machine for a time and explore the doors first thing. I'm beginning to wish to have a talk with those that built it, myself. It's made with marvelous machinery."

Bard stood looking at the machine, a feeling of eerie watchfulness striking him again. He turned his head to look up at the top of the Gate and found a Charwing perched there, looking back at him with dark eyes.

"You're right," Loran agreed with the inventor, "we'll go back, eat and rest for tonight. In the morning we must press on for more answers."

Bard nodded agreement, feeling a touch of relief at leaving the Gate while it was getting dark. But at the same time, excitement began to build at what they might find beyond the doors in the morning.

THE AKARNAN'S 'SOON' was longer than Drifter would have liked. By the meals, he guessed that days passed as he waited in the cramped cell. Only once did someone come in to visit him. Then it was the nurse, coming to make sure that his temperature was correct and his heart still beating. He tried to press her for information, but all he gained was the estimate that the Akarnan had held him, mostly unconscious, for at least a week before the Volka caused a revolt and took him themselves. When Drifter tried to get more from the nurse, she threatened once again to call the guard and have him 'neutralized'.

He could not count the passing of days by when he was awake or slept. He spent much of his time lost in memories or waking visions, or somewhere between the two states. He found that he could relive parts of his life before the Greenspark fall with much less pain now. Gradually, his earlier life unfolded to his mind, set free from the cage where he had kept it. Parts of it were still too tender to touch, especially later parts. These he crammed hastily back into their hiding place whenever they showed their faces. But others, especially from when he was young, came quite easily.

He remembered the school he had gone to, a simple Sector school near his home. There had been a hill between it and his house, a tall, humped thing that boys rode sleds down in the winter and girls went to for the wildflowers in the spring. It was a tiny patch of wilderness in a sea of city. Maples and oaks grew on that hill. Their leaves turned red and gold in the fall. He remembered keenly one red leaf blazing in the hand of a slim, blonde girl of twenty-one when he asked her if they could spend their life together. And she had said yes.

How short that life together had been.

When he was weary of sitting still and longed to be on the move, Drifter would practice his martial arts in the little cell. He ended up breaking the back of the chair this way, with a blow that was harder than he had intended. The next day when he awoke it had been replaced. He had not heard anyone enter the cell or take the old one away.

The meals continued bland, though he eventually got used to the amount of seasonings used in them and even enjoyed a few of the menu items. There was a rotation to them, a pattern always followed that he learned to anticipate. The morning meal, or what he understood came in the morning, was a few bits of meat and some eggs. These could be fried or scrambled, bacon or sausages. The next meal was usually a slice of bread with something on it, anything from meat to jam. The last plate of the day would contain something a little more hearty, such as the mashed potatoes and vegetables. After that there was a long gap, the space of night, before the pattern started over again.

Drifter was not hungry half of the time the food came. With so little to do, he did not use much energy. It seemed a waste to let it go uneaten, but he had the feeling that the people in this place did not care. They had more than enough to keep themselves and a useless prisoner alive.

He often thought of experimenting further with the mysterious relic set in his robotic hand. But after the one outburst, he resisted using it again. The Akarnan leader's warning was clear. He might be watched at all times. And the weapon was the one true edge he had over his captors. As long as they were in doubt as to what it was and what he could do with it, he had a tool, small but significant, to use in gaining eventual freedom.

By the time they came for him, he was ready to meet any incident or action that would follow. The nurse was not there this time, nor the legal little fellow. It was just a pair of guards, weapons against their shoulders and armor gleaming. The lead one had orangish hair, the second black. Other than that it would have been difficult to tell them apart.

"You're to come with us." The one in the lead dropped Drifter's boots on the floor in front of him. Without waiting to be asked, Drifter began to lace them on. Like his cloak, they were clean and shined, a tear in the side even patched without a joint. To himself, Drifter commented wryly that if nothing else, he had gained better clothes from this whole incident.

"The council is waiting," the second guard added. Whether it was to hurry him or not was hard to tell, as it was spoken in a flat monotone.

"Then the joke's on them, for a change." Drifter shrugged, tying his last lace with a touch of truculent slowness.

Once he was ready, he stood up, stamping his feet in the shoes with pleasure to have them back. Now he could go anywhere, in a building or out, without physical discomfort. If he had a knife in his belt he could have lived in any climate and survived.

The guards fell into place, one in front of and one behind him. Impassively, he allowed himself to be led out of the room.

Drifter was taken down the hall, away from the main chamber where the podium stood. At the end of that passage was a door which led into another, wider hallway. This one was draped in crimson banners, each with a different golden symbol centered in a ring of silver stars. Between them were tall, narrow windows of a silvery sheen, looking out on a lawn almost entirely enclosed by walls of the building around it. The grass grew green and short, carefully trimmed into shape. The trees had leaves of startling purple and orange shades on them, though it appeared to be early-mid summer. Drifter watched the wind blowing through the leaves out of the corner of his eyes and wished that he were out in the air and sun, rather than stuck inside.

At the end of the hall there were three doors, one straight ahead and two to the right. The guards took him through the second door on the right, entering a tall, wide chamber with a heavy wooden door at the end. This had its own pair of guards, standing at attention in front of it. A gold symbol was deeply etched into the door. The two separate pairs of guards saluted each other, Drifter's keepers indicating that they were bringing him at the council's orders. The couple at the door nodded and opened it. Drifter was brought into the private council room, where matters between the Volka and Akarnan were discussed away from public eyes. Today, there were only Volka present.

It was a large, half-circular room with the door being set in the flat side of it. The far curve was mostly made up of what at first appeared to be windows looking out on a quiet, hedge garden scene. But It soon became apparent that they were not windows at all. Instead, they were huge screens, set into the walls and made to project gradually shifting images of quiet, outdoors scenes.

To the left of the door was the widest space in the chamber, where the floor was pale cream intersected by black and gold lines. On this floor, facing Drifter as he came in, was a large, arced counter or desk made of variegated red and cream stone. Black and gold stripes ran vertically and horizontally on its face, marking off squares. Behind each square sat a council member. Four men and a woman, all dressed in stiff, formal suits and ties. The bent, balding questioner was there, sitting just left of center. He had his tablet out and was running his finger over it anxiously, counting off something or other. Privately, Drifter thought that it was unanswered questions.

Beside him, in the central position, sat a man in a dark suit with thin, blade-like shoulders stuck stiffly in the air, a long, pale neck and head which looked too heavy for it. His hair was thin, as if the close air in the place made hair grow poorly on the men, and his nose too large. He had an electronic tablet as well, set in front of him with one hand laying on it. His eyes fixed on Drifter with a predatory swiftness.

The other members did not stand out. They all seemed to be cut of the same material, even the woman with her stern hair and tapered fingers. They did not speak in the following interview, just listened and sometimes nodded when the central figure spoke.

Beyond them, the room rose into a set of wooden benches. These were empty, though evidently built so that trials and discussions could be watched by picked members. A guard stood at the base of them, as if to make sure that Drifter did not ruin them in a fit of anger or desperation. The two guards who had been escorting Drifter stayed by the door, one on either side just like their compatriots on the opposite face of the wall. Another pair of guards stood next to an object set in the middle of the floor on the right. This piece drew Drifter's gaze away from the council members for a moment as he came in.

It was a tall, dark arch of smooth stone. Inside of it a door was set flush, a plain pull-handle on its face. It was a dark, shiny material much like the stone and exactly like the material of another door Drifter had recently stood at. The Gate of Eternity.

His eyes narrowed thoughtfully as he looked at it. His memory of what had been inside the Gate was too vague for him to decide if it could have been that very room.

"Take the floor, Mr. Drifter." The lead man's voice was surprisingly sonorous, though it had a sort of dry weariness which grated on the nerves. Drifter's head whipped back toward him, and he paced out into the center of the floor in front of the half-circle desk, stopping there with his arms crossed. He nodded his head once at the little, bent questioner from before. "Just Drifter. As your inquisitor will tell you."

His voice, low and rough but firm, carried well in the room. It was like an uncut stone sitting on a clean paper plate. Out of place and unwanted for its rawness.

The words made the bent man scoot around uncomfortably in his seat, while the central figure drew back his head as if about to peck something with his large nose.

"Very well, Drifter," the central figure continued, "I am Head Councilman Flemming. We have called you here today to inform you of your rights and invest you as a formal ward of the Volka council."

He paused as if expecting an answer. Drifter threw a single word into the gap.

"Ward."

"Yes, well, that means—"

"I know what it means." The loner's glimmering gaze cut him off at head-height. "One, The act of guarding; watch; guardianship. Two, one who, or that which, guards; garrison; defender; protector. What I want to know is how you are using it."

At this the questioner and Flemming had to have a whispered conference. Eventually, the lead councilman nodded his head a few more times at Drifter and humphed. "Yes. We mean it exactly how you explained. Now, to get on with business..."

He picked up the tablet and looked over the words on it, as if unable to keep many of them in his head at a time.

"To invest you as a ward, the council must, by the decrees of the council of Dagor, explain to you the position in which we have found you, inform you of your rights and prove that the council has the right of conquest with which to take wards of state."

Drifter shifted slightly on the floor, face unperturbed. "The Akarnan recycled me when I was near-dead and you have kept me in a cell for days. Is that conquest?"

"That is not what I was speaking of. That is our pseudo-wardship. Now please, silence while I read the decrees." Flemming arched his neck to get a better point with which to view his tablet.

"Item the first. Having found the incumbent, that's you, in a state of helplessness being held by the Akarnan council in violation of the Dagor council, this council, the Volka assembly, has taken upon itself to bring the incumbent under our guardianship, until such time as it sees fit to release the aforesaid. The incumbents state as an Othered extenuates the circumstances so as include infinity, until mortalis, ect. The Akarnan council have, to placate the assemblies; A, made apology to the council for breaking pledge. B, made apology to the incumbent for the same. And C, paid a fine of the agreed-upon value to keep their seat in the assembly."

The councilman gave Drifter a sharp look. "That is the explanation of position."

Drifter made a motion of assent. "Everyone's been paid off and apologized to for my kidnapping. Understood."

With a faint noise of irritation and another command for silence, the councilman went on.

"Item the second. The rights of an incumbent are as follows. Past the age of eighteen the incumbent may make a plea of citizenship before a full assembly. Such personage may also be given legal council, representation and benefits. See items fifty-four B, One-sixty-one G, ect, ect. In the case of an Othered Incumbent, all laws are mitigated. Othereds may not have representation, council, ect. Once made ward of the council they may not plead any cases, nor find representation beyond what the council offers. Othereds must be kept confined in the council building except for under special license, to be granted by full assembly. An Othered ward has no rights, except for that of sufficient nutrition."

Once again Drifter made a sign of assent, a tiny twist of his lips showing what he thought without him breaking the silence imposed on him.

"Item the third." Flemming cleared his throat and drank from a tumbler of water near his right hand. The air in the room seemed to become more still, as if everyone was hanging on his words.

"An explanation of conquest. This is a long item, so I will ask your patience and silence."

If anyone had spoken then, it would have sounded out of place. Drifter did not even nod, face shaded by the overhang of his hood.

"In the year three-fifty of the Ascended Nation, A.N., the Volka council found that the Akarnan had constructed a door or gate in what was to become afterwards the private council chamber. It was not a normal door, as it tapped into strange energy flows only guessed at before. Its construction was a secret up until this time. It allowed the Akarnan to travel, not between time, nor to any physical space in this dimension. In fact, it was a door to secondary dimensions, an idea that the two councils were just beginning to experiment with. The door tapped into a mysterious construct like a series of hall or passageways, very dim and set with many such doors or gates. These had evidently been there for some time and, upon opening them, it was found that they were the exit into these various secondary dimensions."

The councilman shot a look around the room. "I will forbear from going further into the history of the passages or gates. Its exploration is a long, interesting tale but does not bear upon this discussion."

He cleared his throat again and continued, "In the year three-fifty the door was discovered by the Volka council and a full assembly held to decide upon rules dictating the use of this new technology. It was called the Council of Dagor. In it, many binding rules were made between Volka and Akarnan, firstly that it would be kept a secret from all but the assembly, hence the private council room. Secondly, that the 'Othereds', as anyone from a secondary dimension is know as, must not be interfered with unless the full assembly cast a majority vote in the favor of the movement. It eventually came to the Volka's knowledge that the Akarnan had found a portal to another dimension and were already breaking this pact, by introducing 'relics' or great power into it. They had, in fact, built a portal to this dimension themselves, much like the gate in this room, setting it into a blank wall of the passages."

Here Flemming indicated the door and arch at the far side of the room.

"This was dismissed on promise of the action halting, as it had begun before the pact. Eventually, the Volka council decided to make use of this dimension themselves, as it had already been sullied. This they did with perfect legality, the motion being accepted by a margin of six to four. The Akarnan were mostly in the minority."

"The motion was to experiment with a new weapon that the Volka had conceived for warring with the aliens of the neighboring planets. It was first designed to destroy the entire population and life of a planet, therefore rendering it open to resettling. It failed in this, being strong but not yet potent enough to thoroughly destroy a planet's life. It was tested on the dimension that the Akarnan had discovered. As repayment for their votes, the Akarnan demanded that they be allowed to install agents on the chosen world after the destruction, to act as surveillance. Unfortunately, most of these agents soon went insane in the varied atmosphere and have fallen out of contact. The few who survived with intact mentality have just started to contact us, since the gate has been unsealed. As the assembly agreed upon in the motion, once the gate was used to test the weapon it was resealed with the original Akarnan lock so that no Othered could pass it and discover the machine of destruction inside, as the weapon had failed and left a scattering of survivors intact. Unfortunately the Akarnan, unknown to the Volka council, bestowed a single key to open the gate upon the Othereds of this dimension, once again in breach of pact. Because of this, one survivor, *you* sir, were able to unseal the door and open it. In case of such emergency the Volka had built in a protection unit meant to destroy anyone attempting to enter. You know the results."

The councilman set aside his tablet, folded his hands together as if much pleased and looked at Drifter blandly.

Chapter 18: Shadows of the Past

"So what you're telling me," Drifter said slowly, as if unsure of himself, "is that you, the Volka council, are the ones who created the Greenspark fire and unleashed it on my world."

Flemming nodded to the questioner beside him, who smiled back. "That sums it up nicely."

"And you built this weapon to destroy the people and life of a planet, entirely. My world was just a test, which it failed because some of us survived."

"Yes, that is correct."

"So to finish the explanation off." Drifter uncurled his right hand and gazed at the relic inside the palm as if unconcerned. "You were playing a game with us. All those people dead, the cities and landscapes destroyed. Just a test."

"Well now," the councilman blustered, "I wouldn't say—"

"But I would." Drifter's eyes came up, gleaming with an odd light like a sickly fire. The hairs on the Volka council members' necks stood up as they heard the edge of the scorch in his voice. It was there, like a tangible thing in the room.

"Weapons of mass destruction. Fire rained on comparatively innocent people. Death, pain...the scorch." Drifter closed his eyes for a brief moment. "By the powers given to me by the Akarnan. By the bond between the Beasts of Dark and Drifter. By every scorched soul in Apex, I condemn you. The sentence is Death."

Power coursed through the blue stone in his robotic hand, making it glow like an evil eye. Flame and energy soaked the room, blasting almost every living being within it. The screens cracked, the guards melted in their suits. Blue beams swept the desk until it stood scorched and blackened. The walls bore the marks of the flames like swirling, psychedelic ornaments. Because the room was soundproof, the guards outside did not even know what was happening. Eventually, only Drifter stood, gasping and holding his right arm as if to keep it back from more destruction.

A pile of ashes sat where the council members had been. Their tablets and their lives were forfeit. The room had been scorched like an Apex survivor's soul.

Tears marred the toughened, soot-stained skin of Drifter's face. Still holding his own wrist in bondage, he straightened and staggered towards the arch with the gate set in it. Weariness made him stumble at every step, and moisture blinded his eyes.

The black stone was cracking from where he had hit it with power. Smoke swirled around him as he jerked the door open and staggered through. Behind him, it crumbled into a pile of useless pieces.

THE NIGHT WAS CLEAR and cold. Loran lay along the bench in the car, head resting on one door by the window, feet curled next to the opposite. The young men, Bard and Jeroam, had put up a shelter next to Elisha's truck so that everyone would be less cramped. The shelter was made of a large piece of canvas, stretched from the side of the truck down to the ground, where it was weighed with rocks to hold it in place. They had enjoyed themselves putting it up and settling down to sleep. Loran had heard their chatting and laughter from inside the car on the other side of the truck. It gave her a small smile, two boys having fun despite the ruins and wreckage around them. It promised well for the future of Apex. Especially if they found a pair of like-minded young women to join them...

But it was not their jollity which kept Loran from sleeping. That had long since ceased, leaving a peaceful quiet on the little camp. Something was weighing on the woman's mind. She did not know what it was. Perhaps the fact that, in the morning, they would be delving into the secrets she had been hunting down for so long. That would explain the thrill of quiet excitement she felt. But it did not give her satisfaction about the longing on her mind.

Sitting up, she ran a hand across her eyes. There did not seem to be any sleep in her tonight. She felt alert, awake and drawn.

"Trusting my intuition has saved me before," Loran sighed, opening the door of the car. Outside, the air was cool, touching her cheek with its frosty fingers. She stood just outside of the car for a moment, running her eyes over the horizon. Black buildings looming, hazy stars in the sky. A pale moon shed a touch of grayish luminescence on the world. Nothing out of the ordinary.

Carefully, Loran closed the door of the car. She did not want to awake anyone else with her insomnia. With a small shrug of her shoulders, she walked over to the path leading up the hill and started along it. The only sounds were the distant cheeping of some insects and the light swish of her skirt, coupled with the tap of her shoes on cement. Everything had a repressed, distant sound to it, as if the whole world were waiting on some chance discovery. Once or twice, Loran thought she saw red eyes gleaming at her from the dark. But nothing came of it and she told herself not to be so jumpy.

The buildings at the top of the hill loomed up, marking the place where she could cross the fence. Careful not to stumble in the dark, she made her way over it. On the other side of the buildings stood the gate.

It was dark, blacker than anything else in view. The moonlight barely touched glints of gray from its arch. The interior seemed like a hole into utter blackness. It was not simply void of light. It absorbed the light around it. Only the tiny glinting lines of the machine's rails on the inner face of the door broke up the shadows.

Wondering what had called her to this place, Loran moved to stand in front of the Gate. Mystery breathed out of it at her.

"Loran."

The voice chilled her blood. Turning slowly, Loran perceived a figure standing next to the arch. She wondered for the first time in her life if ghosts were real. Hood shading his face, hand outstretched with a Charwing sitting on the fist, was Drifter. His form and way of standing, with pale eyes just glittering in the moonlight, were unmistakable.

"Drifter." Loran finally took breath. Stepping towards him, she saw that he was not thin or ephemeral in the least. His clothes, at least, appeared to be made of reality. The only odd thing about him was that his right hand gleamed a little, as if he were wearing a gauntlet of steel.

"Yes. I made it back." Drifter shrugged a shoulder at the Gate, making the bird on his hand caw, taking to the wing. It disappeared into the night. "From in there."

"I—we thought you were dead."

There was a hint of shadowed smile in his voice as he returned, "I was. In all but mind. The phantoms brought me back."

"Phantoms. You met phantoms in there? What is this gate?"

Drifter shifted and sighed. "It's a portal to a mysterious hall, giving access to different dimensions. No—don't interrupt. I don't understand it much more than you do. The doors in it lead not only to other planets or far away places, but to other universes much like ours. Just separated by walls of...I don't know. Invisible energy. I was taken to one and found out the truth about the Greenspark."

"It was launched from this machine." Loran gestured at the Gate.

"I know. You were right. I should have listened. It's not the end of the world. The Greenspark was not the apocalypse at all. It was just someone's test of a terrible weapon. You were right all along."

Loran shook her head slowly. "I don't understand."

"I'll explain it all, in time." Drifter moved to lean against the arch of the gate, drawing in a breath as if weary. He flexed his right hand in a strip of moonlight, making the metal glitter.

"I learned about the relics and phantoms as well. They are connected, as you said. The phantoms made the relics and put them in our world. They thought we needed a little magic. And they took me captive to prove it."

Loran stood, head bowed in thought. "That is why I've had you in my thoughts. Images of you trapped somewhere...with electric lights and gray walls."

Drifter nodded, agreeing with her picture. "I escaped that dimension and destroyed the door to it, so that we would not become guinea pigs for their weapons again."

He shook his hooded head slowly from side to side. "I've seen another world now, Loran. One not touched by the scorch. And I know there are others out there. Many others. But I must be suited to this one, because I don't want to leave it again. I want to go back to roving in the ruins. And I want you to come with me."

The woman drew in a quick breath, surprised. "Oh, but I can't. I called Elisha and Jeroam to help inspect the machine. We're going to explore the passages with Bard. Who knows what we'll find and learn in there. Secrets and powers beyond what we have been given in this realm. And the boys are keen to learn. Bard and Jeroam, that is. I'm glad Bard is finally fitting in somewhere. I don't want to leave them stranded, without my help."

Her words seemed uncertain, though she tried to put her usual stern coldness into them.

Drifter stepped forward with one of his sudden moves to stand in front of her. "They sound like they will do fine without you. Bard has a good heart, even if he still has much to learn. We can leave them a message explaining some things, so that they won't go into other dimensions blind. But I've seen another world now and know that there aren't any out there that are actually better than this. People are just as cruel and perhaps more conniving in other dimensions. I'd rather have my freedom here, than all the mysterious powers of another dimension and the chains to go with it."

He paused for a moment, seeming to listen to the night, before he finished, "I can survive here better than most, make a living where others die. And, Loran...I want you with me. Will you come?"

Loran only hesitated a few seconds more, looking from the Gate to him, before she put her hand on his arm and bowed her head.

"Yes."

BARD'S SLEEP WAS TROUBLED in the middle of the night. He thought he heard the sound of the car start up and leave silently, but then dismissed it, as there were no headlights. Turning over, he fell back asleep, dreaming of the day to come.

When he awoke, he sat up with a start, hearing voices outside and seeing red sunlight creep in the flap of their shelter. Jeroam was already gone, so he got up and hurried out. Elisha and the young man were standing in the patch of gravel where the car had been. Its tire tracks could be seen, disturbing the gray pebbles where it had been. The tracks disappeared into the pavement of the street.

"What happened?" Bard looked around, blinking away sleep. "Where is Loran?"

Elisha looked grim. "That is the strangest thing, lad. Seems she's run off with a ghost."

Bard held up his hand with a jerk of surprise to take the folded bit of paper which Elisha proffered. It was a message, written in a hand he did not recognize. But how the words were put together seemed oddly familiar.

'The Gate leads to other dimensions, one through each door. Be careful. I've discovered who launched the Greenspark. It was only a test to see if we would survive. Since we did, the world-destroying weapon was a failure. But those people will not be using the passages again. I'm alive and heading back into the city. Loran is going with me. Have fun with the Gate.'

It was signed, *'Drifter'*.

Don't miss out!

Visit the website below and you can sign up to receive emails whenever Rachael S Lucas publishes a new book. There's no charge and no obligation.

https://books2read.com/r/B-A-XHJJ-WJADD

BOOKS 2 READ

Connecting independent readers to independent writers.

Did you love *Drifter's Gate*? Then you should read *Exile Of Dust*[1] by Rachael S Lucas!

[2]

The Dustlands, an arid sweep of waste pocked with fantastic sandstone formations. Under its sunless sky travels Hiram, a teenage boy seeking Nolin, the famous wizard. Nolin is always pushing boundaries. Whether it is in the confines of a slave mine or the magic halls of the Dark Passages, he seeks what others fear to find. Haunted by his past, exiled to the Dustlands, he has become a harsh young man of great power. He refuses to teach Hiram his secrets, frightened that the

---

1. https://books2read.com/u/bQgyPP

2. https://books2read.com/u/bQgyPP

past will repeat itself in another generation. But Nolin can see the spark of Erilaz burning in Hiram. The only way to dissuade the boy might be to tell him everything.

Read more at https://rachaelslucas.wordpress.com/.

Also by Rachael S Lucas

Sarkin
Sailing For Shadow City
A Lonely Wind
The Griffin's Claw

Sci-fi and fantasy short stories
Illusions Of Steel And Sunset

Tales of Civitas Apex
Drifter's Gate

Standalone
Dimensions
Exile Of Dust

Watch for more at https://rachaelslucas.wordpress.com/.

About the Author

Rachael Lucas is a quiet girl from the mountains of northern California, where she works in the woods when they aren't deep in snow. She loves reading, writing, gardening and Asian art among many other things

Read more at https://rachaelslucas.wordpress.com/.

www.ingramcontent.com/pod-product-compliance
Lightning Source LLC
Chambersburg PA
CBHW020319180726
47991CB00018B/73